*Let Jenny Oliver be your ultimate,
indulgent Christmas treat!*

Praise for

JENNY OLIVER

'With gorgeous descriptions of Paris, Christmas, copious amounts of delicious baking that'll make your mouth water, and lots and lots of snow—what more could you ask for from a Christmas novel!'
—*Bookboodle* on *The Parisian Christmas Bake Off*

'*The Parisian Christmas Bake Off* is a charming and warm read, one you will not be able to put down once you start reading.'
—*This Chick Reads*

'…a lovely book, with a beautiful ending'
—*Crooks on Books* on *The Vintage Summer Wedding*

'I thoroughly enjoyed this book. It had a sprinkling of festivity, a touch of romance and a glorious amount of mouth-watering baking! I don't think I have ever felt so hungry reading a fiction book before.'
—*Rea Book Review* on *The Parisian Christmas Bake Off*

'It was a beautiful read with the just right amount of festivities.'
—*Afternoon Bookery* on *The Little Christmas Kitchen*

'What a fun Christmas story!'
—*Fabulous Book Fiend* on
The Parisian Christmas Bake Off

The
Little
Christmas
Kitchen

JENNY
OLIVER

CARINA™

This edition is published by arrangement with Harlequin Books S.A.
CARINA is a trademark of Harlequin Enterprises Limited, used under licence.

Published in Great Britain 2015
by CARINA, an imprint of Harlequin (UK) Limited,
Eton House, 18-24 Paradise Road,
Richmond, Surrey, TW9 1SR

© 2014 Jenny Oliver

ISBN 978-0-263-91760-4

98-1015

Harlequin's policy is to use papers that are natural, renewable and recyclable products and made from wood grown in sustainable forests. The logging and manufacturing processes conform to the legal environmental regulations of the country of origin.

Printed and bound by
CPI Group (UK) Ltd, Croydon, CR0 4YY

Jenny Oliver wrote her first book on holiday when she was ten years old. Illustrated with cut-out supermodels from her sister's *Vogue*, it was an epic, sweeping love story not so loosely based on *Dynasty*.

Since then Jenny has gone on to get an English degree, a Master's and a job in publishing that's taught her what it takes to write a novel (without the help of the supermodels). She wrote *The Parisian Christmas Bake Off* on the beach in a sea-soaked, sand-covered notebook. This time the inspiration was her addiction to macaroons, the belief she can cook them and an all-consuming love of Christmas. When the decorations go up in October, that's fine with her! Follow her on Twitter @JenOliverBooks.

CHAPTER 1

ELLA

Before Ella had checked her emails, the morning had been like any other. The air conditioner was broken and whirring too loudly. The boardroom air smelt of aftershave and strong coffee. Big bushy garlands of tinsel were looped along the wall, baubles hung in bunches like grapes on the windows and a white fake Christmas tree with glittered branches twinkled in the corner. Ella was trying not to look at the new accounts assistant, Katya, who was shambling through a dreadful presentation and would soon be out of a job by the look of disdain on their boss Adrian's face. Ella had wanted to jump up and help her out, do anything to stop the blotches of red flushing the poor girl's cheeks, but instead she'd seen a new message pop up on her iPad and had surreptitiously drawn the tablet down under the lip of the boardroom table so she could read it. She'd presumed it would be from Max finalising details of their anniversary dinner that evening at Claridges. As she opened her inbox, she allowed herself a quick admire of the diamond bracelet on her wrist that he'd given her that morning – rolling her eyes at the memory of him saying, 'Wow, that's nice,' as she opened the box. As they tended to buy their own presents nowadays, it was the first time he'd seen it.

She clicked on the email.

From: Gerald Austin
To: Ella Davenport
Subject: I just thought you should know.

Ella heard Adrian's voice in the background. 'This is all very well, but we've seen it before. And if I've seen it, they've seen it. Come on people. We need a bit more blue sky thinking. A bit more oomph. It's Christmas for crying out loud. Wow them with a bit of sparkle. Ella can you take charge of this one–' He paused. 'Ella… are you with us?'

Ella wasn't with them at all. Her eyes were focused on her iPad as her beautifully ordered life cracked down the centre and her stomach tightened like she'd forgotten how to exhale.

Your partner is having an affair with my wife. Photo attached confirms. Suggest you get yourself a good lawyer. I'm going to annihilate her in court.

CHAPTER 2

MADDY

'I told Mum about the possibility of going to London and she just said no. Said I wouldn't be able to handle it. I think I'd be OK though. Don't you? Don't you think I'd be OK?' Maddy wiped her oily hands on the old rag hanging out of her jeans pocket and then took the hand Dimitri was offering to haul herself out of the boat and up onto the jetty.

'Maddy,' he said, bending down to pick up the board of his windsurfer, the sail already propped up by the side of the taverna. 'You're twenty-four. Don't you think it's about time you just went anyway?' He was about to say more, probably to really make the fact that she should grow up and take charge of her own life hit home, but he got distracted by a scratch on his board. 'Shit, when did that happen? It's those kids isn't? Oi you lot–' he shouted at the gaggle of little kids who were messing around at the end of the jetty, dangling bits of rope into the sea with worms on hooks to try and catch the millions of silver fish that darted around the wooden posts. They looked up all big eyed and terrified when Dimitri yelled, 'Did you mess with my board?'

'No Dimitri,' they all chorused in unison, faces pale and perfectly innocent.

He glared at them for a second, six foot with big, broad shoulders, black shaggy hair and at least three days' stubble, he knew he could terrify them.

'Don't.' Maddy bashed him on the arm. 'They're only little.'

'They've messed with my board. Look at it.'

'You're mean. Stop being mean to them. Look at them.' She turned to wave in their direction, all four kids huddled together, their fishing rods clutched in their hands, their cheeks pink, waiting for their telling off.

Dimitri sighed. 'You stay away from my board. Yes?!'

'Yes Dimitri,' they chorused again.

'And while you're at it, stay away from my bike as well. I saw you the other day sitting on it. Yes. I did, don't shake your heads, if it fell on you it could do some damage. Don't sit on my bike.'

'Can we ride on it again with you, please?'

He narrowed his eyes and shook his head. 'What have I started?' he said to Maddy, and she shrugged a shoulder.

'You shouldn't have been so keen to show off your new toy should you?' she said, nodding to where his beautiful Triumph Bonneville T100 sat gleaming on the cobbled slipway.

Dimitri followed her gaze, paused for a second to admire his bike and then said with a shrug, 'I was excited.'

Maddy shook her head and, still feeling the slight sting of his earlier comment, she turned to the kids and said, 'I'll take you out on this, if you like?' *This* was the sleek white forty foot yacht she'd just repaired the engine of.

'Are you sure Maddy? It's not your boat,' Dimitri questioned, concerned, as the kids all whooped and ran over to jump on the deck of the boat, their shoes leaving tiny, dusty footprints on the gleaming surface.

0

Let Jenny Oliver be your ultimate,
indulgent Christmas treat!

Available from
Jenny Oliver

THE PARISIAN CHRISTMAS BAKE OFF
THE VINTAGE SUMMER WEDDING
THE LITTLE CHRISTMAS KITCHEN

Cherry Pie Island
THE GRAND REOPENING OF DANDELION CAFÉ
THE VINTAGE ICE CREAM VAN ROAD TRIP
THE GREAT ALLOTMENT PROPOSAL
ONE SUMMER NIGHT AT THE RITZ
FOUR WEDDINGS AND A WHITE CHRISTMAS

The
Little
Christmas
Kitchen

JENNY
OLIVER

CARINA™

This edition is published by arrangement with Harlequin Books S.A. CARINA is a trademark of Harlequin Enterprises Limited, used under licence.

Published in Great Britain 2015
by CARINA, an imprint of Harlequin (UK) Limited,
Eton House, 18-24 Paradise Road,
Richmond, Surrey, TW9 1SR

© 2014 Jenny Oliver

ISBN 978-0-263-91760-4

98-1015

Harlequin's policy is to use papers that are natural, renewable and recyclable products and made from wood grown in sustainable forests. The logging and manufacturing processes conform to the legal environmental regulations of the country of origin.

Printed and bound by
CPI Group (UK) Ltd, Croydon, CR0 4YY

Jenny Oliver wrote her first book on holiday when she was ten years old. Illustrated with cut-out supermodels from her sister's *Vogue*, it was an epic, sweeping love story not so loosely based on *Dynasty*.

Since then Jenny has gone on to get an English degree, a Master's and a job in publishing that's taught her what it takes to write a novel (without the help of the supermodels). She wrote *The Parisian Christmas Bake Off* on the beach in a sea-soaked, sand-covered notebook. This time the inspiration was her addiction to macaroons, the belief she can cook them and an all-consuming love of Christmas. When the decorations go up in October, that's fine with her! Follow her on Twitter @JenOliverBooks.

CHAPTER 1

ELLA

Before Ella had checked her emails, the morning had been like any other. The air conditioner was broken and whirring too loudly. The boardroom air smelt of aftershave and strong coffee. Big bushy garlands of tinsel were looped along the wall, baubles hung in bunches like grapes on the windows and a white fake Christmas tree with glittered branches twinkled in the corner. Ella was trying not to look at the new accounts assistant, Katya, who was shambling through a dreadful presentation and would soon be out of a job by the look of disdain on their boss Adrian's face. Ella had wanted to jump up and help her out, do anything to stop the blotches of red flushing the poor girl's cheeks, but instead she'd seen a new message pop up on her iPad and had surreptitiously drawn the tablet down under the lip of the boardroom table so she could read it. She'd presumed it would be from Max finalising details of their anniversary dinner that evening at Claridges. As she opened her inbox, she allowed herself a quick admire of the diamond bracelet on her wrist that he'd given her that morning – rolling her eyes at the memory of him saying, 'Wow, that's nice,' as she opened the box. As they tended to buy their own presents nowadays, it was the first time he'd seen it.

She clicked on the email.

From: Gerald Austin
To: Ella Davenport
Subject: I just thought you should know.

Ella heard Adrian's voice in the background. 'This is all very well, but we've seen it before. And if I've seen it, they've seen it. Come on people. We need a bit more blue sky thinking. A bit more oomph. It's Christmas for crying out loud. Wow them with a bit of sparkle. Ella can you take charge of this one–' He paused. 'Ella… are you with us?'

Ella wasn't with them at all. Her eyes were focused on her iPad as her beautifully ordered life cracked down the centre and her stomach tightened like she'd forgotten how to exhale.

Your partner is having an affair with my wife. Photo attached confirms. Suggest you get yourself a good lawyer. I'm going to annihilate her in court.

CHAPTER 2

MADDY

'I told Mum about the possibility of going to London and she just said no. Said I wouldn't be able to handle it. I think I'd be OK though. Don't you? Don't you think I'd be OK?' Maddy wiped her oily hands on the old rag hanging out of her jeans pocket and then took the hand Dimitri was offering to haul herself out of the boat and up onto the jetty.

'Maddy,' he said, bending down to pick up the board of his windsurfer, the sail already propped up by the side of the taverna. 'You're twenty-four. Don't you think it's about time you just went anyway?' He was about to say more, probably to really make the fact that she should grow up and take charge of her own life hit home, but he got distracted by a scratch on his board. 'Shit, when did that happen? It's those kids isn't? Oi you lot–' he shouted at the gaggle of little kids who were messing around at the end of the jetty, dangling bits of rope into the sea with worms on hooks to try and catch the millions of silver fish that darted around the wooden posts. They looked up all big eyed and terrified when Dimitri yelled, 'Did you mess with my board?'

'No Dimitri,' they all chorused in unison, faces pale and perfectly innocent.

He glared at them for a second, six foot with big, broad shoulders, black shaggy hair and at least three days' stubble, he knew he could terrify them.

'Don't.' Maddy bashed him on the arm. 'They're only little.'

'They've messed with my board. Look at it.'

'You're mean. Stop being mean to them. Look at them.' She turned to wave in their direction, all four kids huddled together, their fishing rods clutched in their hands, their cheeks pink, waiting for their telling off.

Dimitri sighed. 'You stay away from my board. Yes?!'

'Yes Dimitri,' they chorused again.

'And while you're at it, stay away from my bike as well. I saw you the other day sitting on it. Yes. I did, don't shake your heads, if it fell on you it could do some damage. Don't sit on my bike.'

'Can we ride on it again with you, please?'

He narrowed his eyes and shook his head. 'What have I started?' he said to Maddy, and she shrugged a shoulder.

'You shouldn't have been so keen to show off your new toy should you?' she said, nodding to where his beautiful Triumph Bonneville T100 sat gleaming on the cobbled slipway.

Dimitri followed her gaze, paused for a second to admire his bike and then said with a shrug, 'I was excited.'

Maddy shook her head and, still feeling the slight sting of his earlier comment, she turned to the kids and said, 'I'll take you out on this, if you like?' *This* was the sleek white forty foot yacht she'd just repaired the engine of.

'Are you sure Maddy? It's not your boat,' Dimitri questioned, concerned, as the kids all whooped and ran over to jump on the deck of the boat, their shoes leaving tiny, dusty footprints on the gleaming surface.

'Yeah it'll be fine,' Maddy said, pulling on a big red, oil streaked jumper that came down to just above the frayed edge of her shorts. Sweeping away the wisps of hair that the wind was blowing in her mouth, she said, 'And, just by the way, with my mum, it's not that she can tell me what to do, it's that I don't want her to not want me to go. I want her to think that I could cope.'

'It's a pretty expensive boat, Mads.' Dimitri shielded his eyes from the low sun as he took in the huge white yacht.

'Can you see what I'm saying about my mum?' She frowned, kicking one of the posts with her old Nike trainer. Then she added, 'The boat'll be fine. And anyway–' She jumped down onto the stern, taking the rope she'd looped into one of the jetty rings with her to cast off. 'I can't say no now, look at them…'

The kids were all sitting crossed legged at the bow like tiny figureheads, watching expectantly.

'See this is probably what your mum's talking about. You're hot headed – stubborn – you don't think things through.' Dimitri shook his head, tendrils of black hair wobbling like a sea anemone.

'Oh please,' Maddy scoffed as she pressed the button to haul up the anchor. 'She just can't recognise that I'm not going to stay here forever and she's using the whole not being able to cope as an excuse.'

'I think she worries that you've been too sheltered,' Dimitri yelled over the sound of the two hundred and fifty horsepower engine as it sprang to life.

'Well, as you say, it's time for me to grow up. Do it anyway,' Maddy shouted back.

'Maddy, part of being a grown-up is realising when you've made a mistake,' he said, wincing as she started to steer the yacht out of the harbour. The kids were clinging onto the tinsel-wrapped railing at the front, dangling their feet over the edge and laughing as the spray bounced up into their faces.

Maddy ignored him, focusing ahead of her on a view so familiar it was etched in her mind. The wide blue sea, dark like sapphires, the little white horses jumping like skittish foals, rays of low winter sun darting off each wave like silver fish, and all she could think was, *God, I wish this was London.*

CHAPTER 3

ELLA

Ella could hear the pad of Max's Gucci loafers on the beige carpet, and walked into the lounge to see him standing in the doorway, one hand pulling his tie loose.

'I thought you were going to Claridge's straight from work?' he said, his beautiful face innocently perplexed. Arrow-straight eyebrows drawing lightly into a frown, blond hair casually dishevelled.

'Are you having an affair?' She asked as calmly as she'd rehearsed. Infuriatingly, her hands were trembling.

Max paused, his eyes narrowed momentarily, then he swept the tie from under his collar and threw it on the sofa. 'Of course I'm bloody not,' he said, then headed over to where she was standing and raised her hand to his lips. 'You're crazy. It's our anniversary,' he said, looking up at her, all innocent wide-eyes.

The first time Ella had met Max's parents they had been shown onto the veranda by the Portuguese maid and poured iced mint water from a crystal jug. She had stood, awkward and out of her depth, as the still air hummed with heat and the only noise was the sprinklers battering the lush lawn and the ice clinking in their glasses. His mother and father were standing rigidly next to one another, muscles tense, clearly having been interrupted in the middle of a blistering row. Max's father had patted the golden retriever at his feet and trudged off down the garden without even a nod of hello, his mother had looked Ella up and down with an expression of languid distaste, her lips unnaturally plump as she pouted and said, 'When the men in this family lie, their cheeks go a very unnatural shade of pink. Funny, isn't it? It's a gem his mother passed on to me. Comes in very useful.' Then she headed into the house, leaving the two of them alone on the decking watching as the labrador bounded through the jets of water drenching the lawn.

As they stood opposite one another in the lounge, Max's eyes seemed to soak deep into her – but his smile wobbled as if he was nervous and, much as she wished she couldn't, even under his Val d'Isere tan, Ella could see the hint of pink tinging his cheekbones.

'This is too important. I wouldn't have an affair,' he said, looking her straight in the eye.

He smelt of Max. Of the shower gel from the gym mixed with his bespoke patchouli aftershave and perhaps a glass or two of wine. She found herself wanting to believe him just so that the warmth of him, the familiarity, wouldn't disappear from her life. They'd been together since she'd graduated University. They were them. Max and Ella. She couldn't be single again.

'Look,' he said, pulling her by the hand and drawing her out to the hall. 'Look what I just carried all the way here.' In the doorway was a Christmas tree, massive, ten or twelve feet, lying wrapped in white netting, a trail of needles behind it. 'I had to drag it the last bit,' he laughed. 'It was so bloody heavy.'

She could tell he was nervous as he struggled to prop up the tree. 'I thought it was time we had a real one. I know I'm always going on about the needles but I thought, you like them so much, it would be a nice surprise. What do you think?'

'Max?' Ella said, watching as he moved quickly, edgily, trying to rip at the netting to set the branches free.

'I don't want to lose you,' he said without looking up.

She thought about when they'd first started going out. The carousel in her head that had whispered, *what does he see in me?* Max was this cool, good-looking guy who lived his life with the carefree abandon that came hand in hand the promise of inheriting a fortune. She had been in awe of him – at the time herself still a little gauche, though firmly on the path to reinvention. They'd met at a party thrown by her step-mother, Veronica. He had joined her by the fountain in the garden, where she'd slipped away for a breather – an escape from the high-calibre networking Veronica encouraged. He'd done a stupid shadow puppet show with his hands and, to his amazement and delight, she'd laughed.

When was the last time he'd made her laugh?

As Max pulled the mesh off the tree, the smell of pine infused the room drawing Ella back to memories of childhood Christmases. Completely unexpectedly and entirely unwanted. Of sneaking down to see a tree piled high with gifts. Of her dad coming home every year with a tacky gift from the stall outside his office – a fibre-optic angel and a huge, glitzy star. Of the arrival of her new baby sister, Maddy, and the purchase of a nativity set to mark the occasion. Ella and Maddy laying it out every year and fighting over who got to put baby Jesus in the crib. Of sitting at the top of the stairs with her sister, both in their matching red dressing gowns and hearing her dad say, in a whisper so they wouldn't hear, *'I can't do it. Not any longer. Not even just for the kids.'* She'd thought he meant dressing up as Santa. She'd realised how wrong she was the next day when he left and the world fell down.

Pushing the memory aside, Ella watched Max struggle with the giant fir. He'd bought it for her, he'd said. Was she being stupid? Should she just carry on with Christmas, decorate the tree, forget about the photo, hope Max chose her, carry on and on until they had children and they were a family but then one Christmas he might say exactly the same as her dad had said to her mum that night as they sat on the stairs. And she suddenly found herself saying, 'Max, I can't do it.'

He paused. 'At least let's talk about this,' he said, holding the tree up precariously with one hand. 'It's not what it seems.' But then the tree slipped and crashed to the ground, the trunk smashing up against his precious smoked glass coffee table and shattering the right-hand corner. Max swore at the sound, then walked over and ran his hand along the crack. 'Shit look what it's done. Bollocks!'

Ever since he'd bought it at auction for a huge sum of money without consulting with her, Ella had hated that table and he knew it. It was a monstrosity. Now, the way he sat down on the arm of the grey velvet sofa it was as if it was the table and him against the world. As if she had started this in order to ruin the table. As if suddenly Max was the wronged party.

She heard him sigh, saw his shoulders slump. The tree lay sprawled across the carpet like a whale, Max kicked the trunk with his foot and it flopped off the smoked glass to the floor with a thump. 'It hasn't been right for ages.'

Suddenly she realised that she didn't want to hear this.

He ran a hand through his hair. 'I have been seeing someone but it's not an affair. We just get on. Ella, it's not the cause of this, it's a result of… I suppose I just… We get on.'

She wanted to quickly rewind to him ripping the netting and trying to impress her. She wanted it still to be all his fault. 'You get on? Don't we get on?' she said. Everyone

who saw them at parties always said how well they got on, how they were jealous of their relationship – the fact they didn't have to be glued to each other's side every second. They were free to do as they wanted.

'We did get on, really well, once.' Max scratched his head. 'We don't really get on any more, Els. We don't see each other.'

This wasn't what she wanted to happen. Was it too late to realise she could have turned a blind eye?

'We socialise together.'

'Well what do you and this girl do?'

Max paused. 'I don't know. We watch Gogglebox.'

'What? What the hell's Gogglebox?'

'Nothing.' He shook his head. 'Ella she likes me for me. She's not trying to make me better or improve me or make me try harder.'

Ella looked down at his shoes. She had bought them for him. 'I don't think you can make this my fault,' she said.

'I'm not making it your fault, I'm trying to explain that I think you're amazing, but we're not right for each other any more. I don't know you any more.'

'This is ridiculous.' Ella felt sick. She didn't want to be having this conversation. If she was honest she'd thought that Max would suggest relationship counselling, say they could work through it, anything not to upset the status quo – the perfect life they both enjoyed, or she had thought they both enjoyed.

She walked into the bedroom, pulled her wheely case out from under the bed and started throwing in clothes. Then she went to her dresser and scooped up some make-up and toiletries, adding them loose amongst the other stuff. She never packed like this. She grabbed her sleep mask and ear plugs from the bedside table and packed her passport just because it was there as well.

'Where are you going to go?'

'I don't know,' she said, pulling the case over the plush carpet, the wheels getting caught.

'Look, let me help you,' Max said, picking it up and walking with her to the door.

This wasn't the way it was meant to happen. He was meant to take the case back to the bedroom and insist she stay.

'It's probably a good thing if we have some time apart,' she said, her heart racing with uncertainty and panic. She needed to get her control back.

'Maybe you could go and stay with your dad?' Max suggested.

No she couldn't. She couldn't let Veronica see her like this. She couldn't turn up there like a failure, she couldn't face the brusque advice and the dusting down and the get back out there. She needed some time just to be nothing.

Outside it was raining – tipping it down – and the grey sky almost melted into the grey pavements. The Christmas lights on the lamppost outside their flat were broken and flickered on and off like a strobe. Ella stepped forwards and hailed a passing cab.

Max held on to the top of her arm. 'Will you be OK?'

'I'm always OK,' she said.

He narrowed his eyes as he looked at her, but she just gave him a small smile and pulled the door of the cab closed behind her.

'Where are we going?' the driver asked as he pulled away.

Where were they going?

An image sprang into her mind of blue sea and a little white building with terracotta tiles on the roof. A place she wouldn't have imagined running to in a million years. But where else would she go? It was Christmas – not a time to be staying on friends' sofas.

'To the airport, please,' she said, leaning her head back on the headrest.

'Which one?'

'Oh I don't know. Let me just call Dial a Flight.'

When they were on their way to Heathrow with an extortionate last minute ticket booked, Ella stared out the window at the pouring rain, felt the beat of her heart pound in her head and thought, *God, this is all actually real.*

CHAPTER 4

MADDY

The repairs to the yacht were going to cost all her savings and then some.

Her mum had had to top up the rest and was furious. While the unseasonably high winter temperatures had seen a massive spike in profits for this time of year, the flip side was the wild thunderstorms that had swept part of the back roof off and flooded the outhouses – the repairs had cost pretty much the entire summer and winter's profit. Maddy's yacht joyride, which had resulted in a huge dent in the side, had not only cost her mother but had proved her right – Maddy wasn't mature enough to go to London – but she didn't have the money to go now anyway.

Maddy was sitting in the garage. Bored and pissed off. If it was summer, going to work was no hardship. She worked on the boats, jumping from one to the other in an old t-shirt and frayed shorts, feet roughened from running on pebbles and over hot tarmac, face golden, hair thick with salt and bleached at the tips, laughing and shouting, oil streaking her arms, smelling of sun cream and swimming in the sea till sundown. But in the winter she worked in Spiros' garage – a shabby white building with green doors that were cracked and broken at the bottom – sanding, re-painting, fixing engines that tourists had given a beating during the holiday season. She had to listen to Spiros' dreadful choice of music as it blasted out of a paint splattered radio and every day shake her head when he asked her why she wasn't married yet and had no babies.

Spiros was on the mainland today though, delivering an engine, so Maddy was on her own. She had her own music on and the windows flung open that Spiros kept closed because the sun made the place too hot. But Maddy could cope with the heat if it meant having the view – probably one of the best on the island – out over the Mediterranean, a sheer drop down on the cliff edge and, at this time of year, accompanied by the sound of the waves crashing against the rocks.

As she leant on the window sill, looking down at the navy water, she pulled a letter out of her pocket. The headed paper said *Manhattans*, the double t shaped like the Empire State building. The job offer made it clear that the backing singing work was only for Christmas and that while they had been impressed with her audition tape and there might be occasions where she was required to perform solo, there was no guarantee of this. They reserved the right to replace her at any point. The address was in Soho. 15 Greek Street. She'd thought it was fate when she'd written back to accept.

This was her dream – of making it big. Of singing somewhere other than Dimitri's bar where regulars chatted over her and sometimes her granddad got up and joined in. She wanted the big city and the men in suits, the money, the fame and bright neon lights.

Her sister, Ella, had emailed a Christmas card seemingly just to brag that they were celebrating their anniversary at Claridge's. Maddy had Googled the restaurant, Fera, and picked what she would have ordered on the menu.

The '*dry-aged Herdwick hogget, sweetbread, cucumber, yoghurt and blackberry*' purely because she didn't know what hogget was and presumed that her sister would know. She wanted to walk down Oxford Street, go to Selfridges and see a whole floor devoted to shoes. She wanted to see the Carnaby Street Christmas lights for real, not just on her sister's Instagram.

But most of all she wanted to be picked to sing on a stage because someone thought she had talent, not just because they were related to her. She wanted someone to verify what she hoped, that she was a bit better than average, and whoever that was going to be, she wasn't going to find them in a tiny bar on a Greek island in winter.

This letter was the first rung on her ladder.

It was possibility.

And now it was just bits of paper falling from the window down into the sea.

CHAPTER 5

ELLA

The stewardess was wearing a Santa hat. The captain wished them a Merry Christmas after he hit the runway a little too fast. And everyone was handed a Quality Street as they exited the plane. Ella waved a hand in refusal, then paused as she stood at the top of the metal stairs. It wasn't hot like mid-summer hot, but it was certainly warm enough to make her wish she wasn't wearing 100 denier tights. She breathed in through her nose, pushed her sunglasses up on her greasy hair and had to steady herself on the banister for a moment. The smell of airline fuel, the hiss of the bus brakes, a great wide sky – the type you don't get in England. The type that stretches on and on and up into infinite possibility. A wisp of cloud like chalk on a blackboard.

She hadn't been to Greece without Max for over a decade, and suddenly he seemed like a beautiful shield reflecting the attention and keeping her at a nice, safe distance. She felt like she'd left her armour at the Pimlico flat and was standing there naked.

'Can you keep moving please, don't stop on the stairs,' the stewardess called out.

In Arrivals her iPhone buzzed like a starving baby bird. A hundred messages from Adrian about the Obeille mobile phone account. No one could do it but her. They were floundering. They were going to lose it. He knew she was on holiday but could she possibly…

Nothing from Max.

Out the front of the airport was a snaking queue of taxis. As Ella waited for the two drivers at the front of the line to stop arguing she could feel a trickle of sweat down her back and glanced up at the unseasonable sunshine. She looked over the road at the familiar line of palm trees combing the air as a welcome breeze picked up, the weatherbeaten coffee stall where people stood at the counter and drank thick coffee from tiny glasses rimmed with gold, the scratch of grass where a group of men played backgammon in the shade of the palm, and thought how usually there was a driver holding a sign with Max's name on it.

In the car, the driver chatted away almost to himself as she stared out the window watching the landmarks whizz by; a strip of beach lined with a couple of tourist bars, most closed for the season, the school on the bend that she'd been so jealous of Maddy going to while Ella was at boarding school – lonely, confused, forgotten – where she was forced to play lacrosse in the snow and eat liver the colour of petrol.

She was still looking out at other little shops and cafes along the drive she recognised when the driver turned up the road to her mum's village. Ella had to look back to check the sign was right, it seemed too soon. The road was rutted and the drive bouncy. She felt a bit sick as they jumped along, the lush vegetation gleaming in the bright sunshine. As they turned the corner into the main square, she saw Christmas lights hanging from one street lamp to the next and bunting flickering in the breeze around the square. Out in the bay three great statues of boats sat ready to light up at dusk as part of the Christmas decorations. Ella paid the cab and wandered out past a row of shabby white houses on her right draped with the odd sprig of parched brown bougainvillea. Bypassing the church on her left and the shuttered-up tourist shop, she was being pulled to the view ahead of her like the grubby looking dog that limped past, its nose sniffing along the ground leaving a line like a snake track in the red dust.

A half-moon bay curved like a sleeping cat below her. Frothy white horses glistened in the late afternoon sunlight as if flecked with diamonds and rolled over plump, pale pebbles that rattled like bones as the water pushed them, chattering, up the beach. Little fishing boats, the colours you'd paint them in primary school, bobbed on their moorings, just a couple of them like knitting grannies, nodding up and down as the waves gently tumbled. It was impossible to see where the sky met the sea.

She realised that she had never been here in winter before. She was used to two weeks of bubbling sun, flocks of tourists and the roaring hum of cicadas. But as she looked out over the horizon, flecked with prickly pears and plants like aliens, fronds jutting out at crazy angles and precariously perched on the side of the rocks, she realised how silent it was. How quiet. How exposed. How perhaps this was a terrible mistake.

'Ella?' A familiar voice said.

She turned to look in the direction of a dirty big garage, the green doors padlocked and the neon sign flickering. Her younger sister was walking towards her, looking as cool and calm as she always did. Hair pulled into a messy bun, long tanned limbs hanging weightlessly, freckles over her nose, gap between her front teeth that she could slide a penny into. Young, gangly, immature, beautiful Maddy.

'Hi,' Ella said, feeling suddenly sweaty and awkward in her now crumpled shirt and pencil skirt that she'd been wearing at the office. Her feet pinched in her shoes, the polished leather dirty with dust. 'I just arrived.'

'No kidding.' Maddy raised a brow. 'Does Mum know you're coming?'

Ella felt instantly defensive. 'No. I wanted it to be a surprise.'

Maddy gave her a look that Ella interpreted as both mocking and bemused. 'She'll be surprised all right. Isn't it your anniversary? Is Max here?'

Ella shook her head. 'Yes, but we went out last night because he had a big deal come up at work,' she lied, the rehearsed words rushing out too quickly. She paused, took a breath to calm herself down. 'He's flying out later,' she added, and instinctively her hand wrapped around her phone and she looked down to check it again. No messages. In fact barely any signal at all. She could feel Maddy watching her, looking her up and down. She wished that she'd changed into something more casual before getting on the plane. She felt foolish in her work clothes in contrast to Maddy's laid-back ease.

Maddy shrugged. 'I'm going there now. You can follow me.'

Ella nodded, hating the fact she was unfamiliar with the network of back streets. When they came to stay they stayed at the five star hotel at the next beach where bougainvillea poured like cherryade over the balconies, the waiters knew their names and there were aperitifs in the bar at six. Max always hired a boat and they would zoom up to the jetty, an arcing wake behind them, and she would step out wearing a sparkly maxi dress and a big sunhat and Max would tip one of the little kids on the jetty to tie up the boat and make sure it was secure because, while he liked to mess around, showing off in his speedboat, he wasn't the best sailor and had no idea how to moor or when to drop anchor.

But now it was just her. Following her sister. Going to see her mum. And she realised that she was nervous. The thought popped into her head as suddenly as the view of the taverna appeared before her, and, as she pushed it away, she found herself caught. Staring, involuntarily, at the sprawling building. She hadn't looked at it in years. Really taken it in. Seen the terrace that led out into the sea like it was floating on the water and the lattice of vines that stretched up along one wall. The beautiful terracotta tiled roof that curved like waves and thick wooden beams that her mum had strung with coloured lights that swayed gently in the breeze. The stone walls had been whitewashed since she'd last been there but *The Little Greek Kitchen* had been slapped on the side in yellow paint, the same as always.

Maddy had come up with the name and Ella remembered being so jealous. Her suggestions had seemed so lame in comparison.

'Are you coming?' Maddy asked as they reached the front door.

Ella had paused. Realising that she'd already been rejected once that day, she suddenly felt like a glutton for punishment, going in for more.

'Yes,' she said, putting her shoulders back and smoothing down her skirt, refusing to acknowledge Maddy's curious glance.

It was the smell that knocked Ella for six. Warm pastry cracking and bursting in the oven and cheese melting into a soft, spongy goo. Summers spent sitting on the veranda of a villa they rented stuffing little filo pies into her mouth and jumping into the pool while her dad barbecued and her mum sat in the shade rubbing sun cream into Maddy's tiny arms, wearing an old white linen shirt and no make-up, and looking stunning. It was on this island that Ella had dipped Maddy's toes into the sea when she was a baby, it was where she'd reluctantly agreed to go on the donut rides that she hated so that Maddy would have someone with her, where she'd taught Maddy to play the card game *Slam!* and let her beat her just to be nice, and where, on the plane on the way home, she had held Maddy's hand and listed all the good things they were going home to when she cried about the holiday being over.

As Maddy and her mum stood side by side now, Maddy having gone over and tapped Sophie on the shoulder, Ella could see that their likeness had only got stronger as they got older. That even in looks now, she was the odd one out.

'What is it?' Sophie frowned, rubbing her hands clean on a tea-towel. 'Why aren't you at work?'

Maddy nodded towards the doorway.

Ella was standing between her granddad who was snoozing in an old armchair and a big bunch of conifer leaves that had been thrust into a pot of oasis and decorated like a Christmas tree, white lights sparkling, tiny rainbow coloured baubles winking as they bobbed in the breeze, and on the top branch the big gold star her dad had bought bound on with wire.

'Ella,' Sophie said, hair all wild and scrunched up in a knot on top of her head, wearing a pale purple sweatshirt pushed up at the sleeves, and a pair of stone-washed jeans that had gone full circle since the eighties and looked fashionable again. She came round to give her a hug, which Ella found herself unable to reciprocate. Caught off-guard by the gesture, she stood rigid. Her mum stood back and smiled. 'How lovely to see you. What a nice surprise,' she added, as if Ella appearing out the blue was perfectly normal.

'She's brought a case with her,' Maddy said, as if Ella wasn't there at all. A look passed between the two of them like a secret language.

'Are you staying with us?' her mum asked.

Ella was too distracted thinking that she wished for a moment that her mum could look at her like she'd just looked at Maddy and know what she was thinking. Know the crazy emotions whizzing round her head about Max without her having to say anything.

'If it's not too much trouble.'

'It would be no trouble at all. We're fully booked at the moment because of this weather…' Her mum pointed out the window towards the slowly sinking sun, '…but you are more than welcome to share the upstairs room with Maddy.'

'Really?' Maddy, who had been leaning against the larder door chewing on a stick of celery, suddenly stood up straight, her brows drawn together in a frown.

Ella nodded. 'Oh don't worry, I can try to find a room elsewhere.'

Maddy shook her head. 'It's fine.'

'There's nothing, Ella.' Her mum shook her head. 'Of the apartments that haven't closed for the season, there's nothing left. People are even letting out their own bedrooms to cash in at the moment. Honestly, the room upstairs is lovely and quite big enough for the two of you.'

Maddy turned away and stood in the doorway with her back to them.

A yellow-eyed white cat jumped down from the sea wall and sauntered over to weave its way through Maddy's legs.

Before Ella could come up with a reasonable excuse and start calling round the hotel chains, there was a sudden hacking cough from next to her and a snorting sound that seemed to signal her grandfather waking up. 'Jesus Christ,' he said. 'I forgot where I was for a second.' Then rubbing the sleep from his eyes, he sat up further in his chair, reached for his glasses on the table next to him and said, 'Well if it isn't Eleanor, goodness me, look at you. All dressed up for this old place.' He laughed, all croaky and husky, and Ella realised it wasn't just her mother that she hadn't seen, but also him and her grandmother who had gone by the wayside of her life. 'You here, Maddy in London. I don't know. Can't keep up with any of you.'

Ella watched Maddy's head shoot up with a look of horror.

'I didn't know you were going to London, Maddy,' Ella said, wondering whether she would have told her she was in town. Would she have asked to meet up? Would Ella have agreed? Her next thought was that she didn't want Maddy in London. London was hers, she thought. Then much deeper down, a tiny bit of her said that it wanted to make sure that she wasn't going there on her own, Maddy would be completely out of her depth. In the last however many years she'd only been off the island to go to Athens, as far as Ella knew. She ignored that voice.

'She's not going,' Sophie said, emphatically, walking back to the counter, pausing to stroke Maddy's hair absentmindedly as she went past.

Ella frowned as she watched Maddy glance to one side, her jaw seemingly locked rigid in place.

Instinctively Ella reached up and touched her ponytail, greasy now from travelling, and wondered when the last time her mum had stroked her hair was.

Her phone beeped.

She pulled her hand away from her ponytail and was reading the text in an instant.

Max.

Please don't stay away too long. We should talk some more. Where are you?

It was like a scene in ER. The phone defibrillating her heart back to life. Her blood was suddenly pumping through her veins again. Like she'd reached the surface of normality and could breathe.

'I've just got to reply to this, sorry, it's work,' she said, stepping outside for a second.

Believe it or not, I'm in Corfu. I need a couple of days at least to think. Ella wrote.

Corfu? Blimey, you don't mess around. Understood re: time to think. I'll be at the club, flat too weird without you.

She smiled as she put the phone back in her bag. They could sort it out. They could have that dinner at Claridge's and talk it all through. They could get back on track. Back in their perfect life. She would turn a blind eye to this small hiccup. In the cold light of her mum and Maddy's life in Corfu, suddenly home with Max seemed like the only place she belonged, and she couldn't wait to get back.

She walked back into the dark coolness of the room and said, 'I'm only here for a couple of days actually, so Maddy it shouldn't put you out too much.' She was the guest, she was the mature one, and she was blowed if poor little Maddy wanting her room all to herself was going to force her out.

'Lovely.' Her mum smiled, glancing up from where she was dipping little baby squids in batter. 'Do you want a glass of something?' she asked. 'Red wine? Beer? Retsina?'

For a moment Ella thought how lovely it would be to just be able to sit down, pour a glass of chilled white wine into a little glass, pick at a plate of plump purple olives and silver anchovies and gossip and laugh and giggle like she remembered her parents and their friends doing. When she would watch from the door and then her mum would catch her and she would be called into the room and she'd think she was in trouble, but actually they'd offer her something to eat and she'd perch on a chair in her nightie and they'd ask her questions and tell her jokes before her mum would take her hand, soft and warm, and put her back to bed.

But instead she said, 'Do you think I could just go up to the room? I'd really like to get changed, you know I'm here straight from work.' She could feel her grandfather watching her. Could sense Maddy hanging around by the back door listening. Could see the look of disappointment flash across her mum's face before she nodded and said cooly, 'Of course you can. Maddy, sweetheart, can you show Ella upstairs?'

CHAPTER 8

MADDY

Maddy hated seeing her mum upset. Dimitri would always be like, 'She's fine, look at her, she's smiling…' but Maddy could tell by the tilt of her head or the way she would swallow and look away. Maddy's emotions were written all over her face but her mum and Ella, they had a way of just hinting at what was brewing underneath and it drove her crazy. Mainly because they were usually the cause of each other's upset.

'You could have had a drink,' Maddy said as she sat down on the wooden chair next to the dressing table in the upstairs room.

'I wasn't thirsty,' Ella replied without turning round. She'd put her suitcase on the small single bed in the corner that Maddy used as a sofa.

Maddy sat toying with a hair grip on the table. The idea of sharing a room with Ella made her nervous. She never knew the right thing to say to her. Got muddled and intimidated, which almost always led to her saying the wrong thing.

Dimitri once asked Maddy why she let Ella get to her. Maddy had shrugged and said, 'I don't know.' But she did know. Because on the one hand Ella terrified her, but on the other hand Maddy so desperately wanted to be liked by her again.

And it was exactly this awkward desire to please that led Maddy to say, 'You can have my bed.' Pointing towards the big double bed in the centre of the room, white gauze curtains hanging either side like a canopy, the material rippling in the breeze from the open French windows that looked out over the sea.

'No, I wouldn't dream of it.' Ella still had her back turned to her. Maddy watched as she unpacked. A weird selection of stuff, but all of it the most beautiful quality. A kaftan that sparkled in the evening light, a wide-legged silk pantsuit that draped like pouring water, a couple of pairs of jeans and the odd pot of moisturiser. She tried not to be jealous but she couldn't help it, envy seemed to constrict her throat.

'So...' Ella said as she carried on unpacking and arranging, 'Tell me about London.'

Maddy didn't want to tell her. Didn't want to say it out loud because to Ella it would seem so nothing. A couple of nights singing in a bar. She would look at her as if she was crazy. Little Maddy in the big city attempting to follow a dream. She'd probably tell her not to get caught up in a prostitution ring or agree to any topless modelling. The idea actually made her smile a little – she remembered when the two of them sent off for a modelling competition in *Just Seventeen* magazine. Taking each other's pictures and pouting for the camera. Where had they been when they'd taken them? She narrowed her eyes as she tried to picture the photographs. There was cream wallpaper with gold stars. There were advent calendars that said Joyeux Noel at the top in swirly writing. Her dad's flat. They had been staying at her dad's flat in Battersea. They were meant to be having dinner with his new girlfriend, Veronica. When they'd got to the restaurant Maddy had refused to eat anything.

When she looked up Ella was watching her, a collection of toiletries cradled in her arms. 'Oh it's nothing,' Maddy said, shrugging the question off. 'I was going to go but I've had some cash flow difficulties.'

After that neither of them said anything for a while. A hundred different things to say floated in and out of Maddy's head. She wanted to ask how their dad was, whether he was still with Veronica. She wanted to ask why Ella had appeared out the blue without Max, she wanted to know what she'd eaten at Claridge's, if she'd even gone. Most of all though, looking at all of Ella's beautiful stuff, she wanted her to be the kind of sister that she could ask, *will you lend me the money to go to London*. But instead she said, 'I'll get you some sheets.'

Dinner was as awkward as Maddy had thought it would be. Her mum had laid the big table in the kitchen – covered it in candles and white china and sprigs of olive in vases. In the centre of the table was a big, bubbling moussaka and a ceramic bowl of Greek salad, the olives from the grove on the hillside, the feta from Dimitri's goats.

Ella had changed into a long sleeved blue and white striped top, loafers and skinny white jeans with a thin red belt. Maddy thought she looked like she'd just stepped out of the pages of a J Crew catalogue.

'So how's work, Eleanor?' her grandmother asked after they'd all been served and Ella had asked for a much smaller portion so hers had been passed round to her grandfather.

'Great, the company's not doing quite as well as it could but if we can land this new account we'll be sorted for the fiscal year. It's a mobile phone company.'

Her grandmother made a face as if to show she thought that all sounded very clever and important.

'I'll work on it while I'm out here,' Ella added as her
phone rang, almost on cue, and she nipped outside to
answer it.

'Bloody phones,' her grandfather muttered.

'You all right, Mum?' Maddy asked when Ella was out
the room. She'd noticed she was just pushing the moussaka
around her plate and seemed restless, on high alert trying
to do everything to please Ella. The kitchen, Maddy
noticed, was spotless. Not that it was usually dirty, but
it was gleaming. And on the sideboard her mum had put
out the nativity set they'd had as kids and a tacky plastic
angel with fibre-optic wings that Maddy hadn't seen
for years twinkled in the low lighting. They always did
a kind of haphazard Christmas. Her mum would throw a
big party at the taverna on Christmas Eve and do a mix of
Greek and English food and all the locals would come, but
on Christmas Day it was just their family and they'd have
lobsters and fresh fish, and her mum would decorate the
place with lights and glass bowls of pomegranates, she'd
scatter olive branches and hellebore flowers along the
mantlepiece and string mussel shells that she'd gilded with
gold leaf along the windows and glass hearts, almost too
delicate to touch, in front of the mirror.

The nativity set though, Maddy didn't even know her
mum had kept that. It was only seeing it now that she
realised how much their Christmas trimmings had changed.
Or perhaps, she thought, watching her mum watch Ella as
she talked quietly into her phone outside, her mum had
consciously created new traditions.

CHAPTER 9

ELLA

It all felt too much as Ella walked back into the kitchen.

The phone call had been from Gerald Austin, the husband of the woman Max was having an affair with. He'd wanted to know how Ella was going to proceed. He was filing for divorce.

'You know they're together now?' he'd said, his cut-glass accent splitting through her, and she'd hung up.

Inside she noticed the nativity set for the first time and it made her feel even worse. The idea of Maddy and her mum laying it out every Christmas together, the little sheep with one broken leg and the horse that she'd etched her name in the bottom with a safety pin and the Jesus that they'd fought over, that Maddy had drawn a moustache on with felt tip pen and that she'd tried to wash off with Mr Muscle before her mum saw it. She wanted to box it all up and carry it upstairs and stuff it in her suitcase.

As she sat down she felt all eyes on her. Her mum watching expectantly. 'Everything all right, Ella? Can I get you anything? I can heat up the moussaka if it's gone cold, if you want?' she asked, and her polite willingness to please her made Ella even more defensive.

She didn't want to be treated like the guest.

After the divorce her dad had gone to live in a flat in Battersea. Maddy and Ella had lived with their mum who was just about coping with it all. Then a year later their dad had met Veronica and their mum, rocked by this news, was then pushed over the edge completely by the sudden death of her sister. Ella had watched the whole thing from the sidelines, struggling to fit in at a flash all girls' school where she'd got a scholarship and just wanting her family back together and her mum back to normal. But instead of that, her mum upped sticks and moved to Corfu, her dad's business skyrocketed and her parents agreed that it was in Ella's best interests to become a boarder at the school she quietly hated. Her holidays were initially spent on the island with her mum and sister but that changed the more she was picked up from the airport, sitting in the back while Maddy tuned the radio to songs her and her mum knew the words to and Ella had never heard. Never knowing where anything was kept in the cupboards, unsure who the locals were, no idea what was happening in the programmes they watched on TV. The more she felt like the guest. And the more she resented having to go. The more she went on school trips or stayed with her father and Veronica instead, living out of her suitcase in the plush, cream spare bedroom of their swanky flat.

'So Maddy, what was the cash flow problem?' Ella asked, trying to deflect the attention from herself, as she shook her head at her mum's offer to reheat the pasta and played with a slice of aubergine with her fork.

'She smashed a boat onto some rocks earlier in the week. Blew her life savings,' her granddad said without looking up from where he was hoovering up his moussaka. 'Fabulous food, Sophie, as always, just fabulous.'

'It's for the best,' her mum cut in as she leant over and picked up the salad bowl, passing it round the table. 'London wouldn't suit Maddy at all.'

'I am here,' Maddy said, arms outstretched. 'I am at the table you know? And I think I could handle it. I'm not nine any more.'

Her grandmother looked up warily at her mother, gave her the kind of look that suggested that Maddy was right and her mum was wrong. Ella watched the dynamics round the table like she did a boardroom meeting, sussing out allegiances. Her grandfather just gave a snort and went back to his food, pouring himself more wine.

Ella sat back, arms crossed in front of her, wine glass dangling from between her fingers and surveyed the frown on Maddy's face. Noticed how the lines in her forehead were just starting to stay even when she relaxed and her cheeks were more chiseled, less babyish. It almost surprised Ella that Maddy wasn't nine any more.

Her mum was glancing over at Maddy as if trying to tie her where she was with just a look. But Maddy looked like a bird, too big for its nest.

The feeling that her mum had never looked at her like that was as unexpectedly sharp as Amanda's husband's comments on the phone. And it made Ella say, 'I'll lend you the money', without really even thinking about it.

Her mum's head whipped round. Maddy's eyes flicked up. Her grandmother's eyes closed for a second too long. Her grandfather kept eating.

'You won't,' her mum said, quickly.

'Oh my God that would be amazing.' Maddy visibly jumped from her seat but then sat down again because her and Ella didn't hug or exchange physical contact in any way.

'You don't have anywhere to stay,' her mum said.

Ella took a sip of her wine, watched Maddy flounder as she considered her lack of lodgings. 'She can stay at my flat. Max isn't there,' she said.

'Really?' Maddy had to roll her lips together to contain her smile.

Ella shrugged as if it was nothing. Why had she done it? Because, she realised, the memories had hit her harder than she'd expected and, just for once, she wanted her mum to herself. To see what it was like not being the guest. She had never been here on her own, without Maddy, without Max, and she got that feeling, like she did so often at work, that this was an opportunity that she should grab. She had this small window of time to try and understand what it was she had missed. What had been taken away from her. And she couldn't do it with Maddy here. Not with the little looks and in-jokes that passed between them.

The fact that her mum was shooting her a fierce look at that moment would have to be ignored for now.

As Maddy was topping up her wine and toasting with her granddad – who then reached over and touched the top of Ella's glass with his, saying, 'Good on you,' – another male voice cut across the room.

'What are we celebrating?'

Ella turned in her seat to see a guy lounging against the doorway in cargo shorts and a light blue shirt, his sleeves rolled up to reveal a tattoo of a compass that traced halfway up his right forearm. Hair shaggy, dark and wet, either recently washed or he'd just come out of the sea. Stubble not quite obscuring a razor sharp jaw. Nose like a horse's: long and aquiline with a small hook. A nose like that and you either stand proud and tall or wither and die. Eyes too dark to see from this distance but clearly looking her way.

No way could it be, she decided.

If it was, then this could be really embarrassing.

I hope it's not him, Ella thought.

An image of herself at fifteen. Doe eyes and puppy fat.

Cocky, bad-tempered Dimitri who would click his fingers sullenly for the ropes of their boats and eight-year-old Maddy would ask him if he wanted her lemonade, giggling, while awkward teenage Ella crossed her arms over her waist where she was sitting in her bikini and try and look at him from under her eyelashes like she'd seen Princess Diana do in her interview. He would sneer at them and stalk away, hanging around watching with his whispering and laughing gang of friends.

Dimitri sauntered into the kitchen, all louche and relaxed. And Ella looked down at her plate, wishing that he was in Athens, where she thought he was happily settled – never to be seen again. She pursed her lips and put her shoulders back as he came closer, dark and handsome and butterscotch tanned.

'Dimitri, you remember Ella don't you?' Maddy said. She had the wine glass up to her lips so Ella couldn't see if she was smiling.

Dimitri sat himself down in the seat her mum had just vacated like he owned the place, flipped it round backwards and leant against the frame. Then he cocked his head to one side and seemed to study her.

Green.

His eyes were the colour of freshly cut grass.

'Eleanor?' he nodded. 'How could I forget?'

Ella found her mouth would only stretch into the slightest of smiles and thanked God it was dark in there because her cheeks had unexpectedly turned luminous red. 'I think I remember you...' she said vaguely. She saw his lips quirk up and knew immediately that he knew she was lying.

'Of course, why would I think you would remember. Stupid me.' He held out a hand, green eyes dancing like imps. 'Dimitri.'

'Yes of course.' Ella took a sip of water because her throat was suddenly really dry, and then reached forward to shake his hand.

His skin was rough and dry, and his hold on her was completely different to being touched by Max. While her hand was in his it was like she couldn't speak. Like her brain had been momentarily switched off and she was paralysed, like one of those spiders who injects their mate with poison, except nicer than that. And more stressful at the same time.

'Are you hot, Ella?' her granddad asked.

'No not at all,' she said, pulling her hand back and sitting on it. 'It's…' she rubbed her cheek with her other hand and felt the warmth radiating from it, but couldn't think of any reasonable excuse.

If there was one thing she didn't need to be reminded of, it was her fifteen-year-old self.

Dimitri leant forward, seemingly unabashed by the whole previous thirty seconds, and scooped up some moussaka with a spare fork. 'So…' he said with his mouth full. 'What are you celebrating?'

'I'm going to London.'

'Ahh.' He nodded. 'I should have guessed. I suppose you have something to do with this?' He turned again to look at Ella and she found herself having to look away.

'I erm–' she stumbled.

'Ella is paying for Maddy to go,' Sophie said, coming over to the table with bowls full of creamy, white yoghurt and dried figs like squashed bruises and setting them down with a smack on the centre of the table. 'And in doing so taking my best waitress,' she went on as if it was that, rather than just little Maddy leaving, was the problem. She picked up the remains of the moussaka as Dimitri reached up for a last scoopful, her lips tight, her eyes a little red. 'Which no one seems to have thought through at all.'

'Agatha could do it,' Maddy said, her hand stilled on her wine glass, clearly afraid it was all about to fall through because Agatha was so moody they tended to only draft her in when it was super busy, and even then she never took the orders.

'Agatha couldn't do it, Maddy. She can't be front of house. You know that. She scares all the customers away and if there's one thing I need at the moment, it's customers.'

There was a pause.

'Yes.' Her mum nodded. 'Thank you for thinking of me through all this.'

Maddy looked down at the table. Dimitri raised a brow like he'd just walked into a storm and was trying not to smile in the face of the tension.

The white cat trotted into the kitchen and Ella, keen to avoid being a part of the conversation, leant down to stroke it but it darted away, pausing in the far corner of the room where it winked one eye before jumping up on the windowsill to settle down to sleep.

Her mum seemed to be taking her annoyance out on the yoghurt, scooping big dollops of it into little blue and white painted bowls, thrusting them at Maddy who passed them on like a pass-the-parcel.

'Well it's obvious,' her grandfather said, reaching forward to spoon some figs into his bowl, his lip turned up at the corner as if they were all stupid. 'Ella'll do it. Won't she? Won't you? You're here. May as well make yourself useful.'

'Waitressing?' Ella said with horror before she could stop herself.

There was a pause.

The only noise was the hum of the motor that made the fibre-optic angel wings glow.

'Yes Ella, waitressing. If that's not beneath you,' her mum said without looking at Ella at all. And for the first time Ella realised that perhaps alienating her mother wasn't the best way to get her to notice her.

CHAPTER 10

MADDY

The plane had to circle three times before it could land. Snow was causing havoc at the airport and the runway needed to be cleared. No more planes were taking off. The wind was shaking the aircraft, juddering the wings.

Maddy closed her eyes and held onto her armrests. She'd never been on a plane on her own before. The last time she'd flown had been coming back from her one and only trip to visit her dad, seemingly a lifetime ago. And she'd had Ella with her to hold her hand.

She forced herself to open her eyes and look out the window. To marvel at the sight of London below her, like a map speckled with white. *Take it all in, Maddy.*

She glanced at the person next to her and gave them a little smile. The woman turned her lips up but then looked away, as if embarrassed that they'd had any contact.

Maddy went back to looking out the window.

When they finally landed, the captain wished them happy holidays and the flight attendants had Santa's elf hats on and big tins of Quality Street. Maddy paused at the entrance of the tunnel that led them out of the plane and into Arrivals, cramming an orange cream into her mouth and wishing she'd paused over her selection more carefully and got that big purple one with the hazelnut in the middle of caramel. The taste of the chocolate mingled with the residue of fear in her mouth and she rested her hand on the side of the plane just to catch her breath.

'Please keep moving, there's a place to pause as you exit the tunnel.' The flight attendant ushered her forward. But Maddy just moved to the side, let the people in suits and the guys with big Beats headphones and relatives with bags of presents push past her. She took a deep breath and inhaled the stale smell of aeroplane food, harsh chemical cleaner and the sharp tang of fuel, she felt the icy blast of air around the edge of the tunnel and the engulfing heat of the airport and she thought, *this is it, I'm here. I've made it.*

Someone pushed into her back and she stumbled forward, catching her arm on the sharp metal edge and nicking her jumper. The person didn't apologise, they just kept on walking, their iPhone pressed up to their ear.

'Hey, thanks a lot,' she shouted, pulling up her sleeve to inspect the damage to her skin. Someone else sighed when they couldn't get past her and muttered, 'Jesus woman, get a move on.'

She glanced over her shoulder to look at who'd said it, and a small guy with a red sports jacket and a crime novel under his arm stared back at her, eyes wide, 'Come on!' he chivvied again. 'Jesus H Christ.'

Maddy made a face. 'It's Christmas. Be nice.'

He pushed past her.

She shook her head in disgust but made herself forget about it. Some idiot shouting at her couldn't put a dent in her excitement. Ditto her throbbing arm.

The airport was stark but to Maddy it was stunning. Exotic. Romantic. Beautifully monochrome. Outside the sun-flecked grey sky shimmered like granite. Planes on the runway were wrapped in wisps of cotton wool fog. It was no longer snowing but the ground was covered with white, crisscrossed with tyre tracks of black slush.

Inside it smelt like stale air and possibility. Coke machines buzzed bright. Maddy stood on the travelator, flattening herself against the edge so that people could march past with their wheely bags, her hand pressing on her scratched arm, wondering why everyone was in such a hurry, why they weren't pausing to drink it all in. The travelator rumbled on at a snail's pace, allowing her to absorb all the posters advertising perfumes and Scotch whisky, then one came up for the Michael Buble Christmas album, and then another for carols at the Royal Albert Hall complete with fanfare trumpeters, and then there was an advert for Harrods, presents wrapped up in their sludge green and gold, and then Chanel, white snowflakes falling on some really stunning celebrity whose name was on the tip of her tongue. A poster for Christmas markets along the Southbank showed people all wrapped up in scarves and gloves pointing at treasures on stalls in little wooden huts. Maddy could feel the Christmassiness rising up inside her. It was going to be amazing.

At the end of the corridor was a model red bus and a stack of fliers for a London city tour. A man in a chauffeur's hat and a badge saying, 'Ask me about the Christmas bus! All aboard!' was leaning up against the edge of the stand, surreptitiously checking his phone. When Maddy took a flier he didn't even look up.

'Is it good?' she asked, turning the flier over and seeing pictures of Regent Street and the London Eye all glowing with lights.

'Dunno. Never been,' he said, sliding his phone into his pocket and then readjusting his hat. Maddy raised a brow. 'You're really selling it to me.'

He shrugged.

'Well I'll take my chance,' she said with a laugh as she walked away, folding the flier into her pocket – even he couldn't tarnish the shine. She wandered on, joined the snaking queue for passport control and whiled away the time thinking about open-topped bus rides in the snow, walking into the Royal Albert Hall in some kind of full-length gown and pearls, and sipping *vin chaud* along the Southbank while buying trinkets and... what was that picture on the flier? She turned it over – yep, ice-skating in front of the London Eye.

It was going to be the best Christmas ever.

'I'm sorry madam, that's all the baggage that's been unloaded.'

Maddy bit her bottom lip. She'd been watching the hatch, waiting for her luggage to appear for the last forty minutes. 'It can't be. My bag's not here.'

'That's all the baggage that was on the plane, madam,' a woman in a creased white shirt and black trousers said with just enough sympathy to make sure it all stayed official. 'I can give you a form to fill in and we can send the bag to you when we've located it.'

'Well, where is it?' Maddy said, plaintive. Tiredness was beginning to catch up with her.

The woman gave a tight smile. 'I assure you madam, we'll do everything we can to locate the luggage.'

Maddy looked at her name badge. 'Janice. Please. I really need my bag. It has my clothes and stuff.' The bag had Maddy's life in it. It had her music, it had her favourite books, her clothes for her new job. She closed her eyes because for a moment she thought she might cry. She was exhausted, it was late, she was hungry. And, to her shame, she suddenly really missed her home.

She thought back to her send off. Dimitri had appeared with his Jeep and thrown her bag into the back. Her mum had stood in front of her and said, 'If it doesn't work out Maddy, just come straight back. Just get on a plane. OK?'

And Maddy, about to give her a hug, had pulled back and said, 'Why can't you just say, good luck? Why do you have to presume that I'm going to fail?' She'd looked away for a moment, seeing the fronds of the Christmas branches sticking out from the taverna doorway, the big gold star wobbling from its precarious perch on the top, and realised with a jolt that for the first time in years she wasn't going to be home for Christmas.

'I don't think you're going to fail, Maddy, I'm just–' Her mum paused, wiped her hands on her apron, 'I'm going to miss you is all.'

For a moment Maddy had wanted to wave Dimitri away, tell him that she no longer needed a lift. But then Ella had stepped forward out of the darkness and leant against the doorframe, watching. And something had ridden up inside Maddy. The same thing that had made her apply for the job in the first place. The need to prove herself. The need to go and see who she could become, just as Ella had done.

'I'd better go,' she'd said, 'I don't want to miss my plane.' Then she'd smiled and stepped forward and given her mum a hug. Felt the familiar sharpness of her shoulder blades and softness of her waist, the enveloping comfort of Penhaligon's Orange Blossom and Pantene and the warmth of the kiss on her cheek. 'Bye Mum.' She'd had to look up to the sky with big wide eyes to dry the moisture.

'Bye honey. Good luck.' Her mum had taken a step back, her arms crossed in front of her.

Maddy had jumped into the Jeep and when Dimitri had been clearly about to ask if she was OK, she'd given him a look, and he'd slipped into first and they'd driven off up the hill. Her mum and the taverna getting smaller and smaller in the wing mirror.

'Are you all right, madam?' She felt Janice's hand on her shoulder. Her bottom lip wobbled.

Come on, Maddy. She shouted at herself in her head. *Grow up. This is your big adventure. Don't you dare cry. Don't you dare.*

'Yes, thanks, I'm fine.' Maddy nodded.

'Come on,' Janice said, giving her arm a little squeeze. 'I think I've got some mince pies at the desk.'

CHAPTER 11

ELLA

'You tie it up behind you.' Ella saw Dimitri's lips twitch in a smile as she picked up her apron.

'I can see that, thank you.' She thought of her last holiday where she'd stayed at a five-star boutique yurt in the Serengeti. Max had been upset when he hadn't seen all of the Big Five. She stood in the entrance to the taverna, the sky a sharp wintery blue, the remains of old swifts' nests cluttering the eaves of the awning, Dimitri sitting with the ankle of one leg crossed over the knee of his other, sipping an espresso, the smells of home-baked croissants, thick cut toast and gloopy marmalade, strong coffee and cigarettes swirling like smoke through the cool of the morning – making her nose suddenly wrinkle up with unexpected emotion. She had a sudden flash of her ten-year-old self here on holidays, belting into the sea dragging a windsurfer behind her, the only complication in her life being how to get the bloody sail to stay up as she wobbled in the water.

She was fumbling trying to tie a bow in her apron round her back, realising that her white jeans might not have been the best idea for her first day waitressing, when a young, good-looking couple walked past and said, 'Hi there.' The woman was in a thin black cashmere top and long shorts while the man wore chinos and a polo shirt with the collar turned up, a sweater was slung round his shoulders and aviator sunglasses looped into his button hole. They were clearly staying at the hotel round the corner and Ella thought that she and Max had quite possibly had dinner with them one summer. The woman, she thought, was called Susan... no Suki, yes that was it, because that was the name of their cat when they'd been growing up. Suki and Pedro. He was a banker. Big guffawing laugh. Max had played golf with him.

'Hi,' she smiled, pushing her hair out of her eyes and thinking now that she was glad she'd made an effort with her appearance. 'How are you?'

'Fine.' The guy, Pedro, smiled. 'And you?'

'Great, thanks. It's good to see you.'

'You too.' He nodded.

Ella nodded back, still smiling, they all looked at each other for a second or two, but then Suki glanced at Pedro and Pedro looked at Ella and when still no one said anything, Pedro said, 'A table for two.'

'Oh.' Ella felt her cheeks start to pink. 'Of course.' They had absolutely no idea who she was. She grabbed two menus and started to walk towards a table at the jetty edge. 'You know we er–' But she stopped when she saw that they weren't looking at her at all. In fact they seemed to see straight through her, like she was simply a dark outline obscuring their view of the glistening water.

She heard Dimitri snigger as she stopped what she was saying mid-sentence. The couple sat down and Pedro said, 'Boiled egg for me, fruit salad for my wife. Yoghurt on the side, grape juice, one orange – freshly squeezed, a couple of days ago we had the carton stuff and I don't want that again. And a pot of strong tea – real milk, none of that UHT crap.' Then he smiled, handed her back the menu without having looked at it, and slipped his aviators on.

They were dreadful, Ella thought. Is that what she was like? Is that what she'd become? It took her a second to remember that she was doing a job and should write everything he'd said down on the pad her mum had given her.

'Hey Ella,' Dimitri called as she walked back, a little stunned, to the kitchen. 'Tell your mum that Maddy texted, all good apparently, she's loving it.'

Ella nodded, images of Maddy – lounging on her beautiful charcoal velvet sofa, spritzing herself with her Chanel Mademoiselle while breakfast orders were being barked at Ella by her peers – made her lips tighten in frustration.

'Maddy's apparently having a wonderful time,' she said as she walked into the kitchen.

Her mum looked up from where she was grilling strips of thin streaky bacon so it snapped, crisp. Pans of eggs were sizzling and fat red tomatoes spat and hissed in bubbling olive oil. The big table at the end of the jetty was filled by a group of artists who came every winter to paint, and couldn't start without one of Sophie's infamous full English breakfasts.

'Good,' was all her mum said.

The atmosphere between them had been frosty since Ella had offered Maddy the money. Maddy however had been over the moon. She'd booked the next available flight to Heathrow so they'd only spent one night together in the room above the taverna. Ella had got undressed in the bathroom and then got into bed with her book. The only thing they'd said to each other was, 'Night' before rolling over to face in opposite directions.

But when Ella had woken up in the middle of the night, the room so black that she couldn't see her hand in front of her face, she had turned over and heard Maddy say, 'Are you awake?'

She hadn't replied.

'I'm kind of scared,' Maddy whispered. 'Not *really* scared, just a bit.'

Silence.

'You remember that time we flew to see Dad and Mum made us wear sticky name badges with our address and phone numbers on them?' She laughed softly, 'I kind of want a name badge. I think I'll be OK though. I hope so. It's just that when I imagined going I had you there in my imagination. You know, just in case.'

Ella heard Maddy roll over, bunch the covers up around her. 'I suppose there's always Dad…' she carried on, then paused before she said, 'I don't know if he'd see me though.' Her voice going up at the end of her whisper as if it was a question.

Ella still didn't say anything. But she had lain awake for hours afterwards thinking that she should have replied, hating herself for staying silent. But by the time she had decided to reply it seemed too late.

'Ella–' her mum called, 'Can you make the coffee? The jugs are in the corner, remember I showed you?'

'Oh right. Yes.' Back at home Ella didn't eat breakfast, nor did she drink coffee or tea – never had, couldn't understand why people did. She left for work at the crack of dawn, but Max liked a bowl of porridge followed by a bacon sandwich and HP sauce every morning and when he'd realised that Ella could make neither porridge nor coffee or make bacon just the way he liked it, he'd hired Rose – a middle-aged woman with a huge chest who reminded him of his house mistress.

'Ella, what are you doing?' her mum asked as she walked past her carrying a tray piled high with plates of eggs, bowls of glistening mushrooms and stacks of golden, buttery toast. 'That's too much. You take the plunger out before you put the coffee in. Jesus, Ella do you not know how to make coffee?'

The idea that her mum had forgotten that she didn't drink it made her silent.

'I don't know how you and Max live sometimes.' She shook her head. 'Here, coffee, water, plunger. OK?' Then she strode out, clearly stressed, balancing the tray of food while scooping up two jugs of freshly squeezed juice that clanked together as she walked.

Ella's phone rang as she was spooning out coffee powder.

'Max?' she said, the line was crackly.

'Ella?' She heard him say. 'Ella–'

'Hang on Max, I can't hear you. Let me just go outside.' She hurried out the back door and stood by the sea wall, looking out at the fishing boats. 'Max, hi.'

'Ella I think Amanda's husband is going to call you. Don't believe anything he says,' he said, then the signal cut out.

'Damn this island,' Ella sighed, looking at the one bar on her phone.

'Ella!' Her mum was in the doorway. 'The coffee?'

'Oh sorry.' She hurried back in. 'Sorry, I had to take a call.'

'You never have to take a call on your shift.' Her mum's cheeks were pink with stress and her brown curls were falling loose as she took over the coffee making duty.

'Excuse me–' a voice said from the doorway. 'Just wondering on our breakfasts.' Pedro was standing, legs apart, arms crossed.

'Oh shit.' Ella looked down at her pad. 'Sorry I didn't give you the order…' she said to her mum.

'We have been waiting,' he said curtly, glancing at his watch. 'We have a boat trip booked.'

'I know, I'm really sorry.'

'Pedro, I'll make it now,' her mum said with a huge, apologetic smile. 'Don't worry it'll be quick. You'll get the boat, it's – what – at quarter to isn't it?'

Pedro clearly liked the fact her mum knew his name, had remembered him as a customer, 'Thanks Sophie,' he said, chest puffed out.

'Come on,' she ushered him out of the kitchen, taking the pots of coffee with her. Ella stood watching, frustrated with herself for messing up. Wishing that she'd been able to impress her mum rather than annoy her further. 'And it'll be on the house,' her mum added. 'How's the holiday going? Nice to see you off-season.'

'Well, with these prices and this weather, I mean, who can resist. And the hotel's doing turkey. Christ knows where they've got them all. Do they even have turkeys in Greece?'

At the end of her shift Ella slumped down on one of the chairs that faced out to sea, pushed her sweaty hair out of her eyes and retied it in a big scruffy ponytail, then shut her eyes and put her head back. When she opened them she saw all the coloured lights strung above her and the curled brown leaves of the vine.

She had never been so exhausted in all her life. She kicked one of her shoes off and saw that the back of her heel was rubbed raw. Her hand was burnt where she'd pulled the grill pan out without considering how hot it would be. Her arms were stained with splodges of coffee and her fingers sticky from the remains of jam on people's plates.

A shadow fell across her table.

'OK?' Dimitri asked.

'Never better.' She raised a brow then turned to look out at the sea as he kicked a chair out and sat down. 'Please do, join me,' she muttered.

'Woah! Someone's had a bad morning.' He laughed.

Ella was so tired she couldn't really open her mouth properly to reply, so instead she watched the waves, the tumbling, rolling blue as it crashed against the wall. The fishermen sitting on the ledge, their rods bobbing, their hats pulled low. The white cat was prowling the rocks.

She heard the soft pad of plimsolls on the concrete floor, then Dimitri say, 'Hey Sophie.' Then, 'Ooh that looks good.'

'It's Ella's lunch. Hands off, you.' Her mum laughed, sliding the plate of Greek salad, taramasalata, humous and pitta bread along with plump olives, roasted garlic and strips of oily, soft red peppers onto the table, then said, 'Ella, you're back on this evening, so have a break and eat this. You did OK this morning.'

'I'm sorry I messed up Pedro's order.'

Her mum frowned. 'It's fine. Things like that happen all the time, especially when you're new.'

But Ella didn't want to be new. In the same way that she didn't want to be the guest. She wanted to be perfect at this. She wanted to be, as Maddy was, her mum's best waitress. Ella had earned a twenty percent salary bonus last Christmas and was due a lump sum incentive for bringing in one of their most lucrative clients at the beginning of the year, but suddenly being good at this seemed like the most important challenge she'd faced.

'I think she really hates me,' Ella sighed.

'She doesn't hate you.' Dimitri leaned forward and scooped some humous onto an olive. 'She's testing you.'

Ella frowned as she sat forward and dipped a piece of pitta bread into the taramasalata. 'What do you mean she's testing me?' she said, before popping the piece of warm, freshly baked pitta into her mouth and being momentarily stunned by how good it tasted. She had missed this cooking. Next thing she was popping an olive into her mouth, shovelling peppers onto her fork and scooping up thick garlicky tzatziki.

Dimitri sat back, his arms folded across his chest and watched, a smile twitching the corners of his lips. 'Well. As far as I can tell, Ella, you haven't exactly been that present in her life. The stories I heard always involved you jetting in on a speedboat and leaving half an hour later after a cursory chat with the family.'

Ella took a sip of water. 'Go on,' she said. Her spine tingling, defensive.

'And then you appear out of the blue just before Christmas having clearly had a row with your husband.'

'Boyfriend. We're not married. And we have not had a row.'

Dimitri just laughed. Then spread his arms wide like he couldn't care less either way. 'All I can say is, if I was her, I would be wondering why you were here. Whether you were just using the place to run away. And if that was the case, well, I'd feel maybe a little put out. Especially as you've just funded a trip that she didn't want Maddy to take. Which I actually think is a good thing for you to have done, by the way.'

Ella didn't reply. She found herself wanting to go over to her mum and ask for a chat in private. To tell her why she was here and why she had given Maddy the money, but something stopped her. Pride, maybe. Or fear that it wouldn't make any difference.

She looked up to see that Dimitri was staring straight at her and she had to look away. After a second or two he stood up and said, 'I have to go to work. Enjoy your break.'

She watched him lope across the concourse. Remembered how she used to watch him as a teenager, desperate for him to notice her. How she'd make Maddy turn around and walk back the way they'd just come if she happened to see his scooter whizz past them. There had been photos of his wedding on Maddy's Facebook page and Ella had zoomed right in on them, studying one in particular of the bride, her back to the camera, her dress hitched as she walked up the hill to the church and Dimitri, waiting for her, staring down in an open-collared shirt and trousers, a grin splitting his mouth in two.

She had stared for ages, enough time for someone at work to come out and tell her she was late for a meeting, absorbing the expression on his face, inspecting the girl walking towards him. Could she just see the side of her face? If she zoomed in far enough it did look like she was laughing. Ella had felt jealous of women in magazines before; at their perfection, but she'd never before felt jealous of a photograph. Never of an expression.

CHAPTER 12

MADDY

The lost luggage had tipped Maddy over the edge. She'd held it together while filling in the form but then had a little cry in the taxi to Ella's flat. Inside she hadn't been able to find the light switch to the living room and had had to feel her way to the bedroom, so tired that she'd just cleaned her teeth and curled up under the soft white sheets.

When she woke up and left the comfort of her bed to explore the rest of the flat, her first thought had been why was there a Christmas tree on the floor in front of the bookshelves. But that had only caught her attention for a second because, glancing round the rest of the apartment, she realised there was so much more to be astounded by. In front of her was a TV the size of a cinema screen. On her right were three windows, floor to ceiling, opening out onto a balcony that was at road level but set back from the pavement as, she noticed getting up and peering out and down, there was a basement flat below her that had a little courtyard garden. Behind the huge grey sofa was a dining table to seat eight and chairs so gorgeously designed, the wood so soft that they made her need to run her hand along them. Apart from the tree lying on the floor the only nod to Christmas was in the corner, above the table, where a bunch of silver and gold tissue paper pompoms hung from a hook in the ceiling. A huge white rug covered great slabs of floorboard and as Maddy walked barefoot across the varnished boards she found herself in the wide open hallway, a bathroom that looked like it was from a hotel off to her left, the bedroom next to that and then in front of her was the kitchen. She took a couple of steps forward, almost unable to believe quite how stunning it was. Marble-topped work surfaces hugged the walls and in the centre an island unit similar to her mum's but still seemingly fresh out the box. The double oven sparkled, the huge industrial hobs glistened, the white porcelain sink with its fancy taps looked unused. Walking forward, Maddy ran her fingers over the marble, then the kettle that was all dials and lights and see-through, the Nespresso machine, the juicer, the pasta maker, the fish boiler, the bread maker, the Phillipe Starck lemon squeezer, the open shelves stacked with fancy bowls and plates, and crystal glasses. None of it, aside from perhaps the glasses, looked like it had ever been touched. She pulled open the huge Smeg fridge, empty apart from six bottles of Bollinger, a pint of milk, HP sauce and Chanel Rouge nail varnish. Maddy went over to the other side of the room and opened the cupboards behind the kitchen table, one after the other, finding beautifully folded sheets, towels, tea-towels. The other cupboards were empty save for some Quaker oats and a half box of Alpen with no added sugar or salt. On the big glass table was a fruit bowl but in it was a collection of multi-coloured Christmas baubles and a bunch of fairy lights. She stood with her hands resting on the edge of the island and looked around, taking in this beautiful restaurant-standard kitchen and almost felt sad for it, its complete and total lack of use.

'I'll use you,' she said, looking at the oven and hob and all the other appliances. 'Don't worry, your existence won't be totally in vain.'

Then she battled for five minutes to work out how to turn the kettle on.

Finally, cup of tea in hand, she wandered over to the large double doors on the wall adjacent to the fridge and stood looking out onto a communal patio at the back of the apartment block, the ground speckled with dewy frost and trails of bird footprints. Putting her tea down on a little cafe table and chairs that sat in the corner of the room, obviously set up to catch the morning sun, she turned the knob and threw the windows open, a gust of icy air streaming in.

I made it she said to herself as she took in a great gulp of freezing air, felt it travel through her body, making her shiver. Wrapping her arms around her, she stepped out into the frost.

I made it to London.

The patio was stark, there were bins against the back wall and a recycling unit. The little section she stood in was backed onto by three other flats – one the curtains were drawn tight, in the other, she glanced to the right, she saw an old woman sitting at a bureau. Grey hair up in a chignon, glasses on the end of her nose, big white cardigan pulled tight around her waist, the woman was writing a letter Maddy thought, her fountain pen scratching furiously across the paper. She peered forward to see more, the dim room was lit only by the low tones of red and green from the Tiffany sidelight. She knew she shouldn't be looking but she couldn't resist.

In the corner of the room was a Christmas tree, its spindly, half-dead branches draped with raggedy tinsel and old-fashioned decorations that would sell now as antiques, next to it the woman's slippers sat side by side kicked neatly off perhaps as she'd curled up on the dark chintzy sofa. No, Maddy thought, she didn't look the type to curl up. Along the mantle piece were ornaments dotted among sprigs of holly, a newspaper was folded on the marquetry coffee table. As Maddy was on her tiptoes trying to see more, the woman turned sharply in her seat and caught her snooping. The look of displeasure in her eyes made Maddy dive back into the flat, slam the French doors shut and dart back to the safety of the bedroom.

Leaning with her back against the closed bedroom door she took a couple of breaths to calm her beating heart. Her mum was always telling her not to be so nosy, but the lives of others had always been so fascinating. Like their grass was always greener than hers.

She went and sat on the vast bed. Her toes not quite touching the floor it was so high. On Ella's side was a book about marketing and on Max's a car magazine with a Ferrari on the front.

Curiosity led her to pull out the little drawer in Ella's bedside table. Everything was so perfect, so spotless that she found herself wanting to see where she hid her self. The drawer just had a packet of paracetamol and a biro. She was about to close it when she saw the corner of what looked like a photograph. Or what had once been a photograph but was now just scrunched cracked paper, the image of maybe three people, possibly four people, faded and pale. There was just enough colour left to make out a cat. She held it close to her face – yep it was Suki, the cute kitten that had turned into a feral beast as they were growing up. She flattened out the picture, trying to make out what the rest of it, who was in it and why Ella would have kept it.

As she switched on the bedside lamp and held it up against the light, a loud rap on the door made her jump. The photo fluttered out of her hand and she scrabbled to catch it as it fell like a feather back and forth in the air.

Snatching it up, she stuffed it back in the drawer and walked tentatively over to the front door to peer through the spy hole.

The woman from next door was peering back.

'Hello.' She heard her call. 'Hello, I know you're in there.'

Silencing the part of her that wanted to run and hide in the bathroom, Maddy yanked open the door and said, 'Hi,' with a beaming smile, pretending that she'd been neither spying nor snooping.

The woman looked at her over the top of her bifocals. 'Who are you?'

'I'm Maddy. Ella's sister.'

'The girl in the suits and the high heels?'

Maddy frowned. 'Yes. Ella, who lives here.'

'I don't know her name.' The woman shrugged, her lip curled.

'But she's your neighbour.'

'So?'

Maddy, realising she hadn't brushed her teeth and was still in yesterday's clothes, took a step back and positioned herself half behind the door while she felt the woman scrutinise her.

'I thought you were an intruder.'

'No.' Maddy shook her head. 'I'm just staying here while she's away. I'm Maddy.'

The woman ignored her outstretched hand, kept her own gnarled fingers clasped tight in front of her, big diamonds winked in the low lobby light. 'They had a row. I heard them,' she said. 'Did you know they'd had a row? I never normally see them at all – come in late, leave early – but I heard this.' She pursed her lips as if annoyed that she'd said as much as she had. Displayed her interest. 'Anyway. I have things to do. I'd rather you didn't look into my flat. They usually keep the blind down.'

'But then there's no view.'

The woman scoffed. 'It's an ugly space. It's for the bins.'

And when Maddy tried to disagree, the woman turned and disappeared back into her flat leaving her standing alone to consider the preposterous fact that none of the neighbours knew each other. At home Maddy knew the whole village, practically. There was one new family she was less familiar with but that was because they were Portuguese and the language barrier made it hard to chat, but the husband and wife had come into the bar a couple of times. Christ, she even knew the tourists. If someone was there for more than a week, Maddy knew them. That was half the fun of it. So many different stories, so many different lives.

Yet this woman didn't even know Ella's name.

Going over to the fallen Christmas tree, Maddy knelt down and ran her fingers through the branches, the scent of pine rising up through the air. So Ella and Max had had a row. Was that why the tree was discarded on the floor? Rubbing her hands together and smelling the Christmassy sap on her fingers, she pushed herself back up and padded back to the bedroom. It wasn't so much the idea that perhaps Ella's life wasn't as perfect as Maddy always presumed it to be that she mulled over on the way, but the simple fact that at one time they would have confided in each other when things took a turn for the worst. They used to tell each other everything. Ella would sit on the bathroom floor reading magazine problem pages while Maddy was in the bath and she'd give Maddy the low down on everything that was happening at her school – all the gossip, all the drama, all the second-hand tales of snogging and bitching. All Maddy wanted to be when she grew up was Ella. Except a bit cooler. If it was *Sweet Valley High* she wanted to be Jessica to Ella's Elizabeth.

When she got to the bedroom Maddy pulled open Ella's wardrobe and all thoughts of anything flew straight out of her mind.

'Oh my God.' She held her hand in front of her mouth and stared. Before her were row upon row of the most gorgeous clothes she'd ever seen. Maddy actually gasped. Her fingers reached forward to stroke a soft pink cashmere sweater while her eyes had already moved onto a charcoal silk shift with antique lace trim and a pair of snakeskin cigarette pants with Gucci on the label. Flicking through the hangers she was dazzled by names she'd only ever seen in Grazia; Stella McCartney, Fendi, Cavalli. The fabrics rippled and swished, and in her hands had the satisfying weight of expense. Then there were the shoes. She had to bend down to fully absorb them. All lined up on the floor of the wardrobe, some so precious they were in little white bags. Boxes of Manolo stilettos were stacked next to buttery leather knee-high boots and black suede pumps with the double T logo of Tory Burch on the toe.

Maddy just wanted to climb inside the wardrobe and live there. Clothes had never been something she'd spent a lot of money on, but when she'd flicked through the tourists' magazines, her feet up on the railing at the taverna, an ice cold Coke next to her, and imagined herself strutting through the streets of London, these were the clothes that she'd have worn in her fantasy.

It was only as she was speeding through the items, wondering if any of it was actually appropriate for singing in a London bar, that she noticed it was all ranked in order of style. Cocktail dresses at one end, work wear in the middle, then casual clothes and lastly jackets and coats. The shoes she then realised were lined up in similar order. And the clothes folded on the shelves weren't in piles per item but instead seemed to be arranged in outfits. Jeans with belt and t-shirt. Trousers, shirt and cardigan. Then she saw the polaroids stuck on the inside of the wardrobe door. Outfits, categorised. The photographs taken off websites and catalogues. She pored over the pictures – 1. White trousers, yellow shirt, gold loafers, red necktie. 2. Black dress, turquoise pashmina, silver stilettos.

When they were kids Ella was a hopeless dresser. Her jeans were always too short and the waist too high. Her trainers were always super white and her jumpers shapeless. But then fashion wasn't Ella's thing, she was more poetry prizes, maths prizes, trophies for essay writing competitions.

Maddy stared at the polaroids again. Was this how Ella was living? Not suddenly a successful, fashionable WAG but constructed like a paint by numbers. Maddy bit her lip, felt a small ache in her chest.

From where she stood she could still see the Christmas tree on the floor in the living room and it all suddenly seemed just desperately sad.

CHAPTER 13

ELLA

Lunchtime rolled into evening. The boat party seated themselves at the big long table they'd set up at the start of the shift. The artists sat on the promontory in their own little gang. Alexander, the usual evening waiter, in his mid-fifties with hair the same colour as his perfectly pressed white shirt, arrived and immediately allocated Ella and dreadfully moody Agatha the tables they'd be waiting while her mother and grandmother worked tirelessly in the kitchen.

Ella was determined to do better than that morning. She'd gone up to her room after her lunch and changed out of her tight white jeans and into a looser black pair of trousers and a fitted black t-shirt. She'd given her hair a quick wash and plaited it neatly so it was away from her face. Then she had stood in front of the mirror and said, 'It's just a role, Ella. All you have to do is fit it.' She thought of garden parties with Max and his friends, the insincere fawning while people glanced over her shoulder to see who else was walking in. To fit in Max's world she had learnt the laugh, the touch of the arm, the charming compliment, the immediate self-deprecation, the languid blink, the hierarchy.

Why should this be any different?

'OK, I'm ready.' She'd arrived in the kitchen, her apron tied neatly, her pad in hand. Her mum had glanced up and then had to do a double take.

'What shall I start with?' Ella had asked, walking forward to admire the bowls of salads that cluttered the main table ready for serving – tabbouleh, dark green with fresh herbs and pomegranate seeds glistening like rubies, couscous laden down with Harissa and roasted vegetables and heaps of her mum's signature Greek salad, big purple olives torn in half, spaghetti strands of cabbage and great wedges of tomato and cucumber liberally doused in olive oil almost as dark as the olives themselves and razor sharp red wine vinegar.

'Your shift doesn't start for another half an hour.' Sophie said.

'That's fine. I don't have anything else to do.'

'Enjoy the sun for a bit? The island?'

Ella shook her head. 'No. I'm ready to work.'

And for the next few hours she carried plates of big juicy prawns, their long tentacles curled and charred, big carafes of red wine the base dark with sediment and bottles of white sweating with condensation from the fridge. By the end of the evening Ella was darting between tables carrying plates of meatballs and kebabs up one arm and in the other hand a collection of little mezze platters – dropping only one tiny piece of calamari that the cat ate before anyone noticed.

'Mum, table six, one tuna salad, one pork chop – salad no chips, two stuffed tomatoes and one stuffed pepper.' Ella tore off the top sheet of her pad and stuck it on one of the hooks next to the stainless steel island unit.

Sophie paused, a strip of courgette dripping with batter sizzled over the hot oil in her pan, and glanced up at Ella.

'You're getting good,' she said, her head cocked to one side.

Ella shrugged, felt embarrassed by the praise. 'When I'm given a job I try to do it the best I can.'

Her mum dropped the courgette into the oil and it hissed. 'I wouldn't expect anything less,' she said without looking up.

Ella felt a sudden flush of relief and pride. Then felt stupid for feeling it and went back out to take more orders.

As the chill of the night descended, Alexander wound down the storm shutters and encased them all in walls of plastic, heaters glowing down from the roof and the coloured lights stilling as the plastic blocked out the breeze. The artists ordered saganaki and Alexander came over with plates of halloumi sizzling up his arm then, enjoying the showmanship of it, sloshed the cheese with brandy and with a quick flick of his lighter shot the whole lot up in flames. The boat party looked on, gasping with envy, and a whole new batch was ordered for their table.

When her mum was called out for praise by the guests, Ella said that she'd plate up the desserts. 'Honestly, I'll be fine. I'll be good at it. I promise.'

Her mum looked at her then laughed and Ella realised what it felt like to bond over a hard night's work.

As her big knife sliced and cracked through the baklava, the sticky honey gluing her teeth together as she licked it from her finger, the sugary, flakey pastry dissolving on her tongue, the taste was an instant reminder of summers on the island before the divorce. Her whole extended family sitting under the vine canopy of a sprawling holiday villa. Fat, drunk wasps buzzed from grape to grape as her grandfather swiped them out the way and argued with her dad about the cricket. Her Greek great-grandmother would sit in a chair and check that her mum was keeping up with traditions. Was she making Tsoureki at Easter? When her aunt admitted that she bought hers from a Greek shop in South Kensington, along with the traditional red eggs, her great-grandmother had sucked in her breath and done a sharp shake of her head. Her aunt and her mum had giggled like guilty schoolgirls.

Ella would listen to the shouting and the laughing and see the hugging and the boisterous arguments and the swigging of ouzo and the eventual dancing and never presume that this would just be a slice of her life. She had taken such happiness for granted, unaware of its transience.

But as she ate another little honey-drenched cube she thought of the little white boxes of baklava her mum would send her at school, tied with blue ribbon. The first year Ella ate it and sobbed, the taste of the past too strong. After that she would pass it round and never eat it herself. More recently she would hand it straight to Max with the excuse that she was watching her weight.

'Everything ready?' her mum said, standing in the doorway, and Ella wondered how long she'd been watching.

Ella nodded.

'Good. We can relax now,' her mum said as she balanced plates of baklava on a tray. 'The boat's leaving in fifteen and the artists, well they have their coffee with us. Go outside, sit down, I'll do this.'

Ella could still taste the honey on her tongue.

'You OK?' her mum said, pausing on the threshold.

Ella was about to shake her head. To ask her for the first time why she never came to get her. Why had their relationship been allowed to dissolve. But then her mum raised a brow and said, 'Sorry it's not all quite as glamorous as your life!'

And Ella pulled back into her shell.

The artists' table was laden down with desserts. There were pears stewed with raisins and cardamom piled high into chunky white bowls. Big dollops of yoghurt quivered over the sides of little glass pots drizzled with honey and the sticky baklava dripped on the table. Steaming pots of fresh mint tea were carried over by Alexander and then a bottle of Metaxa brandy was added by Dimitri who ambled over after closing the bar.

Ella hovered in the background by the Coke machine, shy to approach the group of strangers, listening to the conversation that was lucid from retsina and more so now the brandy was being handed round.

'My marriage was hideous,' said a woman with her back to Ella, pulling her white blonde hair up on top of her head and then letting it fall again, her arms flapping around wildly as she spoke. 'He just wanted a wife who looked pretty and let him shag whoever he wanted. He's living in the Cayman Islands now. He can't come back here. If he does then he knows I'll take him straight to court.' She paused when Dimitri held up the Metaxa and said, 'Yes, thanks Dimitri, I'll have a glass.' As she took a gulp and grimaced she went on, 'My therapist saved me. Made me look back over all my relationships, break my patterns of behaviour. What I thought was my type was basically just wrong,' she said, knocking back her brandy.

'Ella.' Dimitri lent back in his chair, feet up on the railing. 'Come and sit down. The topic's probably of interest.' He gave a wry grin.

The blonde woman turned round and looked at Ella. 'Ahh, our lovely waitress. Have you been divorced?'

Ella shook her head. 'Oh no. I'm in a very happy relationship, thanks.'

She felt Dimitri watching her, knowing she was lying, and her cheeks started to pink under the weight of his gaze.

'Lucky you,' the blonde drawled. 'Take a seat. I'm Colette.'

As Ella tentatively pulled out a vacant chair the rest of the group introduced themselves. They were loud, boisterous, confident. Their frank openness was in stark contrast to Max's world, where no one ever said what they meant.

The young guy sitting to her left, Pete, who had dreadlocks and was wearing some sort of paint-splattered boiler suit said, 'I never look back.'

Ella poured herself a small glass of brandy and took a sip, immediately coughing with shock from the strength of it.

'You'll have to toughen up, young lady,' one of the artists laughed.

'It's fear.' Dimitri kicked his battered converse off and put his bare feet back on the railing, Ella could see the cracks in the skin on his heels, the dust imbedded in his soles. 'Everyone is afraid. It takes courage to acknowledge your fears, your mistakes, expose your vulnerabilities.'

He's still very good-looking, Ella thought.

'I wrote letters to my dead mother,' said the Irish woman at the other end of the table. 'Notes. One every day. It was the best thing I've ever done. I started all polite but by the end we were rowing, screaming at each other. Eventually I asked her why she'd never seemed to love me.'

Ella felt her back stiffen. She poured more brandy.

The woman carried on, 'She wrote back to me in my head that night. I could hear everything – the complete other side of the story, all the bits I never saw – just how she'd have said it. It made me put myself in her shoes and see it all completely differently. As an exercise it was overwhelmingly cathartic. I talk much more to her now than when she was alive.' She gave a little huff of disbelief, then, seemingly embarrassed by her drunken over-sharing, tucked her t-shirt in tighter and ate a piece of the baklava in front of her. Ella wondered if it was to glue her mouth together in an attempt not to say anything else.

Dimitri took a drag on his cigarette and she noticed he had no wedding ring.

Then she looked around the group and thought, I'm not like you all, I'm just having a little break from a mistake my boyfriend made. I don't need a therapist or to write letters to my mother.

She took another sip of her brandy.

Or perhaps that was exactly what she needed.

'Top up, Ella?' Dimitri asked.

Dear Mum, she thought, the brandy like fire, *why did you forget about me? I used to sit on my bed at school wishing you would come and get me. Why couldn't you have seen past my act? I was young and alone and lonely.*

She thought of her school dorm. Her posters, her trophies, her books. And under her pillow a photo she'd stolen from her mum's album of the world she'd left behind – of Maddy and Ella clutching the cat who was clawing to escape and her dad laughing while her mum held the camera out to capture the four of them in front of their house the summer before her dad said he was leaving. She remembered the tight feeling in her chest when the cleaner had come in one day, face all apologetic, and handed her the rubbed out image explaining that it had gone through the wash, caught up in the pillowcase.

Dear Mum, I wish you had been stronger.

Dear Mum, My boyfriend has been having an affair and I don't know who to talk to about it because I'm embarrassed and ashamed and annoyed and angry.

Dear Mum, I'm scared that I don't know where I fit.

The alcohol fumes smoked round her brain, fuzzing the edge of the coloured lights above her and drawing images on the pebbledash wall of Max and Amanda hand in hand. But then Ella's whole past with him seemed to flash before her. How special she had felt when he'd singled her out. His Ella. He'd lifted her up into his world and she had made herself something more. She had made him more. She had pushed him to be more than just someone who lived off his inheritance and drank champagne all day in private members clubs. In theory it had been a perfect. And it *had* been perfect. But keeping up. Keeping it all together, keeping him engaged and hard-working, she realised as she stared at the wall, had been exhausting.

The subject changed. The mint tea was refilled, another bottle of Metaxa came out, and then some ouzo and then some more Metaxa. Dimitri put his iPod in the speaker dock and the artists danced to the light of the red and yellow light bulbs that swayed above them. One of them swept her mum up and they did a sort of two-step. Ella rested her head against one of the wooden posts and watched through the threads of Dimitri's cigarette smoke that drifted past her. Saw her mum tip her head back and laugh. Remembered the hollowness of her face at her aunt's funeral, Maddy clinging to her legs like a limpet, never allowing her a moment on her own.

Dear Mum, Why have I never thought about any of this from your point of view?

As the night darkened and the clouds skated over one another, slipping past like cardboard cutouts on sticks, Ella found herself pulled up to dance, the guy with his dreadlocks and boiler suit refusing to take no for an answer. She was twirled and twisted as she tried to wave him away but he was having none of it. And as Pete hurled her towards the railing by the sea her phone suddenly beeped, in range of signal.

Ella yanked her hand away and opened the text. Her back to the group, the railing pressing into her stomach. But instead of more hoped for communication from Max, it was another text from Amanda's husband. Another picture. Max and Amanda having lunch at The Bluebird. Another picture. Arm in arm down the King's Road. Another picture. Shadows kissing in the doorway of a Chelsea townhouse.

Another text. *It isn't about money, Ella. It's about revenge.*

Revenge she presumed meant ensuring her relationship dissolved as well. Max could have his cake but he couldn't eat it too.

Someone slipped something into her hand. A shot glass of something. She turned to see the wedges of lemon and salt on the table and realised it was tequila.

Before she knew it, the rest of the night was a haphazard blur of more dancing, more drinking, more drunken confessions. Her mum had slipped away to bed hours earlier, Agatha and Alex were sensibly long gone, the artists decided to see the sunrise but then Colette fell asleep in a chair and Pete claimed the best view was from the top of the hill so they staggered off to see if he was right.

Ella, certain that she didn't want to trek up a hill, found herself left alone. Her vision crooked. She glanced around but saw only piles of overwhelming debris, glasses and plates scattered across the table that she preferred to ignore.

She attempted to walk to her room but found herself dipping and swaying as her legs crisscrossed. She paused. Steadied herself on the back of a chair. Wondered when the last time she had been drunk was. As she tried to think, she felt a warm hand hook under her arm, and looked up to see Dimitri grinning down at her.

'I don't need any help,' she said.

'Of course not.' His tone confusingly sincere. 'But allow me to escort you across the taverna. Just for fun.'

She knew her feet couldn't go in a straight line.

'OK. If you must.'

He nodded.

She felt intensely aware of where his fingers wrapped around her upper arm. Wanted to look down at them but made herself keep staring straight ahead. Eyes focused on the blue door with the gold baubles hanging from a drawing pin.

This close he smelt of Hugo Boss, cigarettes and the sea.

Max didn't smell of any of those things.

At the little door Ella paused. 'Thank you.'

'My pleasure.'

She waited, the fluorescent light flickering, the moths dancing while the geckos watched. She looked up at his eyes, big and green like marbles. Then at his lips, at the dip of his cupid's bow. She bit her bottom lip. She felt suddenly like she was fifteen again, her heart thumping in her ears.

'Where are you going to sleep?' she asked, aware that he couldn't drive his bike home.

He shrugged. 'At the bar.'

She nodded. The flickering lights stung her eyes but she kept looking at him. Seeing each little lash, thick and dark like a raven's wing.

Then, as his mouth seemed to dip fractionally forward she murmured, 'Are you going to kiss me?'

He shook his head. 'No Ella.'

'Oh.' She bit her lip again. 'But I think you should.'

'No, I don't think that would be a good idea.'

'Why not?'

'Because you are drunk and you are arguing with your boyfriend.'

'We're not arguing. He's having an affair. And you shouldn't know that. You should think I'm just someone on holiday. Anyone. Let me be anyone.' She stepped closer, trying to wrap her arms around his neck. 'A girl who just wants to be kissed.'

When he moved back she stumbled, tried to steady herself and bashed into the olive tree that shaded the doorway.

The pain in her shoulder seemed to sober her in an instant. 'Oh my God, I'm so sorry.' She put her hand to her mouth then moved it to cover her eyes. 'I'm so so sorry.'

'It's OK.'

'No it's not. I'm so embarrassed. I shouldn't have said any of that. Shit.' She was flustered. Her body was still drunk but her mind almost totally clear. Her feet wouldn't do what she wanted them to do and she had to steady herself on the gnarled bark of the little tree.

'It's OK.' Dimitri laughed.

'No. No it's not. I'm practically married. God so are you.' She looked at his bare ring finger. 'I think. Oh God, look just leave me here. I'm fine.' She rummaged in her apron pocket for the key.

'Ella, seriously it's not a problem.' He put his rough hand on her arm but she flinched away.

As she fumbled to put the key in the lock she could feel him watching. When she glanced up at him his eyes seemed sad for her.

'God I'm so sorry.' She stopped. Rubbed her hand across her forehead. 'Everything's really messed up. I have no idea what I'm doing.' She saw the little bunch of baubles and sighed, 'And it's bloody Christmas.'

He laughed. 'It is bloody Christmas.'

She shook her head. 'I am really sorry, Dimitri. I'm just not very good at–' She paused.

'At what?' he asked.

She tried for the lock again then stopped, let her arm fall to her side. 'Nothing.'

'What were you going to say?'

'I don't know.'

'Ella–'

'I suppose I'm not sure that I'm very good at…'

'What?'

'Being myself.'

There was a moment's silence as she looked down at the concrete floor, closing her eyes and seeing patterns of colour dancing in front of her eyelids. She felt him take her key out of her tightly clenched fingers and unlock the door. Running her tongue along her bottom lip she wondered whether he'd lead her up the stairs, but he instead he pressed his hand into the small of her back and ushered her forward, placing the key on the inside step and closing the door behind her.

CHAPTER 14

MADDY

In the end Maddy chose one the outfits from Ella's polaroids. Dark blue skinny jeans, gold snakeskin belt, black long sleeve top with a neck so wide it fell off one shoulder. It was all a bit too big but, Maddy decided, made her look chic yet dishevelled and from what she'd read about Soho that should work a treat.

She took the tube to Leicester Square, the bustle of people making her hold her breath. She was pushed and pressed and her hair caught in the doors as they closed. She had Ella's black cashmere coat on and wished she'd had the foresight to take it off before getting on. Sweat was trickling down her back. No one looked at her. No one caught her eye. She smiled at the girl next to her when her hair got caught but the girl looked away. They trundled on. At her stop she pushed her way to the doors but no one moved and as the doors started to shut she had to call out and a man forced them back open for her.

Out in the open she paused for a moment to catch her breath. To look with relief up at the leaden sky. The cold air whipped through her, confusing her body temperature and drying the sweat to ice. Pulling the coat tight around her, doing a quick, subtle check of her A to Z, she started to walk up the Charing Cross Road, gazing into the windows of old bookshops and pausing to admire the cakes in the window of Patisserie Valerie. Just as she was running her tongue over her bottom lip, anticipating the taste of a six tiered concoction with chocolate frills around the sides and raspberries piled high on the top, she tasted her first flake of snow.

It had snowed once in Athens when she'd visited a friend at New Year but it hadn't settled. Now it was falling like icing sugar, dusting everything in sight and reminding her of the little buttery *Kourabiethes* biscuits she sprinkled with sugar every year. Maddy tipped her head back and looked up at the sky, at the haze of flakes that swirled and danced above her. Savouring the sight for a second or two she then pulled her iPhone out of her pocket and took a photo, immediately texting it to her mum, even though she knew she never checked her phone, then took another three and put the best on Instagram. The 3G would cost her but she didn't care, it would make Dimitri jealous.

The thought made her smile to herself. But as she pressed to share her falling snow photo on Instagram another popped up that Dimitri had added last night. A party with the artists. She had a moment of envy then reminded herself that she'd done that last year, and the year before. She'd sat with them and giggled and got drunk on ouzo. Fine. Good. She wasn't missing anything. But then she scrolled down and saw another photo. Was that Ella dancing in the background? And her mum laughing. She tried to zoom in but the app wouldn't let her. Damn it. What was going on? What had she missed? She goes away for a second and they're all playing happy families and having the time of their lives?

Maddy pulled her coat tighter and tried to retrieve the magic of the snow. Of the frosting on the red postbox, of the big red bus driving past, its windscreen wipers pushing the slush out the way, of the Christmas trees jutting out above every building, of the tourists gasping at the flurry as they spilled out of China Town, the streets lit with strings of white lights and miniature lanterns.

And it was, it was amazing. She walked on, the snow billowing against her face, the shoppers and tourists pushing past her – but she was seeing it all a little less, a section of her brain back on the island, back at the photograph, wanting to know what had been so funny. Wanting to be there with them. As she turned up Shaftesbury Avenue, saw the big starburst lights suspended across the road, The Palace Theatre, the Curzon cinema, then Soho House and GAY, all the places she'd read about, heard about, had been desperate to see, she found herself wanting to tell someone, to point them out and coo and take photos. On her own it didn't feel quite real. It was only as she paused to get a coffee from an old Italian deli, stand against the counter and sip it like a local, she realised that she was actually a bit lonely. Even the waiters didn't have the time to smile back at her.

She checked her map again. Greek Street wasn't far. She wasn't here to be a tourist she reminded herself. She was here to work, to make something of herself. She was here for the bright lights and the centre stage. She was here for the unobtrusive heavy frosted glass doors embossed with the Manhattans' logo. For the black and white staircase that led to an underground cavern. For the high vaulted ceilings with the huge chandeliers, for the deep, wide stage with red velvet drapes and massive spotlights. For the bar where the list of cocktails on offer was longer than the entire taverna menu. For the clump of Christmas trees decorated only in tiny white lights. For the doorman with the the hat that he tipped as he heaved on the brass handle as if it weighed nothing. For the expensive soap in the toilets and individual hand towels. For the way she could sashay in, dressed in her swanky clothes and feel like she was famous. For the woman behind the desk with the bright red hair curled like a fifties pin-up girl and the tight black pencil skirt. For the manager who strode over dressed in a cream suit and a pale blue cravat.

'Madeline Davenport?' he asked, looking at her through narrow hot pink glasses.

'Yes that's me. Hi.' She held out a slightly clammy palm wishing again that she'd taken her heavy black coat off before meeting him.

'You said you weren't coming.' He glanced at a clipboard he was carrying.

'Well no actually I emailed again to say that I could. Just the other day,' she said, pointing behind her as if the past was sitting there over her shoulder.

'No.' He shook his head, took his glasses off and folded them into his top pocket. 'I've replaced you. Apologies but I can't be a person down.' He gave a tight smile and his eyes wandered to a scuff on the floor that he polished away with the sole of his shoe.

'Oh no but I have the job.' Maddy looked past him at the big stage, at the technicians playing around with the microphones. 'You said. I'd have it over Christmas.'

'Sorry.' He shook his head. 'No can do I'm afraid.'

Maddy was going to try and plead some more but it was apparent his attention had moved on to other things. In the end she nodded and took a couple of steps back. He returned to his clipboard and then moved to talk to the woman at the desk. Maddy didn't want them to see her eyes welling up so she turned and walked as fast as she could to the toilets.

Standing with her hands on the sink, her face damp from the water she'd splashed on it, she stared at herself in the perfect, flattering light.

Shit.

What now? Go home? Camp out in Ella's flat with no money eating Alpen and drinking champagne?

Her phone rang. She looked at the screen to see it was her mum.

She thought about not answering.

Then she thought maybe it was an emergency and pressed Answer.

'Hi honey. I just thought I'd see how you were doing.'

Maddy turned and leant against the sink. 'Yeah I'm good. All good. It's really fun. It's snowing.'

'Yeah I saw your photo. You'd be proud, I'm keeping my phone with me all the time. Don't get used to it though, it's only because you're away–'

Maddy laughed and her mum paused, she knew her too well. Knew when her laugh wasn't quite right. 'Are you OK?'

'Yeah, yeah I'm fine.'

'You don't sound fine, Mads.'

'That's because I'm in the bathroom. It's all echoey.'

'Oh.' Her mum paused. 'Are you at the place? I got Dimitri to Google it for me. It's very smart, Maddy.'

Maddy looked around the toilet stall, at the gold toilet roll holder and the wooden panelled walls. 'Yeah, it's amazing.'

'Well I was impressed. I thought I should just ring to let you know. I'm impressed. Well done Maddy. Enjoy it.'

'Thanks Mum.' Maddy sucked in her top lip, trying to keep her voice neutral.

'I miss you.'

Maddy nodded.

'Are you sure you're OK?'

'Yes, yes, I'm nodding.'

'OK, well get to work. Go and wow them. Everyone sends their love. Granddad wants you to get someone to film you and send us a video. Can you do that? He says you can do that. Jesus he's nearly ninety and he knows more about it than me.' Her mum laughed. Maddy imagined her in the kitchen, her apron on, the phone wedged between her shoulder and ear as she crushed herbs in the old, chipped pestle and mortar or fed sheets of pasta through the rollers until they were wafer thin.

'I'll see what I can do,' Maddy said. 'I might need to settle in first, you know, before asking people to film me. Could be embarrassing.' She ran the toe of her shoe along a crack in the tiles on the floor, knew it didn't have long before the manager had it replaced.

'Oh absolutely honey, you do what you need to. Don't worry about us at home.' She could hear her mum's smile in her voice. 'I just wanted to ring really to say that I was proud of you. Well done. It looks really good. I was stupid to try and stop you. You go get them. Show them how good you are.'

Maddy had to swallow over the lump rising in her throat. 'Thanks Mum,' she said and her voice broke right at the end but she covered it with a cough.

'Ok honey, oh I've got to go, another boat party have arrived. They're all asking for bloody turkey. Can you imagine? The weather's apparently about to break so I'd better make the most of it. Ring me when you can. I love you.'

'I love you, too.' Maddy mumbled. And as soon as she hung up put her hand over her mouth and silenced a sob.

Maddy, Maddy, Maddy. What are you going to do?

CHAPTER 15

ELLA

A loud thump on the door woke Ella up at – she looked at her phone – ten o'clock the next morning.

A deep voice called, 'It's Dimitri.'

Dimitri. She sat up, ran her hands through her wild bed-hair. Dimitri. Why did the name make her feel a bit sick?

Oh shit.

Ella jumped up out of bed, took a couple of strides towards the door but then backed away, screwed her eyes up tight and shook her hands in fists. *What were you thinking last night?* Glancing round she went back to look at the little mirror above the sink in the corner of the room and squinted in horror at her crazy hair and bloodshot eyes.

When he thumped on the door again she opened it a crack, shielding most of her body with the wood, covering up her bare legs and last night's t-shirt.

'Hi.' Dimitri beamed, looking all tanned and fresh and glistening eyed.

Ella tried to force a smile.

'The forecast says the weather's about to turn so you have maybe one more good day, two if you're lucky. I thought you might want to come on my boat.' He held up a picnic then let his mouth curl up into a wicked grin. 'But only if you don't try to seduce me.'

Mortified, Ella covered her face and he laughed, the deep sound bouncing off the walls of the narrow corridor. 'Let's go.'

Ella shook her head. 'I have to get ready.'

Dimitri took her by surprise by poking his head round the door and looking her up and down, then he stood back and said, 'You have five minutes.'

Ella wrapped her arms tight around her waist, conscious of her near nakedness. 'I need longer than that.'

'Five minutes,' he said, shaking his head. 'As long as it takes me to smoke this.' She watched dazed, cheeks flushed with embarrassment, as he lit his cigarette. 'You are wasting time, no?' he said, flicking his hand in the direction of the room.

Ella wasted another three minutes wandering round shaking her head at the memory of her drunken proposition. In her head it merged with the time all those years ago when she'd followed him around like a puppy, her shameless adoration clear in her every move. *Hi Dimitri, can I help you with that? Hi Dimitri, could you help me carry my windsurfer? Hi Dimitri I like those shorts, they really suit you. Hi Dimitri, I saw you on your scooter in town, you looked so cool.* His valiant attempts to shake her off had been futile.

It had come to a head when clueless Ella had worn her best dress and stolen her mum's lipstick which she'd applied really badly and later found she had some on her teeth, and tried to sashay, the way the coolest girls did at school, down the jetty in her mum's high heels to where Dimitri was waxing down his board in the heat of the blazing midday sun.

Oh God, even the memory of that wiggle walk made Ella feel nauseous. She barely needed to remember the fact someone had scrawled *Ella loves Dimitri* on the

wooden slats of the jetty in chalk. That she had furiously
tried to wipe it off with her stiletto and in doing so tripped,
staggered, teetered and then landed with a belly flop into
the sea, catching the spike of her heel in the gap of the slats
on her way down and twisting her ankle.

Ella went over to the sink. Splashed her face. Mascara
trickled down her cheeks. God it was like looking at her
fifteen-year-old self after Dimitri had dived in to yank her
out and she'd been unable to walk and had lost one shoe
and he'd half carried her, right over the chalk graffiti.
Her dress had gone see-through, her hair was plastered
down over her face and after mumbling a thank you, she
had limped away catching sight of herself in a window,
mascara all over her cheeks and lipstick smudged across
her chin, and the sound of all the boys sitting on the stone
wall – their sniggering ringing in her ears.

Face washed, foundation plastered on, teeth brushed,
Ella skimmed through her wardrobe. She needed her cruise
outfit – white blazer with gold buttons, navy trousers, red
striped shirt – but that was at home. She wanted something
that would make her look aloof, thin and rich enough not to
care about her humiliating behaviour the night before. Her
fingers stopped on a black and turquoise kaftan that Grazia
had put on their Holiday Power Dressing page.

When she opened the door ten minutes later in her
billowy chiffon, Dimitri looked her up and down and said,
'You'll be too cold.'

She didn't have anything else. She didn't have her
polaroids. She had a work shirt and skirt, smart t-shirts and
cardigans made of thin, delicate mesh. She sat back on her
heels as she rummaged through her bag realising quite how
poorly she had packed.

Twenty minutes later they were walking down the
jetty to the boat, Ella wearing her white jeans, that were

slightly stained from the breakfast shift the day before, and some crappy red jumper of Maddy's that she'd found in a drawer. Feeling hungover and embarrassed, she took the opportunity to distract herself with emails while she had signal. Dimitri was strolling ahead in army trousers cut off at the knee and a black wooly sweater, carrying a picnic and a canister of petrol, a glowing cigarette dangling from his fingers precariously close to the fuel. The wood of the jetty, warmed by the morning sun, cracked and groaned underneath their feet. A scuba diver broke the calm surface of the sea as he chucked his harpoon and a bag of octopus onto the jetty and then heaved himself out. Dimitri saluted a wave and the diver proudly held up the largest octopus, its pink suckers pulsating as he stretched the tentacles wide.

'That's disgusting,' Ella said with a sneer.

'It's his dinner.' Dimitri raised a condescending brow as he looked back at her.

The diver then held the octopus by its tentacles and thwacked it hard on the wooden post to kill it.

'Oh Jesus Christ.' Ella covered her eyes.

Dimitri laughed as he held onto the rope of his boat and jumped on. 'You need to get out of the city more.'

'What, so I can watch more animal massacres?' She grimaced, hands on her hips.

He rolled his eyes at her then jogged across the hull and started to loosen the anchor. 'Do you need a hand to get on?'

'No I'm fine,' she said, looking dubiously down at the bobbing bow, unsure about making the jump but not wanting any help, especially from Dimitri.

'Really?' he said watching her, his hand shielding his eyes from the late morning rays.

'Yeah I'm fine.'

'If you say so.'

Slipping her phone into her pocket, Ella took one shoe off and then the next, chucked them forward so they landed in the boat with a bounce, and then lowered herself down tentatively so she was perched on the edge of the jetty, her feet still a foot above the prow of the boat. Still gripping onto the wood she slid herself down until one toe touched solid ground and then the other. Half suspended however, the pressure of her feet started to push the boat away and she found herself caught, hands still holding on, feet moving away underneath her.

'Let go,' Dimitri called.

'No.' She shook her head. If she let go there was a chance she'd just fall on her bum into the water. Sudden flashbacks of her youthful tumble made her close her eyes. *Please not again.*

'Just push yourself forward with your hands and let go,' he said as he was lowering the engine into the water. 'It's bloody cold in there this time of year so you don't want to fall. Push yourself off! Now, Ella. Look wait, I'll give you a hand.'

'I'm fine. I don't need a hand.'

'Why are you so stubborn? You're just like Maddy.'

'I am not.'

'Oh for God's sake, just let go then,' he called as he started tapping another cigarette from the pack.

The boat was moving further away from Ella as she mentally counted herself down to let go and jump, but when the time came she was frozen. Stretched between the jetty and the boat.

'OK fine, help me!' she shouted in the end as the boat drifted further and she was almost diagonal.

Tucking the fag behind his ear, Dimitri loped over and stood looking up at her, while she struggled to stay upright. 'Please?'

'What?'

He shrugged and started to turn away.

'OK, fine. Please. Please help me,' she huffed, and he bent down and scooped her up with both arms, depositing her with an ungainly thud on the red leather passenger seat.

'There you go, Princess,' he laughed, walking back to pull up the anchor while he leant forward to turn the key and start the engine. 'That was hard for you, wasn't it?' He said as two-hundred horsepower roared violently to life.

'What?' Ella asked, pulling out her phone.

'Asking for help.'

She rolled her eyes instead of replying and looked away as if it was all beneath her.

Five minutes later, while Dimitri was jumping about like an exuberant dog – untying ropes and pushing the boat off from the mooring, kicking away other boats from either side, wiping sweat off his forehead, Ella started replying to all her emails. She'd put out some petty work fires and sent some off-the-top-of-her-head thoughts about the mobile phone campaign, when she heard Dimitri cough, seemingly to get her attention.

'What?' she said, glancing up.

'Have you seen the view?' he asked somewhat bemused.

'Where?' she asked.

He pointed out along the coastline to where the olive groves ended and into the distance rows and rows of lemon trees took their place; each varnished leaf shiny and glistening in the sunlight.

'Oh yes, very nice.' She nodded.

'Jesus. You and that phone.' He jumped down to the end of the boat and fiddled with some of the switches and leads. Ella crossed her legs and looked around, wondering if she should help at all. When he didn't say anything more she refreshed her emails again – there'd been nothing more from Amanda's husband. She didn't know whether to be annoyed or relieved.

'What can be that important?' Dimitri shouted over the sound of the engine.

Ella didn't look up. 'Work. You wouldn't understand.'

'You're missing the view,' Dimitri said as he jogged back up to the steering wheel. When she looked up at him to roll her eyes he was pointing towards the rows of little villas nestled into the olive groves on the hillside. Occasionally a car mirror or motorbike picked up the sun and shot back a beam from between the trees like a satellite.

Her phone buzzed with an email. Max@internationalsolutions.com. Her heart thumped like it might break through her ribs. Her fingers hovered over the open button. Was it another pleading request to trust him or was he about to admit the truth? She shocked herself by thinking she barely knew which she'd prefer, which would offer the most relief.

But just as she was about to open it up, before she could answer her own question, long, tanned fingers plucked the iPhone out of hers and hurled it overboard.

'What the hell!'

'Look at the God damn view.'

'That was my phone.'

He held his arms wide in a shrug that said he didn't care. Ella scuttled to the edge of the boat and stared down into the sheet of blue beneath them. 'Go and get it.'

'Get real.' He made a noise somewhere between a snort and a laugh and took the cigarette from behind his ear and lit it.

Ella leaned right over, scanning from side to side to see if she could make out the shape of her iPhone as it sank. 'That was my phone.'

'So you've said.' He cut the engine and sauntered back to drop the anchor where they bobbed, fifty metres or so out from the shore, smirking to himself as he tied the knot.

When he turned around she was glaring at him, hands on hips, expression thunderous. He shrugged. 'It is something to hide behind.'

'Don't give me that crap. You don't even know me.' Ella sneered.

'And here I was thinking we were very well acquainted,' he said. 'Last night you tell me that you have trouble being yourself.'

'Let's not talk about last night.'

Dimitri shrugged. 'Seems to me, if you have less to hide behind, you're more likely to be yourself.'

Ella shook her head. 'You've just made that up right now. You're backtracking for throwing my phone in the sea.'

'If you say so,' he said and she did a big sigh, stalking away from him, flopping down cross-legged and angry as far towards the prow of the boat and as far away from him as she could get, the icy spray hitting her face like pinpricks.

She sat there fuming. She could hear Dimitri pottering about but she didn't turn around. She felt the wind begin to pick up, lapping the water into tiny waves. She thought about her phone lying amongst the seaweed, the email from Max unread. She wasn't hiding she was just using her technology. It was strange though that in the short time she'd been on this boat with Dimitri, from the octopus bashing to the almost falling in, to sitting here now, she felt more alive, more herself, more relaxed and honest than she had in years at home. She had felt confident and assured at work, but rarely had she been so casual with her remarks, so spontaneous, when with Max or their friends. What she was about to say had more often than not been rehearsed and rehashed in her head a few times before she said it.

As she was thinking, staring out at the blue sea ahead of her, a fishing line whipped over her head with a crack making her jolt back with surprise. Then – as the bait bobbed in the water – hairy, tanned legs squatted down next to her. 'I'm sorry I threw your phone in the water.'

Ella didn't say anything.

Dimitri looked back at the sea. 'This is where you say, it doesn't matter, it's only a phone. I'm sorry I am sulking and ruining the trip on the boat.'

She tipped her nose up and glared at him. He cocked his head to one side and smiled, 'My mother used to say that the wind would change and I would stay like that.'

'Looks like it did,' she said, one eyebrow raised.

'Ooh Ella. That's cruel. My poor heart.' He clutched his chest.

She rolled her eyes and tried to hide a smile. He leaned over and bashed her shoulder with his and then settled down next to her, his legs dangling over the edge of the boat as he leant against the metal guard rail. They looked out at the sea, watching the fishing boats as they bobbed and dipped with the waves.

'Do you want to tell me about your boyfriend?' Dimitri asked after a while, his fingers teasing the fishing line as the waves pulled the float back and forth.

'No.'

An insolent smile spread across his face, making Ella's defences rise. 'Do you want to tell me about your wife?' she said back.

'She died.'

Ella put her hand over her mouth. 'Oh God I'm so sorry. I should have thought. Sorry. God you must have been devastated.' She thought back to the wedding photograph on Facebook. Her envy at that look.

Dimitri shrugged a shoulder as he tied the fishing line to the metal rail and then turned and smiled at her, perfect white teeth on a dirty tanned face. 'We had our time,' he said. 'She came into the bar – Anya – and I knew the moment she came in that I would be with her, just like that.' He clicked fingers wet with sea water and engine grease. 'So I just leant over the bar and I said, we're going to get married. I promise you, we are going to get married. You have to go with your instincts, don't you?' He grinned, 'Like the lion.'

Ella rolled her eyes.

'And we did. We married up at the church on the hill, see it... just up there.' He pointed behind them and Ella twisted round to see the top of a castellated white bell tower, the big brass bell glinting in the sun. She didn't want to tell him that she had analysed his wedding photographs like some sort of CSI, that she knew exactly where he got married and when.

'I thought she was beautiful, Ella. Absolutely beautiful. And do you know her best trait?' Dimitri didn't pause for an answer. 'She could pull me out of a really bad mood,' he said, smirking to himself.

Ella was starting to feel envious and hating herself for it. He had lost something so precious. Yet he had had it in the first place.

Had she had that with Max? Would she be able to tell a similar story? What would she say? That Max suited who she had become?

The summer Ella finished school her father announced that he and Veronica would be moving to Paris and would she like to go with them. It wouldn't be forever but long enough for her to go to University there. For Ella it felt like the perfect opportunity to start afresh and an excuse not to have to go and be the outsider in Corfu. And she had loved it. Loved their apartment, the boulangerie on the corner, cycling to her lectures, visiting all the galleries. But most of all she had loved living with Veronica. She had watched her as she sipped her black coffee and ate brie by the slice with no bread, spoke about politics and the economy, told her father when he was wrong, wore perfect make-up and kid gloves and had a different coat for every occasion. And when Ella had finally plucked up the courage and asked her for help, asked her to get her the same confidence that she had, Veronica had stubbed out her cigarette, looked her up and down with a lazy smile and said, 'I thought you'd never ask.'

She had shown Ella how to be who she wanted to be. To take her out of the shadows. She had given her the best books to study, taught her the best food to eat, wine to drink, newspapers to read. She had whisked her to Galeries Lafayette and paid for a make-over – watched as they slicked on foundation, lined her lashes with brown – not black, never black, far too harsh – tinted cheekbones she never knew she had with liquid rouge, plucked her eyebrows into pencil thin lines, pierced her ears, curled her hair, dyed it from mousy to chestnut dark, shaped her ratty nails into perfect ovals and lacquered them with Chanel Rouge. And then they had shopped. My God they had shopped. Veronica had skimmed through rails laconically holding designer outfits up against her with a scowl or the occasional smile. And Ella had been kitted out from top to bottom. Her feet had been slipped into Louis Vuitton ballet pumps while the sales assistants had unfolded jumpers in the softest angora and jeans that stopped mid-calf like Audrey Hepburn.

'*Et voila…*' Veronica had smiled. 'Ella she has come of age, finally.' When she smiled, her bright red lips spread right across her face and her eyes sparkled. 'I look at you and I think she is my own daughter. And I am glad that I can help you.'

The image of them side by side was reflected in one of the full-length mirrors, Veronica's arm draped over her shoulder, and Ella saw in herself finally someone she was happy with, happy to be.

'You are a lovely girl, Ella,' Veronica whispered into Ella's hair. 'You are lovely even without these things, remember that, *oui*? These are just…' she paused, 'I do not know the word. In French it is *glaçage*.'

Ella shook her head, she didn't know what it meant. Veronica turned to one of the sales assistants and asked her what it meant in English.

The girl shrugged.

Veronica huffed out a breath. 'The cake, it is the top of the cake. *Oui*?'

'The icing?' Ella asked, unsure.

'Ah, yes, that is it. The icing.'

Dimitri ran his hand through his hair, smearing a line of grease across his forehead. Ella pointed to it but when he tried to wipe it away he missed so she leant forward and swiped it off with her thumb. His skin felt softer than she had expected. And she found herself momentarily shocked by rush of feeling.

He rubbed his forehead again, as if making sure the mark had gone, then looking back out to sea said, 'Do you know, we had three of the most brilliant years of my life. Then she got cancer and she died very quickly. Just like that she arrived and just like that she went.' He clicked his fingers. 'But–' he turned to look at Ella and said, 'I loved her very much and I would not swap it for the world.'

Ella rubbed her temple. She wanted Dimitri's story to go away. She wanted not to have been told it. She wanted it not to shine so clearly on her own relationship and see the many flaws reflected back.

The icing, she thought as she sat there in Maddy's holey jumper and barely any make-up. She had been warned but she hadn't listened. Instead she had seen the way her life had changed after her coaching from Veronica. How she had flourished and blossomed in Paris and had come back stronger, sharper, cleverer but also more guarded, more poised, more painted. As long as, it seemed to Ella, her lips stayed glossed with Dior and her clothes remained the envy of the girls who trailed behind Max like he was the Pied Piper, she became someone worthy of his gaze. She had become Ella. Striking, poised, award-winning. And he had become Max, no longer a loafer in the city who visited his hateful parents once a month, but someone who sailed at seven in the morning on a Sunday, started his own business, did an MBA. They had made each other more. But, she wondered as she glanced out across the sea, had that come at the expense of being themselves?

'Your turn,' Dimitri said with a glint in his eye.

Luckily, before Ella had the chance to think of a reasonable excuse not to tell her story there was a violent movement on the fishing line that had Dimitri jumping up, whooping with excitement. 'You're saved,' he said, glancing back at her as he untied the line and started reeling it towards him, 'By a bloody great fish.'

CHAPTER 16

MADDY

Maddy had been into every bar and club in the area. Her shoes pinched, her back ached, her eyes were sore from holding back tears and one of her hands was constantly frozen because she'd dropped a glove somewhere between Dean Street and the Choccywoccydoodah shop and she was alternating with the one she had left. After a spate of brusque rejections she'd had to go into Liberty to look at beautiful things while she warmed up. But after circulating the stationery department a number of times she started to get suspect looks as if she was a shoplifter and left, stepping out into Carnaby Street where even the lavish Christmas lights couldn't cheer her up.

Deciding to cut her losses and go back to Ella's and open one of the bottles of Bollinger, she started to schlep her way back through the slushy snow. This time she didn't see the picture-postcard views of snow-capped London but instead noticed the pile of rubbish dusted with white outside the shop where she bought a soggy cheese and tomato sandwich, the half-frozen overflowing manhole of a burst water main, a tramp with a dog shivering from the cold who thanked her with big pale eyes as she handed him half her lunch.

Morose, tired and now hungry, she took a wrong turn and found herself down one of the seedier Soho streets.

She hurried past girls standing in doorways, nervous and out of her depth, but then paused because there on the corner was one bar she hadn't tried.

The name *Big Mack's* flickered in neon. Maybe it was fate, Maddy thought as she looked up at the sign and remembered every New Year's day her dad bundling her and Ella into the car and taking them to McDonalds. Her mum thought it was a horrendous tradition and refused any part of it, but her dad had a soft spot for a Big Mac, Ella adored filet-o-fish and Maddy would have chicken nuggets and a vanilla milkshake. Only ever at New Year though, his once yearly treat to mop up a raging hangover. They'd eat it in the car, parked so they could look over the river and her dad would put on his *White Christmas* soundtrack, turn Bing Crosby right up and say 'Just one more time, and then I'll admit that Christmas is over.' And they'd sit eating their McDonalds, watching the swans and the ducks, and sometimes the snow, and listen to the last song of Christmas.

She put her hands on the high window sill and pulled herself up a touch to see inside. From what she could see it was an old American-style piano bar. Maddy pressed her nose against the darkened window and saw amongst the faded posters on the wall and the dark velvet booth seats, a small baby grand and a dilapidated stage.

She jumped down and stood for a minute, contemplating whether to go inside. She watched a businessman head into the massage parlour adjacent to the bar. Saw a group of teenagers huddling round their cigarettes scuffing the snow with their boots. Then a man across the street shouted, 'What d'you think you're looking at?' Startled and a little afraid, Maddy found herself backing into *Big Mack's,* the wooden door swinging open much easier than she'd imagined, causing her to stumble and making her entrance much less demure than she'd hoped.

It didn't matter. She could have skidded inside and done a little dance and no one would have batted an eyelid. As it was there was one guy mopping the floor and a girl wiping down the bottles that sat four deep behind a mirrored wall on the bar and neither glanced up at her arrival.

Maddy took a couple of steps forward. Inside it smelt of dirty washing up water, Lynx and stale beer. Some obscure Bluegrass played softly out of two wall mounted speakers and a TV screen flickered with an old black and white movie. The only light was from a couple of overhead spots and one of a pair of gold sconces, she wondered if it was because all the other bulbs had blown. A rather forlorn poinsettia sat on the brass bar and strands of coloured beads hung haphazardly from the three pillars that seemed to separate the bar area from the stage.

'Hi there. Hi. Excuse me.' She took another couple of steps forward into the murky shadow of the bar.

The guy mopping the floor looked up.

Maddy took another step inside. 'I'm actually looking for work. Just over Christmas. I'm–' she paused as the guy looked back down at the floor. The girl behind the bar moved on from the whiskeys to the vodkas. Maddy sucked in her bottom lip, wondered whether she should leave but then she heard someone, she thought the guy, mumble, 'You need to see Mack then.'

She watched as he squeezed out his mop and kicked the bucket over to behind the bar, swept some keys off the shiny surface and disappeared through swing doors at the back.

Maddy wondered if she was meant to follow. And when nothing happened she backed up a couple of paces thinking it might be better to cut her losses.

But what then?

Another season on the boats. Another winter in the garage. Another year of sitting on a chair in the corner of Dimitri's bar with her guitar as everyone she knew chatted amongst themselves while she provided the backing track.

She looked over to the corner of the room, to the tiny stage with two spotlights on the ground pointing up towards a microphone and a ripped velvet star curtain, the fairy lights that worked twinkling.

'You need a job.' She heard a man say as he pushed open the swing doors and strolled over to the bar, mid-fifties trying to look younger, receding hair quiffed back, collar of his pink shirt turned up. He pressed a button on the till and started counting the notes.

Maddy watched, biting her lip, shifting from one foot to the other. 'Yeah. Yeah I do.'

'What can you do?' he said, sifting through the notes, one after the other and turning them so they all faced the same way.

The girl dusting the bottles paused and turned her head slightly to look Maddy's way, sizing her up like a hyena.

'I can sing,' Maddy said, doing a half-hearted point towards the stage. 'I'm pretty OK at singing.'

The man, who she presumed was Mack, kept on turning the notes without looking up and said, 'Pretty OK is no good to me.'

'Well. Actually I'm pretty good.' She started to walk forward towards the bar. 'I'm really good, I hope. You know, it's hard to judge your own talent.' She did a little laugh. Mack glanced up, stony-faced.

'Ever done any bar work?' he said, going back to the notes.

Maddy realised if she was going to get anywhere she had to change tack. She rolled her lips together, straightened her shoulders, ran her hand through her snow-damp hair and pulled her confidence back up from where it was draining out through her toes. 'My mum owns a restaurant back home, my best friend has a bar, I've worked in both. I can make most cocktails, I can pour three pints at once, I can carry a table's worth of food and I can sing brilliantly.'

She saw the corner of Mack's mouth curl up as he slammed the till shut, rolled up the notes and shoved them into his back pocket. 'I can't help you I'm afraid.'

Maddy watched him pick up a spreadsheet on a tatty piece of paper and peruse what she assumed were the shifts his staff were working. He glanced up after a second and seemed surprised still to see her standing there.

'Yes you can,' she said. Thinking about everything it had taken to get here. 'You have to.'

Mack laughed almost as if taken by surprise, a deep rumbling that echoed around the empty room. He put his elbows on the bar and leaned forward, watching her, his chin resting on the knuckles of one fist. 'Where's back home?' he said after a second.

'Corfu–' she said, awkward under the spotlight of his stare.

'I've been to Kavos, twice, years ago,' he said, cutting her off. 'Don't remember any of it. I was plastered from the moment the plane touched down.' He rubbed his hand over his forehead. 'Bad days,' he said, then stared at her again silently.

Maddy didn't say anything. He seemed to be deciding what to do with her.

'OK. I'm a man down tomorrow night.' He straightened up, ran his hand up and down his neck beneath his upturned collar. 'I'll see what you're like.'

Maddy pressed her lips together to hold in her smile. She was going to make it here.

'Don't get too excited,' he said, bending down to swipe a Coke from the fridge. 'It's just dirty, sweaty bar work.'

CHAPTER 17

ELLA

The sky blackened in the afternoon. The waves had got up and the sound as they rumbled the pebbles along the beach filled the soupy grey air.

Dimitri was just tying the boat to the jetty when the looming clouds split at their seams. The water came down so hard it was painful, battering Ella on the back as she ducked her head and clambered off the boat. Her clothes were drenched in seconds, Maddy's woollen jumper hanging down almost to her knees with the sodden weight.

'Oh shit I forgot the fish,' Dimitri shouted over the noise of the clattering rain.

'But it's pouring.'

'Go inside,' he called as he jumped back onto the boat, scooping up the fish in soaking wet arms.

But Ella found herself waiting for him. Reluctant somehow to go back to the taverna alone. Like there was now a fragile connection between them. A bond made of fine gold thread that came from time spent alone together. After he'd caught the fish there had been a kind of euphoria in the air, Dimitri on a high casting more lines until the front of the boat looked like a spider's web. 'I never catch anything, Ella. Never. I am the crappest fisherman on the island. Probably in the whole of Greece.

They say that even with bloody dynamite I wouldn't catch anything. Look at it.' He'd held the giant fish aloft. 'Look at it! You're my lucky charm.' He'd laughed, ruffling her hair with a hand that she preferred not to remember had just been holding a fish. She had been so consumed by the feeling of liking his attention, their easy camaraderie, that she hadn't flinched when he'd messed up her hair.

They hadn't caught anything more. Not one float even bobbed with the hint of a bite, but they had lain, calm and relaxed along the two benches moulded into the plastic of the boat, felt the waves roll them as they talked about things that weren't to do with husbands or wives or relationships. She told him about her work, he talked about the bar.

When she'd said, 'So what do you want to do next?' he'd looked at her quizzically.

'What do you mean, next?'

She'd sat up and leant on her elbow. 'You want to run a bar forever?'

Dimitri had laughed, put his hands behind his head and stared up at the darkening clouds. 'Nothing's forever, Ella.'

'No I just mean, you know, do you want a restaurant? Do you want to open another bar on the mainland? You know – don't you want to grow?'

'No,' he'd said, a slight shake of his head. 'I think the world has enough trouble with people wanting growth, expansion, all that rubbish. I have my bar, I have my customers, I have my friends, I have my surf board, I have my bike. What else do I want?'

Ella screwed up her face. 'I don't know. But what about ambition?'

'What about ambition?' He glanced her way. 'You think these aren't ambitious goals? Friendship? Happiness? Fitness? You want me to have more lines on my face?'

'No,' she said, trying to reformulate her point in her head. To make him see that a bar on this island wasn't enough. Couldn't be enough. That he had to be trying to be better. But her argument was faltering in her head. She felt confused. The lull of the boat and the openness of the sky making him seem more right and her more wrong. So she said instead, 'You don't have any lines.'

He smiled and sat up to point to the grooves next to his eyes. 'What are these then?'

'I think those ones are OK.' She felt her mouth quirk up in a half smile.

'You like my wrinkles?'

'They're OK.'

'Well who'd have known,' he said, lying back again and grinning up to the clouds, 'She likes my wrinkles.'

They hadn't talked much after that. Just lain there. Ella forcing herself to relax and enjoy the silence, the nothingness. Trying to ignore the thousand thoughts in her brain and just look up at the clouds.

'It's getting cold,' she'd said after about five minutes. Dimitri had got up and thrown her a blanket.

'What happens if it rains?' she'd asked later as the sky inked over. 'If there's lightning, isn't being on a boat the worst place to be?'

'Ella.' Dimitri had opened one eye and then held his finger to his lips. 'Ssh.'

Now, as she held the rope for the boat, pulling it close so that he could jump back easily, the rain pummelling her like hail, she wanted this moment to last forever. To keep out the real world. She wanted to wrap the day up and hold it close. Back in the taverna she would go and find a computer and read the email from Max and feel everything that would come with it, Dimitri would fall back on his smart remarks and play up to the attention of her doting mother which she would watch jealously, unable herself to move beyond polite.

She watched him as he hooked the fish's gill with his finger and held it aloft with a grin, the rain plastering his hair to his head in wet tendrils, dripping off his nose and eyelashes. She watched as he tipped his head back to the sky and opened his mouth wide, watched as he laughed out loud as he slipped jogging to the end of the boat. Watched as he stumbled and held out a hand for her to steady him. Felt his strong grip in hers, his fingers tightening as the weight of him lurched to the side but then steadied. Felt the pull of resistance along her arm as she helped to tug him up to the jetty. Saw the lightning flash in the distance. Heard the thunder roll loud and heavy above them. Saw Dimitri's eyes distracted by the stunning fork of light on the horizon.

'Oh shit, I'm going in,' he said as he slipped again, instinctively tightened his grip on her hand as he skidded off the side of the boat.

'No. No. Let go.' She tried to pull away, tried to lock her toes against the wood, tried to balance herself with her free arm, but it was no good. Her bare feet paddled frantically against the jetty, her body tipped forward and she felt suddenly that there was no ground beneath her. Until she smacked the surface of water like she was breaking through ice, submerged in the sharpest, coldest water she'd ever been in. Her skin tingled like it had been stung. The breath stuck in her chest like she was about to have a heart attack. She gasped and inhaled, water icy in her throat, while seaweed wrapped around her ankles like fingers drawing her down, the sodden jumper engulfing her frozen limbs as she tried to push herself to the surface.

Then, as she struggled and kicked and gasped, she felt Dimitri's arm around her. 'Calm down, Ella,' he said, voice bemused. 'We're only in about ten feet of water.'

Ella opened her eyes, stopped struggling for breath as she found herself heaved upwards and cradled to Dimitri's chest while he sidestroked towards the shallows.

'Like old times.' He winked.

Immediately Ella recoiled, humiliated as she remembered her poor young self floundering in the water. Feeling desperately sorry for little her in her memory. Wanting someone to have been there to help her out. Wanting her mum or anyone to have seen and made her laugh at the memory rather than scrunch it up into a little ball and keep it tight in her chest. She shoved her hands against Dimitri, the movement surprised him and he lost his grip on her just as a great roll of waves crashed through them. Ella felt herself panicking again as big arcs of frigid sea bashed against her head and a huge rumble of thunder brought with it a greater deluge.

'It's OK, Ella. It was no big deal,' he shouted over the noise of the battering rain as he tried to steady her.

'It was to me,' she gasped, arms trying to tread water, burning with cold, feet sliding on the seaweed. It had been everything to her younger self. It had been one of the reasons that added to her not wanting to come back to the island. It had been burned on her retina when she went to sleep for months after the event. In retrospect it was silly and insignificant but to that little girl it had been everything.

'No, don't be daft.' Dimitri hooked his hand under her arm and yanked her upright. 'It was funny, sweet.'

'Yeah, hilarious.'

'Let me help you.'

'No.'

'Can you swim?'

'Yes,' she mumbled, the cold paralysing her bottom lip so she could barely speak. 'Just not very well.'

'Get that jumper off. It's pulling you down.' Dimitri tried to lift the sodden wool over her head.

'I'm fine.' She pushed him away as a massive wave smashed into her head, the water gushing into her mouth as she tried to speak.

'For God's sake, let me help.' Dimitri gripped her arm again, and then she felt him pull her towards him and she was too cold and too shocked by the force of the wave to stop him. She felt his hand on the skin of her waist, closer, tighter than before, so she couldn't kick away. She could feel her cheek pressed against the damp material of his t-shirt, smell his skin and the feel the graze of his stubble on her forehead. She tried again to free herself, too aware of him, befuddled by the icy ocean, the rain hammering down on them, her mouth tasting of salt and raw from gulps of seawater, but his arms locked her hard against him.

'Chill out,' he shouted.

'Let me go you great oaf.'

'No. You're slowing us both down and I'm freezing cold.'

'Well leave me here.' She struggled again.

'Yeah right.' He laughed and she could feel the rumble of his chest against her face as she tightened her lips together in a sulk.

The waves tumbled against them as he half-swam, half-walked them forward, the drag of the water with each receding wave drawing them back like they were in battle. Dimitri huffed with exhaustion. Ella felt her body go numb. The rain seemed to get heavier, hitting the water with great thumps.

And then finally they were shallow enough to stand. Dimitri blew out a breath. Ella opened her eyes and saw him shake his hair away from his face. But as she reached up to swipe her own matted hair from her forehead, Dimitri tipped her up and dumped her down with a splash.

'There you go, you can walk now,' he muttered.

'What are you doing?' Ella shouted as she batted about in the waves trying to right herself. When she stood up, straightening her clothes with an indignant huff, she glared at Dimitri and added, 'That was totally uncalled for.'

'What was?' he asked, hands out wide as if he had no idea what she was talking about, rain and lightning and thunder all clashing about on the horizon.

'That.' She gestured towards the water. 'You didn't have to drop me.'

'Jesus Christ woman. One minute you don't want me near you the next you don't want me letting go. You're fucking nuts.'

'Don't you swear at me.'

'Why not? Someone needs to.' He ran his hands through his hair, slicking the water away down his back as the rain kept pummelling. 'Christ I thought we'd got past this. You know, had a good day. You are unbelievable,' he said, storming past her through the water to the shore.

Ella watched him go, feeling the opportunity to say, *we did, we had got past it,* slipping away. She was embarrassed, her pride had been dented and she had felt momentarily paralysed by the memories, so she had fallen back on her stubborn aloofness. Unable to backtrack now, she just pushed after him through the water, wobbly on feet numb with cold.

A moment later she saw him smack the water and shout, 'And I lost my bloody fish.'

CHAPTER 18

MADDY

There was a spring in Maddy's step as she picked out vegetables from the market stalls along Berwick Street. She was so pleased she splashed out on steak at Whole Foods, then got overexcited by the self-service section and filled the little paper bags with shrivelled charcoal peppercorns and fleur de sel, earthy brown rice and scoops of flour, then she moved onto the spices and sampled a pinch of fennel – squeezing her eyes shut at the bitter tang. Her basket already overflowing, she balanced a box of flashy Earl Grey tea leaves on top and, thinking about breakfast and the possibility of making croissants, cut a slab of butter and snapped up a bar of the darkest chocolate they sold.

When it came to paying she decided not to think about the cost. She'd had a shitty day and there was nothing like good food to cheer herself up. She was going to go back to Ella's, cook up a feast, drink the bubbles and then maybe soak in the huge tub with the fancy taps.

It was only as she passed a pop-up stall outside the tube station selling cheap tinsel and terrible baubles that she thought about the tree lying on the floor.

'What can I get you love?' the stall-holder said through lips clenched around a cigarette.

'Enough to decorate a tree for–' She rummaged in her pocket and pulled out the note she had left. 'Ten pounds.'

The guy laughed. The cigarette wobbled up and down. 'Better be a pretty small tree.'

Maddy made a face. 'It's massive.'

He shook his head. 'I can do you a bunch of tinsel.' He held up a big, furry red and green clump. 'And a couple of these.' Boxes of pink spangly baubles, some shaped like hearts, some like lanterns.

Maddy made a face thinking of the decor of Ella's flat. 'What about those instead?' she asked pointing to the box of much more stylish silver stars.

'No can do, love, they're much dearer.'

'OK. Fine, yeah, let's go with the pink.'

'And d'you know what I've got, actually? I've got these.' He bent down and rummaged under the material skirt of his stall for a second before pulling out a box of dented gold decorations, baubles with white frosted scenes of pine trees and kids skating. 'Dumbo here dropped them this morning–' He pointed to a younger guy, face red with spots, just coming back with two Starbucks coffees. 'And one of those bloody rickshaws drove over them. I'll throw them in if you like. And that's probably the best I can do for you.'

Maddy glanced wistfully over his stall, at the boxes of fairy lights that flashed ten different ways, the silver strands ready to pour delicately over tree branches, big glass orbs with paper cut-out scenes inside and rows of decorations frosted with glitter and shaped like flamingoes and London buses. 'That's great, thank you,' she said, mustering up a smile as he handed her the bag of gaudy trinkets.

'It'll look great. Don't you worry.' He gave her a wink as he folded the tenner into his money belt.

'I'm sure it will.' She nodded.

'Oh don't look at me like that.' He held his hands up in the air. 'Go on then, go on. Pick something. Anything. Go on, I can't have those sad eyes on my conscience. Pick something.'

His young sidekick looked up shocked over the rim of his Starbucks.

Maddy paused. 'You're sure?'

'Yes, yes, I'm sure. Come on, lady. It's Christmas. Go on. Pick something. Just make it quick before I change my mind.' He blew on his fingerless gloved hands. 'Quick.'

Maddy bit down on her smile, her eyes dancing as she looked up at him and he rolled his eyes and shook his head.

Then she looked at everything on his stall. It was too much. She didn't want to pick one of the expensive looking glittery ones because that felt like an abuse of his generosity nor did she need any more hideous bushy tinsel. But after a moment of indecision her eyes landed on a star just like the one back home. Big and gold but a bit battered and old. The clip-on light shining down on the stall reflected in bursts off the chipped metal of the filigree fronds. It looked like it had been languishing on the stall for years, like it needed a good home.

'Can I have that, please?' she asked, pointing in the direction of the star, remembering the giggle of delight she'd shared with Ella when they'd watched their dad present nearly exactly the same one to their mum.

'The star?' He looked over to where it sat, half covered with a fake-Disney pack of streamers. 'And I thought I couldn't give that thing away.' he said, reaching forward, his large belly brushing the piles of tinsel in front of him. 'Take it. With my blessing.'

'Thank you,' she said, clutching it to her. 'I love it.'

He shook his head. 'Merry Christmas.'

'You too,' she laughed.

Back in the flat it was cold and dark. The emptiness hit her with a jolt. She put her bags of decorations and food down on the kitchen table and went around switching on lights, moving quickly from room to room, flicking switches and then turned the radio on in the kitchen. The station was playing *A Candlelit Christmas* live from the Royal Albert Hall, she turned it up then went in search of the central heating.

Once it was piping hot, she had a bottle of champagne open, the lights were blaring and *Good King Wenceslas* was booming from the radio, it felt a little less lonely.

Heading to the living room she decided to tackle the tree first. With no stand to hold it in place, Maddy had to balance the vast fir against the bookshelf and tie it in place with some string she'd been surprised to find in the cupboard under the sink. Threading it round and round till she was certain it was secure and knotting it with the same clove hitch that she used for the boats, she then went back to the kitchen and sliced up beef, onions and mushrooms to whip up her mum's infamous stroganoff, a recipe she knew so well she could probably do it with her eyes shut. She felt like all the appliances were watching in awe and excitement. The hob flared to life like a bonfire. She smiled as she took a swig of champagne and left the pan bubbling with satisfying pops to go back into the living room and start looping the gaudy tinsel from branch to branch.

She'd just moved onto adding the squashed baubles when the oven timer bleeped. Darting through to turn it off, she gave the sauce a quick stir, flicked on the kettle for the rice and was about to go back to the tree when she glanced out the window and saw the woman from next door pretending not to watch from the window.

Maddy paused.

The woman looked away, moved her head to make it look like she was perusing her book shelf.

Maddy frowned. Took a sip of champagne. She ran her tongue along her teeth wondering what to do. The woman's flat looked dark and a bit cold, she had her cardy wrapped tight around her thin limbs. Out in the courtyard it had started to snow lightly again. Maddy put her glass down, swept her hair up into a ponytail and headed over to the big French windows.

Throwing them open and stepping out onto her balcony she tilted her head and looked up at the snow as it fell, letting her mouth stretch into a smile. After a second she dropped her chin and turned to look in the direction of the woman's window. She was still there, her finger tracing the spines of her books.

Maddy stared till she looked her way and then waved. The woman didn't wave back. Maddy pointed up to the sky. The woman gave a cursory glance and then went back to her books. Maddy kept on looking her way. In the end the woman flung open her window and said, 'I thought I asked you not to look into my flat. I find it very intrusive.'

'This is my first snow in, like, fifteen years,' Maddy said. 'Well apart from some really fine flakes once in Athens.'

'Excuse me?' The woman made a face.

'This is my first snow since I was a kid.' Maddy laughed. 'I think it's beautiful.'

The woman looked, like she'd never really thought much of snow at all. 'Well,' she said, pulling her cardigan tighter. 'As I said, I'd prefer you didn't look into my flat.'

'Well you see I'm celebrating with a drink and I've just decorated my tree and made dinner and I thought, you know, maybe you might like to pop over for a glass of something. You'd be welcome to eat as well.'

The woman narrowed her eyes, suspicious. 'No I don't think so.'

'Honestly, I have loads and I can't eat it all myself.'

A movement at the window next to Maddy caught both their attention and they looked to see a young guy in a baseball cap glance at them then pull his curtains tight with a scowl.

'People don't want to communicate here, do you understand. We like to live our own lives.' The woman nodded towards the shut curtains as if proving her point.

'I'm just being neighbourly. Friendly.'

'The fact we are neighbours is incidental.' she said. 'It certainly isn't a prerequisite to friendship.' Then she closed her windows and walked away.

Maddy stepped back from her balcony and wandered back to the stove. She stirred the thick, creamy sauce distracted by the conversation, tasting a little on her wooden spoon and instinctively adding more paprika while thinking about being rebuffed.

The timer to say the stroganoff was ready went off just as Maddy was standing on her tiptoes on one of the living room chairs trying to hook the star onto the top branch. She jumped down and looked up to see that it was tilting wonkily to the right but decided to correct it later because she was starving. One half of a cheese and tomato sandwich and some champagne was not the kind of sustenance she was used to. It wasn't piles of spinach pies, glistening vine leaves of salty Dolmades or warm bread with gloopy olive oil the colour of straw.

But the image of the woman at the window ruined the first taste of her stew. The idea that she was too set in her ways, too stubborn to join her infuriated Maddy. Along with the notion that she could so easily turn down a hand of friendship without even getting to know her.

In the end Maddy stood up, leaving her plate untouched, and went to the sink to rinse out the plastic container that the mushrooms had come in. She spooned in piles of fluffy rice then topped it with the stroganoff, a sprinkling of flame-red paprika and flakes of chopped coriander before sealing the lid and nipping out into the hall to ring the woman's bell, leave it on her doorstep and run back to her own flat before she saw her. When she went back to her own dinner it tasted as fabulous as it was supposed to, the bitter taste of annoyance gone.

The next morning Maddy was making a cup of tea in one of the thin-rimmed, beautiful white Sophie Conran mugs, wearing Ella's White Company waffle dressing gown and waiting for her croissants to bake while wondering whether a job in the seediest street in Soho counted as making it, when her doorbell went.

The woman next door was standing on her step. Immaculately dressed in coffee-coloured trousers and a cream polo neck. She had on a slick of lipstick, which Maddy hadn't seen her wear before, and a dusting of rouge on her cheekbones. She reminded her suddenly of Veronica, the clothes almost an identikit of her dad's mistress's wardrobe.

Mistress.

Veronica would be furious if she heard herself described as his mistress. As 'his' anything. She'd terrified Maddy with her feline eyes, their perfect flick of black across the lashes, her sharp, clipped French accent, her stories of growing up in Paris, Montmartre, of how the girls were too dependent, too spoiled, not their own people. For women to survive in this world they needed to be strong, independent, streetwise. Able to stand on their own two feet, she'd said looking pointedly at Maddy who was clutching the tatty scrap of blanket that she wouldn't give up even at nine years old.

'Good morning,' her neighbour said in a tone a touch nicer than curt.

'Morning,' Maddy said, holding her cup with both hands as an icy breeze from the hallway curled its way into the flat.

'I'm returning this.' The woman held out the empty mushroom container.

'Oh.' Maddy looked at it. 'You could have just recycled it.'

'I wouldn't want to presume,' the woman said, thrusting the plastic box at her.

'Did you like it?' Maddy asked. 'The stroganoff.'

'Yes. Very much,' the woman said, her lips tight. 'Although I can't bear coriander. It's the devil's herb.'

Maddy snorted a laugh, 'Well I'll make sure I don't use it again.'

'Don't do anything on my account,' the woman replied.

The door across the corridor opened and a man in a suit walked out.

'Hi,' Maddy said.

He looked up and around as if unsure if she was talking to him.

'Hi I'm Maddy. I'm staying here for a while.'

He looked confused, his blond brows drawing into a puzzled frown.

'And this is–' she pointed at the woman.

'Margery. I'm Margery. Margery Pearce.' she said, almost nervous Maddy thought.

The businessman smiled. 'Hugo. Pleasure to meet you.'

'You too.' Maddy smiled. 'Perhaps we can all have a drink sometime.'

Hugo laughed, incredulous. 'Perhaps we can,' he said, and chucking what looked like his gym bag over his shoulder, strode out of the building.

'So Margery Pearce–' Maddy said, 'Can I tempt you with some freshly baked croissants?'

Margery wrapped her arms around her, looked left and right and then said, 'Well, I don't know.'

'They're Christmas ones, I add slivers of cranberry and orange zest to the chocolate. My mum says they're the best she's ever tasted. Come on. Please.'

'Oh very well,' Margery said and stalked in past Maddy, who smiled into her teacup as she took a sip.

CHAPTER 19

ELLA

The taverna was the closest and most obvious place to go to dry off, but Ella had watched Dimitri head towards it so she had carried on up the hill in the direction of the supermarket. There she had bought a beach towel and ten minutes worth of internet on credit.

To: Ella Davenport

From: Max

Darling, Unfortunately I think it's definitely over. I know. I know. I'm sorry. I'm a shit. (I blame my parents... come on, go with me on this one. You've met them!) It's just all this God damn lying, and messing about, it's exhausting. I'm no good at complex. You've seen me try and work that bloody kettle. Are you smiling at that? I want you to smile. You have a very beautiful smile that I will miss, but I hope actually that I'll see it again because you won't hate me and see that I'm a spineless bastard who just loves two women.

The problem is, I find, as always, I want both. But, I have come to realise that I am just a person with simple pleasures – I don't have what you see in me. You're too good for me. (Christ even I can see that's a cliche but because it's true and I can't think of better I'm not going to delete it. *shows that I'm simple* Is that what those

stars are for? Fuck I have no idea. *Simple* No, I'm not
convinced that I've got this star usage quite right. I'll have
to ask someone from our IT department.)

Anyway. You see I'm nervous. I'm rambling. Going for
cheap laughs. Christ, this is probably the longest thing I've
written since English GCSE. Amanda, I think, is happy
with me as I am. I have no pressure to be better, which is
actually quite a relief (but I'm not saying it's your fault.
Not at all. You were right to push me. I'm just weak. I'm a
man! Ha ha.)

OK, so enough with the rambling. Time to wrap this
thing up. Keep the flat. I'll take the cars and the place in
Suffolk – that seem fair? If not, let me know.

Hope Corfu is superb. Heard the weather is awesome.
Have an ouzo for me, pumpkin. (There's actually a tear in
my eye. Honestly.)

Max x

As she sat on the concrete step out the front of the
supermarket on the top of the hill, watched kids playing
football in the street, an old guy in a workshop bashing
away at a bit of metal, saw Dimitri in the distance bailing
out his boat, watched her mum, through the plastic rain
covers, chatting to a table of customers, Ella realised just
how wrong she had been for Max's world. His view was of
cocktails on his dad's yacht, taking the dogs to the shoot,
getting his top hat out for Ascot and his old school blazer
for Henley. His view was all rose tinted.

What affected her most deeply was that after reading
– after staring at the email with tears in her eyes until the
ten minutes timed out and a box popped up asking her if
she wanted to extend her session, after closing it all down
with shaking fingers and asking the shopkeeper to add a
Fanta Lemon to her tab – her presiding emotion, after the
initial shock, was relief. A sense that she had been walking,

trudging, for the last few years along a very beautiful path, but carrying with her a huge suitcase with no handle. She realised, as she picked the label off her Fanta, that while holding the suitcase in her arms she hadn't quite been able to look over it, only peek round the side. As a result, she realised, she wasn't quite sure what her view was.

She looked across the bay at the heaving clouds hanging low over the water, exhausted and plump with the promise of more rain. Then down at Dimitri, bent over with a bright yellow children's bucket in his hand chucking water out into the sea, cigarette dangling from his lips, red sou'wester flapping over his khaki cargo pants, rain-soaked shaggy hair flopping forward over his eyes. She reached up to her own hair, half dry since her soaking in the sea. She found her touch was unaccustomed to the thick waves she felt beneath her fingers. And it suddenly occurred to her that she hadn't put her head under the water when she went swimming for more years than she could remember. Blow-drying her hair straight afterwards was too much of a pain. Instead she did this terrible girly swimming, her chin jutted out and her eyes glaring at anyone who made a splash as they swam past.

The yellow-eyed cat from the taverna appeared next to her, wound his way through her feet and paused just out of reach of her hand, watching.

Ella couldn't stop thinking about her hair.

'Ella?' She was snapped out of her memories by her mum calling up the road from the taverna. 'I think I'm going to need some help.'

None of the planes or ferries were leaving because of the forecast storms. Bus loads of people were arriving for a dinner that they didn't have the capacity to cater for. Her mum had frozen in panic.

'How can I help?' she asked, a touch out of breath.

'God Ella, I just don't know,' her mum said, her hand on her chest like she couldn't quite catch her breath. Ella peeked out the kitchen door to the tables packed with people, the plastic rain covers bowing as chairs pushed against them and more tourists tried to squeeze round the edges. 'I've never had this many people here out of season. If it was the summer I'd have four people working. I don't even know if I have enough food,' she said, then patted her heart and added, 'I can actually feel the panic – here, right here in my chest.'

If there was one thing Ella knew about it was taking control. It was being calm under pressure and formulating a plan. She pushed her mop of wavy hair back off her face and said, 'Calm down. Let's think about this rationally.'

'I feel a bit sick,' her mum covered her face with her hands and took some calming deep breaths.

'Well for starters, how about we open up the kitchen? We've got the fireplace and the tree. We'll make an occasion of it,' Ella said just as her grandparents ambled inside, eyes wide at the flock of guests waiting outside. 'It'll be all self-service. Gran you sort the wine and the drinks, lay it all out on this table here with the glasses.' As Adrian said nearly every board meeting, Ella never failed to make something out of nothing.

Ella looked at her grandmother expectantly, who in turn was looking slightly perplexed at Ella's mum and shaking her head while saying, 'Well yes I could. But we've never had people in here before.'

'Well you've got them now. Let's get moving. Grandpa, you'll need to light a fire.'

He glanced over at his wife and Ella's mum, clearly quite taken aback at having been asked to do something. When neither of them told him not to worry and just sit down, and instead he was faced only with Ella, hands on hips and one eyebrow raised in challenge, he reluctantly pushed himself back up to standing and shuffled towards the big stone fireplace. 'Let's get it all festive, make a show of it,' Ella went on. 'People can come in, warm up, have something to drink while we put together some sort of set menu. How would that work? Would that work?' she asked, looking back towards her mum.

'Well I think that sounds like a marvellous idea,' her grandmother said, collecting the glasses from the cupboard.

Ella watched as her mum went to look through the doorway at all the people, study the scene for a moment running her hand back and forth over her mouth and then glance back at the big table.

'Yes,' she said, looking again from the doorway to the table. 'Yes we could lay out some bread, cheese and I've made some onion marmalade for Christmas, we can have that. There's cheese and spinach pies and I can just quickly fry up some calamari. I suppose if it's all finger food then we can have bowls of tzatziki and humous and I have some meatballs I can fry up. OK. Yes. I think we can do that,.' She made a face towards Ella who nodded as if to say the more the better.

'It's good we've got you with us, Eleanor,' said her granddad as he shuffled over to look for fire lighters.

Ella paused for a moment, consumed by a sense of pride that she was useful in her own right. This wasn't her filling Maddy's best-waitress shoes or being the polite house guest.

'And how about we have *melomakarona* afterwards? I haven't made them for yonks?' her mum said, looking directly at Ella as she suggested it.

Ella glanced up, surprised. Thought about the melt-in-your-mouth little cookies, super sweet and unbelievably moreish that her and her mum would make together while watching *Santa Claus: The Movie* or *Scrooged* and she'd love it because no one else wanted to watch with them. It was their thing. Their little tradition. Her dad and Maddy only liked proper Christmas films like *White Christmas* or *It's a Wonderful Life*, which they'd watch in the other room while decorating the tree. The taste of *melomakarona* in her mouth, of the honey spiced syrup on her tongue, wasn't just the taste of Christmas, but the taste of one of the few times in her life that it was just her and her mum, alone.

'OK.' Ella shrugged, pretending to be all casual.

'OK,' her mum replied with just the hint of a smile. 'Maybe you could make the syrup,' she added as she walked over to the work surface. 'You were always good at that.'

Ella turned to see her mum shrug and then look down to start sorting through some ingredients. She wondered if she was pretending to be casual as much as Ella.

After a moment's pause, Ella nodded and put down a teetering stack of glasses her grandmother had handed her to go and join her mum. She was unsure when the last time she'd cooked was, but knew that by taking those tentative steps to walk and stand next to her mum on the other side of the island unit she was crossing into territory that she hadn't ventured into for years.

As she took the first few paces, the smell of the fire starting behind her and the oil in the pans sizzling, the noise of the tourists outside and the rain smashing against the windows, it felt more important than anything else that was happening in her life. That, stupidly, taking the steps towards baking those sticky little biscuits was a small act of courage.

One foot in front of the other. Hand trailing on the stainless steel surface. Mum looking up from under her hair, all frizzy and wild from the rain and the stress, the expression in her eyes expectant, possibly nervous. Warmth from the flames that crackled and hissed weaving its way through the air. The corner of the work surface sharp on her hip as she misjudged the distance. Her mum reaching her hand forward to check that she was all right but stopping before she touched her. Ella shaking her head to say it's nothing. The sound of her grandmother outside telling the tourists what was going to happen, the dinner rules. Her mum smiling as she listened. Ella smiling as she listened. The two of them looking at each other, sharing the joke. And then suddenly the moment was breached.

They were side by side.

So easy. So quick.

Yet as Ella reached forward to pick up a bowl it wasn't only that she noticed her hand was shaking, but it felt like all the strength in her arm had disappeared. She was exhausted. The effort it had taken for her not to walk the opposite way, not to leave the cooking at a safe distance while she led and organised – maybe even nipped upstairs to get changed and do her hair – to peel off a layer of defence and stand next to her mum unguarded and equal, seemed almost overwhelming. Everest-like. And for a second, as her mum handed her a sieve and the weighed out flour, she thought she might cry.

CHAPTER 20

MADDY

'Christmas, young lady, is shit.'

Maddy put the pint of Guinness down on the bar and waited for the man to fish around in his pocket for change.

'I like Christmas,' she said.

He blew out a breath. 'You're delusional. It's crap. If I could just go to sleep for week and wake up and it was over that would suit me fine.'

'Still going, Walter. Change the record.' Mack glanced over from where he was changing the optics, swapping the normal vodka and whiskey for cheap Russian imports because it was two-for-one night, as he'd told Maddy during her brief induction.

Walter was one of three customers in the bar. He was in his mid- to late-sixties she thought, dressed in a black jumper and grey woollen coat. His hair was white and crazy like a mad professor and his glasses had red frames. Maddy had arrived, been snubbed by most of the other staff members, given her *Big Mack's* black t-shirt and sent to work the far end of the bar where Walter sat. Where apparently he sat every night of the week.

'No I just love Christmas.' Maddy shook her head. 'All the lights and the atmosphere and, my God, you've even got snow here.' She pointed outside to where tiny flakes had been falling like bubbles, drifting weightlessly through the air. Walter didn't turn and look. 'And have you seen Piccadilly Circus?' Maddy went on, 'I saw it today. Eros is in a giant snow globe. I think that's amazing. I've Instagrammed it.'

Walter took a sip of Guinness and narrowed his eyes at her. 'And you noticed the advertising round the bottom I take it? You know the globe popped last year, burst in the storms. Like a metaphor.'

Maddy heard Mack laugh and turned around to watch him unscrewing the top of a Russian gin and say, 'A metaphor for what?'

'Hot air.' Walter reached into his pocket and got out a pipe, putting it in his mouth unlit. 'So–' he nodded towards Maddy. 'Why are you here? You're far too young and innocent for this place.'

'I tried to tell her–' Mack called over from where he was battling with a broken optic.

'I needed a job.' Maddy shrugged. 'I wanted to come to London. See if I could make it.'

Walter gave a snort of laughter.

Maddy looked down at her hands, embarrassed at her admission. The door opened and a group of three young guys walked in, went straight over to one of the velvet booths and hunched round a menu. The icy chill that accompanied the slamming door made Walter wrap his big grey overcoat tighter round him. He was turning his collar up when he said, 'You know "making it" is a myth. A fallacy.'

'Blimey, you're full of Christmas cheer aren't you?' Mack poured himself a whiskey and turned to lean against the bar, his arms crossed over his belly, his gold signet ring glinting in the dull light. 'Don't listen to him, he's a washed up old hack.'

'Are you a journalist?' Maddy asked.

'No.'

'He's a writer,' Mack said.

Walter gave a dismissive wave of his hand.

Mack snorted. 'He wrote those books, for kids. You know he was a regular JK Rowling in his day.'

'You're not Walter *Brown*?' Maddy tilted her head to the side and studied him, the deep grooves in his face, the white stubble, the slanting green eyes.

Walter turned his head to stare at the door. Maddy looked back at Mack who nodded.

'I loved your books. I read them all. My sister adored them. Oh my God. You can't hate Christmas, all you wrote about was Christmas.' She held her fingers to her lips remembering her dad coming home from work with the last book in the series. They'd snatched it from him before he'd even had a chance to take his coat off and were upstairs reading it, Maddy doing voices for all the different characters and feeling a silly sense of pride when she made Ella laugh. 'I loved your books.'

'They're shit,' Walter said, taking a gulp of Guinness.

'He's never managed to write the Great British Novel,' Mack said, seemingly loving the wince on Walter's face.

'What do you mean?' Maddy asked, confused.

Mack laughed, 'He's got a chip on his shoulder about writing for kids. Wants to write a proper book.'

'But I loved them.'

'I promise you–' Walter leant forward and tapped the bar with his index finger, ignoring her question. 'You will never make it.'

'Jesus, thanks a lot!' Maddy laughed.

One of the guys got up from the table and came over to the bar with the menu. She made a move to serve him but the sullen girl with the hyena stare, who she now knew was called Betty, shooed her away and took the order herself.

Walter hadn't stopped talking, he was waving the pipe in the air as he carried on. 'Because you'll always want more. Stands to reason. It's the addiction of the dopamine rush. You'll never believe that you've made it. Ever. Look at you. Tall, pretty, seem to be reasonably funny, you look smart, you have good teeth, you've made it already. What more do you want?'

Maddy got a cloth and wiped down the bar, just for something to do, she didn't want Mack to think that all she did was stand and talk to Walter all shift. 'I want–' she started, then got embarrassed. 'What did you want? I don't know what I want.'

Walter put the pipe back in his mouth and said through clamped teeth, 'Yes you do.'

Maddy screwed up her mouth and then said, 'OK. I want people to hear me sing. I want that to be how I make my living.'

'Mack, this girl does not want to be a barmaid.'

Mack nodded where he stood, reclined by the bar, sipping his whiskey and checking his phone. 'I know that Walter.'

'Well put her on the stage.'

'I don't need another person on the stage, tonight.'

'Why the hell not? Look at her, she's much more attractive than anyone else you usually put up there.' Walter pointed at Maddy with his pipe and then fumbled in his pocket for some matches.

More groups of guys walked in, more frigid air accompanied them. As the windows darkened and the street lights outside started to come on, big groups came in straight from work and all squeezed into the tiny booths, stealing chairs from other tables so those that didn't fit on the velvet benches could perch at the end. That was when Betty finally relinquished her stronghold on customers and Maddy began to feel the pressure. When she had no idea where something was, like the flashy champagne or a vintage malt, Walter would lean forward from his stool and point it out for her. Betty certainly wasn't interested in giving her a hand, and Mack was out front, circulating, chatting up the ladies and laughing with regulars, a bottle of what he called *Christmas Spirit* in his hand that he poured free shots of into empty glasses. Maddy had had a sip of it early and involuntarily shuddered while trying to stop herself coughing and it coming back up out her nose.

'He gets them so damn pissed they stay all night and spend a fortune,' Walter said, watching as Mack worked the crowd. 'They love him.' Then he looked back at Maddy and said, 'Don't you worry. I'll get you on the stage.'

Maddy was trying to pour three pints at the same time and open a bottle of slimline tonic so couldn't look up when she asked, 'Why? Why would you help me?'

'Because I want to see someone realise their dream,' he said with a wry smile.

Flicking up the beer pump handle, Maddy gave Walter a massive, toothy grin and said, 'I'd really appreciate anything you can do.'

An hour later, as the crowd had started to get more raucous, the music blared full volume and the whole place smelt of alcohol as strong as lighter fluid, Mack leant over the bar and said to Maddy, 'OK, you're on.'

She looked from Mack to Walter, who cocked his head as if to say *I told you so*, and then back to Mack who clapped his hands and said, 'Come on, you've got about fifteen minutes to get changed.'

'OK,' Maddy stammered. Untying her apron and squeezing past Betty and the other barman whose name she'd forgotten, and joining Mack where he'd followed her to the far end of the bar. 'Thanks Mack,' she shouted above the noise of the crowd. 'Thanks, I really appreciate it. I really do.'

'Save it,' he said, putting his hand on her shoulder and pushing her through the swing door into the back room.

The corridor was a dirty cream with scuffs all over the walls and floor, a strip light flickered and stacks of boxes half blocked the way. As the doors swung back they muffled the noise outside and the quiet made her ears ring.

'I didn't want to put you on because I don't think you're right for it. But–' Mack was marching her forward. 'I owe Walter a favour and well–' he shrugged. 'You're old enough I suppose to decide what you want.'

She frowned up at him as he led her into a dressing room where four other girls were busy putting their make-up on, slicking back their hair and straightening the seams on their fishnet stockings. In the corner a plastic Santa was shaking his hips to a tinny version of *Rockin' Around the Christmas Tree*.

'It's up to you if you want to do it or not. I thought you seemed a bit too–' Mack paused. One of the girls looked over, her dressing gown hanging open, underneath was a red satin bunnygirl suit with white fur trimming. 'Innocent, I suppose. But who am I to stand in the way of someone's dream.'

CHAPTER 21

ELLA

The Little Greek Kitchen cooked up a feast as the rain poured. The tourists milled in the fire-warmed kitchen and watched with delight as Ella dipped little *Melomakarono* biscuits into sticky syrup while Sophie dropped batter into bubbling oil to make golden honey puff *Loukoumades*. She then bathed the donuts in thick honey and cinnamon while piping hot and handed them round on pieces of kitchen towel. Her grandfather was up from his chair and holding court where he stood, leaning against the fireplace, chatting about the move from England to Corfu – how he'd never looked back, how they should all do it – and the tourists nodded with wide eyes drunk on holiday memories. The Christmas branches sparkled and the gold star winked in the light of the flames while the fibre-optic angel's wings rainbowed through all its different colours. The guests had feasted and drunk and were happily having their little glasses topped up with rich, black coffee with its lacy froth and scalding their mouths on biscuits straight from the oven. Ella's mum pushed her hair behind her ear with the back of her hand, nudged Ella on the shoulder and gave her a wink, a newfound camaraderie brought about by stress and success. And Ella bit down on a smile, feeling for the first time that she was part of it. Part of *this* life with her mum.

As the first of the buses hissed back into life, crammed with stranded tourists, their accommodation now sorted by harassed, understaffed reps, Sophie pulled up a stool for Ella and said, 'Here look, take a break, sit down, there's not much more we can do.'

The second bus load were filing out, all waves and smiles as they ran through the rain, and the kitchen held only the final dribs and drabs of tourists who had not yet been found a room.

'No, no I'll help you clear up,' Ella said, her legs heavy with tiredness but her mind radiating with an adrenaline-fuelled excitement similar to how she felt after one of her client pitches. They'd pulled something off, together, made a fair whack of cash and it had possibly been better than had there been a full complement of staff and table service. She didn't want it to end. Wanted to hold onto the moment where the evening had peaked, where they'd laughed together when hot oil had spat or a donut had come out a bizarre shape, or one of the tourists had had to shut their eyes in pleasure from a taste.

'Ella.' Her mum put her hand on her shoulder. 'Sit down. We can clear up later. Have a coffee. Oh no–' She put her hand over her mouth. 'You don't drink it do you? God, how could I forget?' She shook her head. 'You know sometimes it is really hard for me to equate the Ella now with when you were a little girl.'

Ella swallowed. She poured herself a glass of red wine for something to do.

Her mum stirred a spoonful of sugar into her coffee. 'It was lovely to cook with you again. I'd forgotten how good you are.'

'I'm terrible,' Ella said, quickly.

'No you're not. Just out of practice.'

Ella took a sip of wine. 'I haven't really cooked anything since I stopped living with you.'

Her mum paused. Ella watched her run her hand over her mouth. She looked exactly as Ella remembered her from being a kid – dressed in a white shirt, the sleeves rolled up, blue Levi 501s, cream Converse hi-tops and a gold necklace with St Christopher on it. Ella had the same necklace, her mum had sent it to her in Paris on her twenty-first birthday, she never wore it but she did carry it in her purse.

Ella's comment seemed to hang in the air, the words dancing about like little pixies, then when there was no answer, drifted off through the open back window and Ella felt like a door that she had tentatively opened swung shut in the breeze.

Her mum took a sip of her coffee. Then, as she placed it down on the surface next to the ripped packet of sugar, said, 'I like your hair like that. It suits you.'

Ella turned to catch sight of herself in the door window. Scrunching her hand into her loose curls, she made herself look at her reflection. Made herself stare. Her eyes wanted to narrow at the sight. The curls had always been a reminder of the self who didn't want to be at boarding school, who didn't want to win the maths prize every year, and the art prize. Who didn't want to walk alongside Maddy when she came to visit in the holidays, her sister all lithe and brown and freckled with her huge gappy smile and long straight sun-kissed hair. Ella with frizz from the sun, white-skinned from an English summer, her brain packed with knowledge about her dad and her life with him that she couldn't talk about because it made her mum shut her eyes for a moment too long and then get up and put the kettle on. When she went home her dad and Veronica would ask politely about Corfu but never really listen to the answer. So her experiences sat, caught, trapped like bugs in a web.

'I'm sorry you didn't cook again,' her mum said.

Ella was taken by surprise that her mum had brought the subject up again. 'It was no big deal.'

'It must have been sort of a deal, you used to love cooking.'

Ella shrugged a shoulder. 'I had other stuff to do. School. Uni. And when I was at home Veronica cooked.'

Her mum snorted. 'I'm surprised she knew how.'

'She's OK. She's an OK cook,' Ella said, wanting to defend Veronica but also wondering why on earth she'd ever mentioned her name.

Her mum raised a brow in disbelief. 'All that woman knows how to do is look good. She bedazzles. That's her trick.'

Ella tried not to roll her eyes at the word bedazzles.

'She got your father–' Her mum carried on, 'And then she turned you into a little carbon copy.'

Ella's hand stilled on her wine glass. 'She didn't turn me into anything,' she said quietly.

'Oh come on, Ella.' Her mum blew out a breath to get her hair out of her eyes. 'Look at you.'

Ella sat up straight. 'She helped me.'

'She ruined you.'

Ella felt her mouth drop open slightly. 'No she didn't.'

'You were lovely. So lovely, so pretty, so clever and then bam, you follow after her like a duckling and you're suddenly all Parisian chic and then going out with a man who–' her mum paused, almost realised suddenly what she was saying and who she was saying it to.

'Who what?' Ella asked.

The chair in the corner creaked as her grandfather got up and walked as quickly as he could manage outside.

Her mum sighed. 'Who didn't know how lucky he was to have you.'

'That's not what you were going to say,' Ella said.

'No, probably not.' Her mum shook her head. Outside it looked like a curtain of black had been drawn over the sky, birds were twisting in the wind, the sea was a rain-flattened grey. 'I was going to say–' She picked up the coffee cup and then put it down again. 'That it didn't seem that he loved you for you. It always felt like you couldn't be yourself around him.'

Ella licked her lips.

She heard someone appear in the doorway, and when she glanced over she saw that Dimitri had stopped on the threshold. He'd clearly heard what her mum had said, and was trying to back away as quietly as he could.

Ella realised she was on the verge of tears. She couldn't think straight. This was the other side. This was her mother's point of view. But it was too much. Too exposing. It threatened to undermine too much of who she was, and she wasn't ready. She was only just shoring herself up against Max. 'I'm sorry. I can't talk to you about this now.'

CHAPTER 22

MADDY

'Why are you back here?' Walter asked as Maddy sloped back behind the bar. 'Why aren't you up there?' he said, pointing to the stage where the girls were lined up on chairs, all lounging and lazy eyed, dressed in their Christmas corsets, lips slicked red, breasts spilling out, long satin gloves up their arms, black stilettos like skyscrapers, singing a sultry version of *I Saw Mommy Kissing Santa Claus*.

'Because that's not the kind of singer I want to be,' Maddy muttered, cheeks red, embarrassed that she'd had to come back past Betty with her smug smile on her lips, humiliated that she'd had to shake her head at Mack and run away from the girls in the dressing room, angry that Walter was sitting there with a big grin on his face.

'You said you wanted to make a living out of it. That was your dream.'

'You set me up. You made me look like an idiot.'

Walter laughed. 'You've never met me before. You know that I'm a grumpy old man and yet you trust me to help you. It's bizarre behaviour. And now you're angry with me. I gave you the chance to realise your dream. Handed it to you on a plate. I even cashed in a favour I was owed.'

'But that wasn't my dream.' Maddy shook her head, felt the annoying, unwanted prick of tears.

'It's never going to be how you want it to be,' Walter said, packing his pipe with tobacco and staring across at her with a look of pity in his eyes. 'It's like Christmas. A mirage. Get there and it's just like any other day. Young Madeline–' he said, sliding himself off his stool and opening his arms wide. 'You're already living the dream.'

At the end of her shift, the night bus deposited Maddy two roads away from Ella's flat. It was dark and the snow was falling thick, wiping out her footprints so when she turned around it looked like she'd never even been there. The main road was busy but the side street she turned down was deserted and, spooked by the stillness and aware of her aloneness, she wrapped her coat round her, pulled her hat down low and almost ran to the front door.

The light in the hallway never turned off. While she'd thought it completely un-eco, as she turned the key and slid through the doors into the warmth of the municipal space, she was suddenly grateful for the twenty-four hour blaze, the scary, dark city outside shut out for now. It was only when she was in the flat with the door shut that she allowed herself a moment to wallow in her naivety. In her stupid, hopeful sounding innocence. In her absolute terror of the girls, all casually confident, in the dressing room. She was out of her depth, sheltered, trusting. At Dimitri's bar they played backgammon, they watched X-Factor on YouTube, they flirted with tourists and added the shot after the mixer so the seasonal customers thought they were getting a super strong holiday drink, they spent their tips on locally brewed beer, they ate bread warm from the bakery when they walked home at four in the morning and ate prickly pears that she held in her jumper and skinned with a pen-knife, they watched the sunrise on the jetty and, when it was really hot, lay down on the boat to sleep. When she sang she had her guitar. She wore her holey jumper and her hair scrunched up on top of her head. Her grandfather would cut in midway through a Bob Dylan cover and people in the crowd would whoop and cheer.

Maddy leant her head against the back of the front door and tried to ignore the smell of stale beer and vodka that infused the air around her, seeping out of her clothes. Rolling her head to the side, she saw the dark shadow of the Christmas tree and felt a moment of calm, like it stood steadfast, familiar, welcoming. Still with her back pressed against the door she slid downwards so that her fingers could reach the plug, and flicked on the fairy lights she'd taken from the decorative fruit bowl in the kitchen and wrapped around the tree.

In an instant it glittered like gold dust.

She reached a hand out and touched one of the branches.

She wondered what her mum and Ella were doing. Whether they were talking and what they were talking about. In her imagination they were baking together, like they used to do on Christmas Eve, watching their crap films – Ella making witty little quips at the expense of their mum who would bellow with laughter. Maddy would sit in the living room listening, trying to be as funny with her dad but never quite getting it right. When it was all of them together Maddy was like a little entertainer, she could have them in stitches while Ella stayed quiet. But in smaller groups, Ella came into her own, when she was given the space to talk, to be herself. At the time she'd been jealous, but now when Maddy remembered those moments she had a feeling the same as the snow falling outside, like if she could she would capture it in a jam jar and put it in her pocket.

Staring sidelong at the tree she realised that she was really homesick. Alone, everything seemed so serious. So important. But had she someone to share it all with, she was in no doubt she'd be laughing by now. She thought about phoning, but her pride made her decide it was far too late in the night to ring. Instead she pulled her horrible alcohol sodden t-shirt off and walked across the moonlit living room to the vast wet room and tried to power shower the evening off her skin.

Clean and dry, Maddy wandered into the kitchen wearing Ella's pyjamas and a huge puffa jacket she'd found in the cupboard, her wet hair in a towel turban, her guitar tucked under her arm. Opening the French windows she sat half in half out, her woollen-socked feet resting on the balcony and watched as the snow fell silent. Over the back wall she saw the Christmas lights attached to the lampposts switch off and heard a car drive by, its tyres churning up the slush. Margery's lights were off but in the other flat she could see the flicker of a TV screen through a crack in the curtains.

She had intended to just sit there, not play her guitar but just let it rest on her thigh, feel its weight, its comfortable familiarity, but her fingers didn't listen. Her right hand strumming lightly, the sound floated out into the soft silence of the falling snow. She started with her favourites; Janis Joplin, Joan Baez's *Plaisir d'amour*, a bit of Dolly and then made herself smile by playing *I Will Always Love You*, which her mum adored. But it suddenly became a bit much – too sentimental, too foolish when she compared it to the girls in the stilettos who held the room in the palms of their hands. So she changed to Christmas carols, *O Little Town of Bethlehem, Away in a Manger, Silent Night.* Over and over she played them, like lullabies.

She stopped when the snow got heavier and her feet felt frozen to the balcony. Her hands were too cold to play and snow had drifted in and landed on her eyelashes. Brushing it away, she leant the guitar against the glass, stretched her back and pushed herself up to standing. It was only then that she saw the TV was no longer flickering in the flat next to hers. The window was ajar and the guy with the baseball cap was standing, watching, leaning against the frame.

Maddy jumped, shocked, then immediately apologised about the noise. 'I'm sorry if I kept you awake. I thought all the windows were closed.'

'Mine was,' the guy said, the light behind him silhouetting his outline. 'I opened it to listen. Sorry. Sorry. I should have said something.'

'No, no you're fine,' Maddy said, suddenly realising that she still had the towel turban on and trying to untwist it surreptitiously while also holding her puffa jacket closed so she wasn't standing there in her pyjamas.

'I wasn't watching,' he added. 'I promise. I'm not some creepy watcher or anything. I was just listening.'

'No honestly I didn't think you were.' Maddy's hair was hanging cold and wet around her face.

The guy nodded, his hands thrust in his pockets. 'OK then. I'll go in.'

Maddy pointed inside her flat. 'Me too.'

'OK. Yeah.' The guy held a hand up in an awkward wave and reached forward to pull the windows shut.

'OK. Yeah,' Maddy said back, but stayed where she was.

'It was good.' he added just before the French doors clicked shut. 'The playing.'

'Thanks.'

'You have a really beautiful voice,' he said, then nodded and pulled the curtains closed. Maddy watched, her front teeth biting down on her bottom lip, unsure whether she was embarrassed or flattered.

When she went to bed though, her audience of one seemed to somehow make up for anything that happened at the bar.

CHAPTER 23

ELLA

Ella was walking as fast as she could out the taverna, out into the sheets of rain, swiping it from her eyes and feeling it soaking through her skin.

'Wait.' She heard a voice call as she kept marching up the hill, no idea where she was going, rain soaking her shoes so they squelched like suckers onto the tarmac. 'Wait!'

She slicked the water off her face and looked back over her shoulder. Dimitri was jogging up the hill.

'Go away,' she shouted.

'Where are you going?' he shouted back.

'Up here,' she said.

'You can't,' he said with less of a shout now he was nearer. 'The mud has slipped and the path is blocked that way.'

'Well fine, I'll go up there.' Ella pointed towards where the road forked and kept marching.

'Wait. Wait. Stop for God's sake. Just stop. Let me say something.' He was next to her, his hand reaching for her arm.

She shook him off and kept her eyes fixed forward. 'We're not talking, remember.'

'I know. And I'm perfectly happy with that. I have no wish to talk to you. I just wanted to say one thing.'

He ran forwards a couple more steps so he was in front of her, jogging backwards.

'That's talking,' she snapped and Dimitri laughed. The rain had soaked through her clothes, her top sticking to her body, her white jeans now a dirty wet grey as her feet kicked up the muddy water that flowed down the hill.

'Just wait. Wait. Please.' He held up a hand.

'What?' She stopped, hands on her hips, water dripping from the end of her nose.

Dimitri had his sou'wester on, the hood up over his face half obscuring his eyes. He'd rolled his cargo pants up and was in bare feet. As he started to talk she looked down at his toes, slippery and black with mud.

'My father always used to say this one thing to us when we were growing up. Courage, he said, Dimitri, is not found in acts of bravery but in acknowledging your fears.'

'Very profound. Can I go now?' Ella said.

He laughed again.

'Don't go, Ella. Go back.'

'Piss off.'

'Honestly.' He reached out and put his hands on her arms. 'Go back. Go back and talk to her.'

'No.' She shook her head, felt the rain get harder, painful as it slammed down on them. 'Why should I?'

He shrugged. 'To be brave.'

'I don't want to be brave.'

He made a face as if to say that wasn't true. 'Well, to be happy.'

Ella shrugged his hands off her arms and pushed past him to carry on up the path. Ahead of her were olive trees, branches shaking with the force of the water, orangey brown mud running in rivulets over the stone walls dividing up the grove. The strings of Christmas lights bounced as the rain hit them.

Dimitri didn't follow her, but stayed where he was and she heard him sigh, exasperated, then shout, 'Your boyfriend is having an affair, you've run away to the family you claim to hate and your mum thinks you've never truly been yourself. What else have you got to lose, Ella?'

'How dare you!' She spun round, wide eyed and shocked. Then marched back down the slope, her shoes slipping as she tried to attempt downhill, so she slid a couple of paces, having to right herself with her arms. 'How dare you,' she said again when she was closer to him.

His eyes glinted with humour. 'I think you're afraid to find out that what you think about your mum isn't actually the way it is. Because if that does happen then everything you've done for the last however many years will have been a complete waste of time. I saw you with that guy when you came here. What's his name? Max? It was all show. All bravado. He was a prat.'

'Oh get lost. We're not even meant to be talking,' Ella scoffed, but she had been struck – he'd got her. She knew now, as the artist had said, there were two sides to every story. That, like the view out to the frothy waves, and the slate grey sea and the charcoal sky, not everything was black and white.

'Talk to her, Ella,' Dimitri said, more softly.

'Why do you care?'

'Because she's my friend.' He nodded back towards the taverna, rubbing his hands together against the cold of the rain. 'And, well…' He shrugged. 'I like you. I've always liked you.'

'Well.' Ella was embarrassed. Suddenly a bit tongue-tied by the simple compliment. 'Well,' she said again.

He just stood there looking at her, water dripping from the peak of his sou'wester hood.

Ella had lost all her words.

As they both stood there with nothing to say, a great wall of lightning lit up the horizon followed by thunder that boomed like an earthquake.

'We need to get inside,' Dimitri shouted over the noise.

'Fine,' she shouted back.

'Shall we go back to the taverna?'

'Yes. Fine.'

He held out his hand.

'I don't need your hand. We're still not talking,' she shouted and slid-slipped her way down the slope as the muddy water rippled past her feet, the sheet lightning flashed, the thunder roared, thinking about her mum back in the warmth of the kitchen, the smells of *Melomakarono* infusing the air, and trying her best to ignore the fact that Dimitri had just said he liked her. Always had.

CHAPTER 24

MADDY

Maddy was woken by a shaft of light streaming through a gap in the curtains right into her eyes. She got up to yank the material closed, to stay in the cocoon of dark oblivion, to forget she had to go back to the bar tonight, that she was lonely, that she was exposed as naive and innocent, and to top it all, that she still didn't have her suitcase, but her eye was caught by the sliver of view.

Outside the street was inches thick with white.

Jumping out of bed, Maddy stood with her hand holding the fabric of the curtain, looking out at the piles of snow teetering on the lip of the black railings, and branches that bowed under the weight of frosting. A spider's web across a panel in the window shimmered with beads of ice like diamonds. On the window sill was a little trail of bird footprints, on the pavement a freshly built snowman, twigs for hair and sweet wrappers for eyes. A kid in red gloves was throwing snowballs at passing cars. Icicles hung like daggers along the eaves of the building opposite. All around it was like the world had been coated in marshmallow. The sun that had woken her was dazzling off ice crystals in the air and making the snow sparkle like the crest of the waves back home. Maddy was entranced. The glass in the window fogged as she pressed her nose against it to stare out at the wonderland of white. Never in her life had she seen anything quite like it. A world of silence where glitter danced in the air.

'Maddy? Hello?' The sound of Margery's voice accompanied by a familiar sharp rap on the door made Maddy tear her eyes away from the scene.

She jogged over to the door and yawned. 'Hi Margery.'

'Are you not up?' Margery said, glancing at her wrist.

She seemed to Maddy to be all dressed up in soft leather boots, and a woollen knee length navy dress. There were pearls looped around her neck and a brooch in the shape of a basket of flowers pinned just above her right breast. Maddy fleetingly wondered if they were real rubies and sapphires as she ignored the comment about getting up late and said, 'What can I do for you, Margery?'

'Well you see–' Margery said, turning her back to Maddy, 'I wanted you to zip me up.' She pointed to where the back of her dress was half open and did a little act to show how she couldn't reach any further to do it up.

'Yeah, no problem.' Maddy leant forward and zippered the teeth together. 'There you go.'

'Oh thank you.' Margery said, then smoothed the dress down with her hands. 'That's lovely. Thank you.'

Maddy waited but Margery didn't say anything else, just ran her fingers down her sleeve, feeling the material and straightening the cuff.

'You look very smart, Margery. Are you going somewhere nice?'

Margery glanced up, 'Oh no. Nowhere. I just–' she paused, smoothed down the material again. 'Well. I haven't worn this dress for years. My husband gave it to me.'

'It looks lovely.' Maddy said with a yawn that she tried to disguise, wondering if this was going to be a long chat or not and hoping she could cut it short so she could creep back into bed.

'I haven't been able to zip it up on my own.' Margery said, her mouth tilting up into a half smile that seemed suddenly to make her vulnerable and shy.

'Oh.' Maddy frowned, realising in that instant that Margery had no one else. Maybe had acquaintances at her club or something like that, but no one who helped her, who came round and saw her. It was just her in her flat. And without Maddy she hadn't been able to wear her dress. As she wondered for how many years it had hung unworn in the wardrobe, Maddy stepped to the side and said, 'Do you want to come in for breakfast?' Awake now, pulling her hair into a bun and rubbing the sleep out of her eyes, she added, 'I can make pancakes with maple syrup and bacon.'

As she said it the door opposite opened and Hugo came out in his suit with his briefcase and gym bag again, and drawled, 'Sounds like heaven.'

'You can have some too if you like?' Maddy shrugged. 'You're more than welcome.'

'Couldn't possibly.' Hugo waved a hand in dismissal.

'Of course you could,' Maddy told him. 'Come on.' She ushered Margery inside and then held the door for Hugo. 'It's only pancakes and a chat!' she said as though he was scared to come inside.

Hugo cocked his head, his brow raised and then with a bemused laugh headed inside, 'OK then, why not? I tell you though, I like my bacon cremated.'

Maddy followed them in, set them up at the big table and went about mixing up batter and popping the pods into the Nespresso machine for the coffees. Margery and Hugo had absolutely nothing to say to each other without Maddy's intervention, so she fired off some questions in the hope that they might pick up a thread of conversation here or there and let her get on with the cooking. As luck would have it, Hugo's upcoming golfing holiday seemed to spark Margery's attention and they were up and running by the time Maddy was pouring the first ladle of creamy batter into the pan.

As the pancake bubbled and Maddy was slotting in the next Nespresso capsule there was another knock on the door. 'Margery, can you get that?' she asked.

Margery stood up and, brushing the creases out of her dress, seemed quite delighted to be given the honour.

When she came back in she looked distinctly unimpressed as she was followed by a middle-aged lady with thin black hair and a shelf-like bosom encased in a tight black turtle-neck. 'I don't mean to intrude–' the woman said, 'But was someone playing the guitar last night? I just, well, it was very late and I was trying to sleep. I'm not saying it wasn't lovely or anything but it was very late.'

'That was me,' Maddy said, glancing up from where she was flipping the pancake with a deft toss of the pan. 'I'm really sorry. It won't happen again. It was late and totally inappropriate.'

'Oh.' The woman gave an unsure half smile, seemed to deflate as she exhaled, almost as if she was geared up for much more of a fight.

'Would you like some pancakes and maple syrup?' Maddy asked, scooping the first pancake out with a fish slice.

'Oh no. No. I couldn't trouble you,' the woman said, shifting from one foot to the other.

'It's no trouble. I'm Maddy. Please, have a seat.' She waved the fish slice towards the table, 'This is Margery and Hugo, my neighbours.'

'Well I–' The woman glanced towards the door but seemed caught as to whether it would be ruder to stay or go. Clearly deciding that the more polite option was to stay and eat, she scuttled over to pull out a chair at the end of the big table. When she sat she pushed her hands under her thighs, like she was trying to be as unobtrusive as possible so she didn't take up too much space in the world. 'Hello. Hi. I'm Stella Cummings. I live upstairs.' She looked up at the ceiling then after a nervous pause said to Hugo, 'I think I've seen you sometimes, leaving in the morning.'

'Hi, yeah,' Hugo said, arm hooked round the back of his chair, iPhone in his hand as he checked his emails. 'I haven't seen you, sorry. I don't know anyone in the block.'

'I think I've seen you,' said Margery with a tight nod.

Maddy watched them all, trying to hide a smile at their ridiculous awkwardness as she dished up the thick, fluffy pancakes, crisp streaky bacon, charred for Hugo, and lashings of maple syrup. 'Here you go,' she said, balancing the plates up her arms and depositing them in front of her guests. 'Enjoy.'

By the end of breakfast, Hugo was going to fix Margery's living room light and email her re: golfing breaks, Stella had apologetically invited them all up for a cup of tea, and Margery had said that she could feed Stella's cat if she ever went away and if she made sure that there was enough food because she didn't want to have to go out and buy any. They'd consumed the stacks of pancakes Maddy had made and Hugo left saying that he'd be more than happy to pop round again if she ever had surplus.

The whole experience made her feel like she'd recaptured her *joie de vivre,* so by the time she was getting ready for her shift Maddy was feeling good again. Nothing at *Big Mack's* could bring her down.

'Maddy you're on *Christmas Spirit* duty!' Mack shouted from across the other side of the bar where he was standing on a stool taping some tinsel to the ceiling, his belly visible where his shirt had untucked. It was a big night for them he'd said as he'd gathered the staff for an impromptu meeting. It was office party night.

Betty had rolled her eyes and sloped outside for a fag, the others started to prep the bar for the upcoming rush. Maddy had tried to stay out of everyone's way and make herself look busy without having to make eye contact with anyone.

Walter was already in situ – looked like he'd been propping up the bar all afternoon. He'd given her a sidelong grin as she'd walked in but otherwise she'd ignored him. Today he was dressed in a white suit, white shirt and black tie. His shoes, that rested on the brass foot-rail running around the bottom of the bar, seemed shined especially.

'Madeline, darling, I have dressed up as an apology for my behaviour yesterday,' he said, leaning over the bar to where she was looking dubiously at the bottle of *Christmas Spirit*. 'I wanted to make an effort so that you might forgive me.'

'Ok, Walter.' Maddy shrugged without looking at him, then walked away. But when she heard him laugh she couldn't resist the urge to glance back over her shoulder, narrow-eyed, to show him that she wasn't impressed.

'Oh go on, forgive me. I like you. I like this small-town thing you have going on. It brings me endless amusement. Please. Don't hate me.'

Maddy shook her head. 'I can't believe I used to love your books. I'm so disappointed.'

Walter put his hand over his heart and feigned devastation as Mack jumped down from his stool and, reaching into the box next to him, hurled something in Maddy's direction.

'New outfits tonight guys. Don't worry Maddy, nothing too revealing!' he joked just as Betty was coming back in and Maddy saw her lips twitch in amusement. 'But something just to liven it up a little in here, help get the cash flowing.'

Maddy watched as the guy whose name she still couldn't remember tore open the plastic bag Mack had thrown his way and pulled out a sleeveless red and white checked cowboy shirt and matching neckerchief.

'What the hell is this?' he said, holding it up to Mack.

'It was the most Christmassy thing they had that wasn't an elf costume. You should be thankful.' Mack snorted a laugh and went back to hanging more tinsel.

Maddy gingerly unstuck the plastic flap on her bag and tipped out the contents. A cherry red boob tube with see-through plastic straps, neckerchief the same as the boys and an alice band with two gold stars that wobbled on springs. It wasn't terrible, but it wasn't exactly what she wanted to stand behind the bar wearing as she served toxic liquor to drunken office parties.

'I think you'll look marvellous,' said Walter, lifting his drink in a salute to the outfit.

'Up, up, up,' they were all chanting. Betty took a swig of tequila and then hoisted herself up onto the bar top where she tipped the two bottles she held upside down, splashing sambuca and tequila into the mouths of the eager punters, wetting their faces, soaking their shirts and stinging their eyes.

Maddy looked on dubiously and, deciding that the top of the bar wasn't the place for her, backed away and snuck out to do a circuit of the room with the *Christmas Spirit* bottle. Squidging through the mass of sweaty bodies, she pushed her way through the throng, shouting over the music to ask if anyone wanted a free shot.

'Just pour the bloody stuff,' Mack yelled from where he was cajoling a group of men in suits to down the last of their Taittinger and get in another magnum.

As Maddy felt herself being crushed and squeezed, two blokes behind her decided that the stars on her headband were a source of endless amusement. As they flicked them back and forth with their fingers she pictured the London life that she'd imagined; the darkened stage of Manhattans, rousing applause, cocktails after work with a host of new friends, lunch in some cool cafe as she read a paperback and sipped an espresso, strutting up Regent Street with armfuls of Christmas shopping. Trying to steer herself away from the pair wobbling her stars in every direction, holding the bottle of *Christmas Spirit* aloft and pouring it haphazardly into any glass she could find, she wondered if Walter was right. This, *Big Mack's,* was the dream.

Her feet slipped on the damp floor, elbows backed into her and knocked the bottle, soaking her boob tube in *Christmas Spirit,* the game to flick the stars on her head caught on with nearly everyone she passed. What was she going to tell her mum? What was she going to say when she sloped home in the new year? Someone pulled her hairband, making half of her ponytail fall loose. Not having a hand free to retie it, she wedged the bottle between her knees and attempted to plait it back up, but as she tried, she suddenly found herself lifted off the ground, three maybe four pairs of hands holding her tightly aloft. Looking down she saw the heads of the men in suits with the champagne. Out the corner of her eye she could see Mack, who winked and raised his glass in her direction, and as they crowd-surfed her forward Maddy was deposited on top of the bar to the cheers and delight of the already hammered punters.

'Oh God,' she said, her feet tripping on the beer taps.

'Enjoy it,' she heard Walter shout from the end of the bar. 'You're only young once,' he laughed.

Maddy glanced over to where he was giving her a double thumbs up. Below her was a sea of open mouths like fish waiting for the *Christmas Spirit* to cascade over them. The girls in corsets were up on the stage, mouthing, she realised, to a booming *Santa Baby*. A couple in the corner were snogging – an office party cliche. One girl was sobbing in a booth, her legs skewed like Bambi and her tights laddered. A tall man in a suit the colour of an aubergine was yanking down the tinsel and wrapping it round his neck like a shimmering scarf. The barman, whose name she didn't remember, was lighting sambuca in his mouth. Mack was spraying the room with a shaken magnum of champagne. And as she watched from up high, Maddy decided maybe she should just relax. Relax and presume that things would work in the end. Relax and notch this all up to experience. Because this was the dream, in a fashion. This was her, living her life. Egged on by the crowd, she tipped the *Christmas Spirit* bottle up and poured a shot into her mouth, the clear liquid dribbling down her chin making her shudder and shut her eyes and feel it burning up her nose. She could hear Walter cheer as she spluttered a laugh.

'Happy Christmas, everyone.' she shouted above the noise, the heat of the liquor fizzing through her, the drunken baying deafening, the frenzy as she poured the liquid down onto the laughing, whooping crowds of office workers who got crazy drunk together once a year, making her feel like she ruled the world.

'Maddy?'

She heard the voice as the music lulled and glancing down almost fell off the bar. It was Walter's hand who steadied her as she looked at the person who'd said her name, and the woman behind him who watched her with a calm, feline gaze.

'Daddy?'

CHAPTER 25

ELLA

'All I can say Ella, is that it was the hardest time of my life.'

The kitchen was empty except for the two of them. Ella and her mum. They were sitting next to one another at the big table. Ella was using her fingernail to carve the grooves in the wood deeper.

'I know.' Ella swallowed. 'I know it was. I can see that now. I can see it. It was just so lonely.'

Her mum exhaled slowly. 'I think the thing was, Ella, was that everyone thought you were much older than you were. You were always such a serious little thing that I think we just presumed, wrongly, that you could cope. That you would cope. Not like Maddy who couldn't be left anywhere on her own for a second,' she laughed, softly. 'We knew Maddy had to come with me. And well your dad had a new life and he was so busy that he couldn't take care of a child. Ella, I could barely take care of a child myself and as a parent I should have been better. I should have put you first, I should have done and it's a giant regret of mine because by not putting you first I lost you.'

Ella put her hands over her face.

Behind them the fire crackled and through the window she could see the rain drops merging together in rivulets down the window.

CHAPTER 26

MADDY

The music kicked off again as Maddy slid down from the bar, wiping her sweaty, alcohol laced hair back from her face and awkwardly readjusting her boob tube as her mind ran through better scenarios for bumping into her father.

If he cared about the setting he didn't show it, bridging the gap between them he stepped forward to hug her, but as he did Maddy took an uncertain step back, bumping into the bar and holding out her hand to shake instead.

The perfect gentleman, her father just smoothly took hold of her hand, his fingers cool and his grip strong, and said, 'It's good to see you, honey.'

Maddy gave her boob tube another awkward tug and glanced at Veronica standing behind him dressed in what looked like Chanel.

Before she had a chance to say anything back, Mack appeared and slapped her dad on the shoulder saying, 'Edward Davenport. Well I never. Didn't think I'd ever see someone of your calibre grace my humble abode.'

'I'm here to pay a bar tab for that lot.' He nodded towards the big crowd of suits in the middle of the room swigging champagne straight from the bottle and lining up the tequila. 'This is where they chose for their Christmas drinks,' he said, looking around with a slight wince.

'Well come again anytime. Maddy darling, get this man anything he wants,' Mack said.

Maddy tucked her hair behind her ear, watching Mack in awe of her dad, realising how well-known he was, Veronica standing back, her perfect hair, couture black dress and huge jewelled necklace seeming out of place in the chaos of the bar, yet somehow she still managed to radiate an aloof magnetism that had every man in the place glancing her way. Unable to think of what was appropriate to say, Maddy found herself starting to ask what drinks they wanted.

'Do you know, actually–' Her dad held up a hand to stop her. 'What I'd really appreciate is a couple of minutes just to chat to my daughter.'

Mack thought he was having a laugh. Then when her dad shrugged to show it was no joke, Mack turned to Maddy and said, 'Why the bloody hell didn't you tell me?'

'I didn't know.'

'What, that he was your father?'

Maddy rolled her eyes. 'No, that you would know who he was.'

'Everyone knows who he is. Christ, if you want to be a singer why haven't you gone straight to him?'

Maddy scuffed the floor with her foot, mortified. Telling her dad she wanted to be a singer was like telling the Queen she wanted to own Buckingham Palace someday. It was his industry, his contacts, his business. Edward Davenport was CEO of one of the largest talent agencies in the UK. A business he'd scrabbled to grow from nothing, supported by Maddy's mum who'd made sandwiches and cakes for local cafes and offices, taken in ironing and made curtains while their dad sat with the phone glued to his ear and Maddy and Ella had watched TV and lived off lentil soup in a house that had cracks in the windows and carpet repurposed from the closed-down department store up the road. Now her dad built megastars, branded icons, plucked boy bands from Butlins obscurity and made them global phenomenons.

He was the last person Maddy wanted to know about her tiny precious kernel of a dream.

As her dad took his usual confident control of the situation, ushering her to one of the empty booths at the front of the bar, Maddy remembered him leaning over, tucking her mum's hair behind her ear and saying, 'One day I'll buy you a mansion.' And her mum had held his hand and said, 'I'm totally happy as I am, Ed. I don't need a mansion.' Maddy had thought that the most romantic thing she'd ever heard, without quite understanding that all it showed were two massively diverging dreams for the future.

When she'd reminded her mum of that moment, one day when she was too young still to realise that they didn't really talk about her dad any more, her mum had paused, her hand resting on the neatly pressed shirt she was folding on the ironing board and sighed, 'God, that was probably the exact moment where it all started to go wrong.'

Maddy couldn't forget the feeling of not being able to put right something her dad had destroyed in his wake. Him bulldozing through life getting whatever he wanted no matter the cost, her mum the dreamer, the poppy getting crushed in the cornfield.

Behind her she heard Mack say to Walter, 'Now they say it, you know, there is a similarity there. In the eyes.'

The first thing her dad said when they sat down was, 'Do you need money? If you need money I can give you money.'

Maddy shook her head. 'I don't need money. I have a job,' she said, pointing back to the bar with a self-deprecating little laugh.

Her dad sat back, his fingers twirling a beer mat on the table, his black eyes watching her through the same thick dark lashes she'd inherited. 'What are you doing working here?' he said, incredulous, a slight smile on his lips, and she felt herself bristle.

'I needed a job,' she said, eyes narrowed, defensive. Wishing that this wasn't how he'd seen her the first time. Wishing she'd been doing something more impressive.

'Well why didn't you come to me?' He raised his hands wide in a gesture that implied that that would have been the most obvious course of action. Sweeping away years of no contact bar Christmas presents that arrived in the post, picked by his secretary or in a last minute dash to Selfridges. She hadn't sent him anything.

Maddy didn't answer. Felt herself retreating inwards. Any bravado and self-assuredness she had day to day just slithered to the ground now she was sitting here opposite her father, especially when the watchful eye of Veronica was thrown in as well. It was like she was nine again, wanting just to go home. Needing her mum standing between them like a shield, telling her she never had to go back. Fighting for her on the phone with the door shut so she wasn't meant to hear. Ignoring Ella's furious looks.

'I should go back to work,' Maddy said after a pause, glancing back towards the bar where Mack was now serving and a couple of drunk blokes had jumped up on the bar, shirtless and tinsel clad, to dance with Betty.

'I think they'll manage without you for a few minutes, Mads. I haven't seen you for–' He didn't have the number of years off the top of his head and she could see him counting.

'I'm going to go back,' she said, sliding out of the booth.

'Maddy, wait–' He put his hand on hers. As she felt his palm on the back of her fingers she suddenly felt like she couldn't breathe. Remembering that this was her dad. That he would kiss her goodnight, hug her when it thunder-stormed, check behind the curtains that there were no monsters.

'Edward.' It was Veronica who put her hand on his sleeve and pulled his arm back. 'We should go. Leave Maddy to her job.'

Maddy hated that she was grateful.

'Maybe you could meet in the morning. Take Maddy for breakfast. Take her to The Ivy.' The corners of Veronica's mouth curled into what Maddy assumed was a smile. 'Come on. Let's leave her to it.'

Her dad's lips had pulled into a thin line as he looked from Veronica back to Maddy and then across to the antics at the bar. 'How are you getting home?'

'On the bus,' she said, not meeting his eye.

'Oh for God's sake.' He shook his head.

Veronica unclipped her purse and pulled out a fifty, folding it in two and handing it to Maddy. 'Take a cab. A black one.'

Maddy didn't want to take Veronica's money but her dad looked like he might settle in for the night otherwise and wait to drive her home himself.

'So can I take you for breakfast?' her dad asked, hopeful, as he unfolded his coat from where he'd had it draped over his arm and started to stand up.

Maddy nodded.

'I can pick you up,' he said quickly.

'No.' She shook her head. 'I'll meet you there. Where was it?'

'The Ivy,' Veronica said as she curled up the collar of her camel coat and knotted the belt. 'Leicester Square tube.'

Maddy nodded, eyes trained on their collars rather than their faces as she backed away with a wave and then turned and headed towards the safety of the bar. She ignored Walter when he leant over and tapped her on the shoulder for the gossip, and refused the hand of one of the men dancing on the bar. The moment was past. She felt hollow, like her insides had been scooped out.

As she stood there, her feet sloshing in a river of beer and spirits, she realised that no, she wasn't hollow, she was lopsided. And the half she'd convinced herself that she didn't need, didn't want, had just walked out the door.

She watched the back of her dad's coat disappear as the door closed behind him with a feeling she hadn't expected bubbling up within her. She put her hand on her chest. Felt the St Christopher that hung on a long, thin gold chain just above her breast bone. Felt a moment's guilt when, against her better judgement, breakfast suddenly held as much excitement as the snow.

CHAPTER 27

ELLA

As her mum topped up their wine, Ella turned her head to look at the fire and seeing the flames licking the last of the blackened wood, she pushed her chair back and went to the stack to pick up two great logs. As she chucked them into the grate she watched the fire jump and dance with greedy excitement, then crouched down to prod the ash and wood with the poker as the yellow-eyed cat sauntered in and edged its way towards her. She didn't touch it, just rocked back onto her heels and let the cat weave its way in front of her. It stretched itself out long, sparks jumping towards its fur as it rolled as far towards the grate as possible, and Ella watched silently, her flip-flop clad toes tickled by soft white fur as the cat inhaled.

'You know once when I was here I went and sat on those rocks over there...' Ella turned and pointed to a promontory. 'And I sat for the whole day waiting to see if you or Maddy would come and find me. I hid myself behind an olive tree and I waited. And no one came.' She laughed at how ridiculous it sounded. 'And then in the end I got cold so I came back and Maddy was watching TV and you were tutoring some little kid English and you just looked up and said *"Did you have a good day, honey?"* and Maddy said, *"Shit Mum, she's just killed him"* because she was watching Eastenders – which I didn't watch – and that was it! That was my great protest, over. And no one even knew it had happened.' She ran a hand over her mouth and laughed again. 'What an idiot. All I wanted was to be noticed. And wanted. And I know you hate Veronica but she noticed me. And I like her. She's really nice. See look you flinch so I can't talk about this.' Ella sat crossed legged on the floor and looked over at her mum. 'I need you to step into my shoes for a second. I need you to see her and Dad not as who you know them to be in your mind, but who they are to me. There are all these stories and things in my life that I can't tell you because this wall comes down and it's so hard and it's just an extra wedge. We've just had all these wedges between us. God, and then there was what I said before the funeral.' Ella put her head in her hands for a second.

Her mum leant forward, her forearms resting on her knees. 'Ella, you don't still think about that do you?'

'I think about everything!' Ella said, looking up to meet her mum's gaze.

Before her mum had moved to Corfu, before their aunt's funeral, before she'd even passed away, Maddy and Ella had gone to stay with their dad for the weekend. When they'd arrived back home on Sunday night their mum had sensed something was wrong. Not from Ella, Ella had perfected a look of calm neutrality. But Maddy was all red-nosed and snivelling, refusing to look Ella in the eye. Before they'd walked up their mum's drive, Ella had grabbed Maddy's shoulder and pulled her back into the bushes and whispered, 'Just don't mention Veronica.'

Maddy had flung herself into their mum's outstretched arms and said, 'Daddy's met someone else. She was there. She's awful. She's French and her name's Veronica.'

Ella had had to close her eyes for a second. She hadn't wanted to see her eyes widen just a fraction, the split-second freeze of her body, the half-smile that showed her teeth, the tightening of her arms around Maddy's skinny little waist.

'Well that's OK, honey,' her mum had said, pushing Maddy back, her hands resting on her shoulders so she could look her in the eye. 'He's allowed to move on. We're all allowed to move on.'

'I hate her.'

Her mum had smiled and pushed Maddy's hair back, tucking it behind her ear. 'She can't be that bad,' she'd said softly.

The cat rolled over so that its tummy was across Ella's feet. She could feel all its ribs as it breathed. The fire kept her there, mesmerised. The wood cracking from the heat, the flames licking up the chimney breast.

When her mum had come in to kiss Ella goodnight she'd paused while folding her clothes up and said, 'Do you think it's serious? No actually, sorry, I shouldn't have asked. Don't answer that.' Then she'd left the room. Ella had crept out of bed and watched her mum standing in the hallway, her shoulders rising and falling, wondering if she was crying and not really knowing what to do.

Ella had immediately liked Veronica when her dad had introduced them. She'd liked how she'd stood back when their dad had walked with them, liked how she'd listened when Ella had told them about the English essay she was working on. She'd felt herself bristle when Maddy had played up, refusing to look Veronica in the eye, refusing to even acknowledge her.

'I really like her, Ella,' her dad had said that evening when Veronica had gone out on the balcony to have a cigarette and Maddy was in bed.

'You do? That's good.'

He'd nodded. 'I loved your mother, I really did. But this–' He'd bitten down on his lip and shaken his head. 'This is something I didn't know was possible.' He'd glanced across to where Ella was standing next to him, both of them in front of the big sliding glass doors of his apartment. Outside Battersea Bridge sparkled with white lights, the reflection wobbling in the choppy water of the Thames. 'I shouldn't be telling you all this. I'm sorry. It's unfair.'

'No it's OK, I like her.' But it was unfair. She'd been torn between liking being trusted with the information and wanting to put her hands over her ears and la la la. The only benefit was that it all seemed very *Neighbours* and her friends at school would devour it.

'You do? So do I. I really like her. I just–' He ran his hand through his hair.

To Ella he was almost like a stranger, she'd never seen him this excited, this happy, this relaxed.

'I really love her. And it means so much to me that you like her, El.' He'd winked at her and the shared confidence had made Ella feel all grown-up. She'd taken a sip of the cup of tea she was holding and beamed back at him but he was already looking away, back to the sliding doors were Veronica was stepping inside from the balcony, the faint smell of cigarettes entwining with Chanel No 5.

'OK. No. Tell me. Is it serious? How French is she?' Her mum had asked later that week. Then she'd put her hands over her face and said again, 'No. Sorry. Don't tell me. I shouldn't ask. Sorry, Ella.'

Ella had looked across at her, seen the desperate need in her eyes and, walking to stand next to her had said, 'No. He said he doesn't. You know he actually said he really misses you–' And before she knew it she'd spun a whole new reality, one that seemed to make everything better.

CHAPTER 28

MADDY

Her father had left instructions with the doorman to show Maddy up to the Piano Bar which was part of the private members' club of The Ivy. She was ushered further up the road from the main door to a flower shop where a discreet entrance, opened by another doorman, led her to the club rooms above the restaurant. Maddy hadn't been able to sleep the night before and, after being up for hours, decided to make use of the spare time by hiring a Boris Bike and cycling from Pimlico along the river, up The Strand and into Covent Garden where she'd got hopelessly lost and had to ask a Big Issue seller directions to The Ivy in exchange for buying one of his magazines and a coffee from Pret which he said he didn't need but it was so cold Maddy ignored him.

The cycle had been stunning. The snow melting around her in the low morning sunshine. The river a sparkling reminder of her view of the sea, the sound of the gulls and the honk of the cruise ships. She'd gone past Westminster Abbey and Big Ben. Seen the Houses of Parliament dusted with white and heard the bell chime as the clouds merged grey over the spire like candy floss on a stick.

Now, as she headed up to the Piano Bar, she pulled off her hat and fumbled nervously with her gloves as she took the stairs. She cringed when she looked down and realised that her shoes, wet from the cycle, left footprints behind her. As she tried to wipe them away with her toe the doorman angled his head and said, 'It's not a problem, madam.' Which just served to make her more embarrassed and unsure. Then as the door opened to the Piano Bar she was immediately grateful she'd swiped Ella's snakeskin Gucci cigarette pants and red cashmere sweater.

The people were impeccable.

A gentleman with perfect olive-skin and designer stubble, wearing loafers with no socks and a blazer with a crest on the pocket, was sipping a cappuccino with a woman dressed head to toe in beige with matching highlights. Alone in one of the armchairs, a lady, rotund in fur with a tiny dog in a Louis Vuitton carrier, was doing the crossword over her bifocals. In the centre table four businessmen were having hushed chat over eggs Benedict and by the window a blonde woman with massive sunglasses sat tapping on her iPad. Maddy was certain she'd seen her on the front of yesterday's Times, which was delivered to Ella's door every day. Her first thought was that she wanted to take a picture for Dimitri, but knew this wasn't the place to start getting her phone out for a quick celebrity-spot snap. Instead she did a sort of crab-like sidestep to the bar in the hope that she might remain inconspicuous and be able to survey the area for her dad.

It was as she was about to perch on a stool and pretend to look over the breakfast menu, that she heard her name called from a table over by the window.

'Walter?' she said, surprised as she looked towards the voice.

'Madeline, Madeline. Don't you scrub up well?' Walter said, lounging back in his big leather armchair, a black coffee steaming on the table in front of him. 'Your father's over at the corner table with his rather stunning companion.'

'Oh God, I didn't think she was coming.' Maddy bit her lip and shielded herself behind the art deco screen.

Walter took a sip of his coffee. 'I've never seen Edward Davenport look quite so nervous. It's marvellous.'

Maddy peered over the top of the screen to where her father and Veronica sat. 'You think he looks nervous?'

'Oh absolutely. Terrified. Whatever you've done to him it's certainly worked.'

'I didn't do anything.' Her tone sounded childish as soon as she said it.

'I bet you didn't.' He laughed. 'Go on, shoo. Go and play happy families.'

Maddy sighed, suddenly deflated by the whole idea, wishing that he hadn't brought Veronica.

Walter watched her over the rim of his coffee cup. 'You should make the most of it while you have it, my dear. Believe me, when it's gone it's terribly lonely.'

She glanced back to see if for once he was actually being sincere but Walter wasn't looking at her, instead he'd put his cup down and was flicking through The Independent.

'Walter?' she started but he waved a hand at her.

'Go on, go away,' he muttered without looking up. 'I have important things to do.'

Maddy walked tentatively along the edge of the art deco screen that divided the room, past the table of businessmen and the woman who she was sure was famous and paused just before getting to her father's table.

He hadn't seen her and she took the opportunity to watch him. His black hair was greying at the temples and just starting to recede. He'd hate that, she thought, remembering when she'd stand on the toilet seat and comb his hair for him. He didn't have many wrinkles but his skin looked thinner, paler, like maybe he was doing too much exercise. He did look nervous, she realised, playing with the ring on his finger, checking his nails were clean, checking his watch. She noticed that he still wore his grandfather's old Timex which surprised her because she'd expected him to have upgraded to a Rolex.

Veronica was reading a magazine, her hand resting on his arm. She looked amazing, hair pulled back tight, neutral make-up, black polo-neck and tiny pearl studs.

In a couple of steps Maddy was next to their table, they still hadn't seen her so she coughed and her dad shot up, hand on her arm, smiling nervously. 'Sweetheart, you made it. God you know part of me thought maybe you might not come. No. Yes. No I'm glad you're here. Sit down.'

He moved round to pull out one of the big leather armchairs for Maddy. As she went to sit down he leant forward to pass her the menu and they collided. He apologised, she claimed it was her fault and then perched awkwardly on the edge of the seat.

'The eggs are legendary,' her dad said as he went back round the table to his own seat, 'The smoked salmon is beautiful. Veronica always has the granola.' He was scanning the menu and then looking up at Maddy with each suggestion. 'You might want the pancakes. Not as good as Mum's but–'

She looked up, startled that he still called her Mum. He didn't notice, just kept reeling off possible options.

'I'll just have a coffee and a croissant, please,' Maddy said.

'Almond? Raisin? Chocolate?' Her dad was rambling.

'Just plain please.' Secretly she wanted everything on the menu. There were dishes on there that she'd never tasted, like haggis on toast or Burford Brown soft-boiled eggs. There was smoked haddock which she adored and eggs Arlington which she saw from the plate on the table next to their's that the poached egg came wrapped in smoked salmon. But she wasn't relaxed enough to enjoy anything she ordered, and a plain croissant seemed like something Veronica couldn't say anything about.

'OK. OK.' Her dad held up a hand. 'I'll be back in a sec.'

He dashed off to the bar to order which caused much fluster amongst the waiters and Maddy wondered if he'd gone because he needed a breather.

Veronica sat silently over the other side of the table, her fingers thrumming on her closed magazine. Maddy glanced up at her and then across, pretending to admire the art on the wall behind her while wondering what she was thinking.

After a moment, Veronica sat back in her chair and crossed her legs. Maddy noticed the red soles of her Christian Louboutin boots.

'So you have grown up at last,' she said, her expression unreadable.

Maddy was so astonished by the comment that she didn't reply. Just floundered, wondering if she'd heard her correctly.

'I have been waiting for this for a long time. For finally you to grow up.'

'Well I don't see that that's–' Maddy started, her voice full of affront.

Veronica held up a hand to cut her off and leant forward, pointing to her across the table. 'Don't you start. I have lived with your ghost for years. You were young and I understand that it is hard when your parents split up but you waited too long to fix things. And even now pff–' She blew out a breath. 'You come to London and you don't even see him?' She shook her head. 'If you were my daughter I would have had words with you long ago.'

'Well it's lucky I'm not isn't it?' Maddy said tartly, eyes narrowed.

'Don't start, Madeline. Don't be defensive. Last time I see you, you have pigtails in your hair and you are shouting to him to choose between us. That is the behaviour of a spoilt child. I don't want you in his life because you have made it unbearable. It was unbearable for him to choose. Imagine–' She rested her chin on the palm of her hand. Maddy watched as the five or six gold bracelets she wore fell with the movement to rest midway down her arm, her skin tanned the colour of caramel. 'You imagine now what he lived with?'

'Well he bloody chose you didn't he.' Maddy curled her lip and slumped back, arms crossed in front of her.

'No you stupid girl. He made the choice not to let you dictate his life. Who should have to live by the rules of a nine-year-old? You were just too stubborn to see it. Like your mother.'

Maddy gasped. 'Don't you dare bring my mother into it.'

'Oh.' Veronica waved a hand in dismissal. 'Such melodrama. Always with you.' She glanced over her shoulder to see Maddy's dad coming back to the table holding a tray of coffees, beaming at them. 'This is your chance, Madeline, to show whether you are still a spoiled child or finally a grown woman.' Veronica unclipped her purse and pulled out a mother-of-pearl cigarette case. 'I wonder which one you will choose.'

'Coffees. All round. I've never done this before,' her dad said, holding up the tray. 'Quite novel, really. Darling, there's no granola so I got you avocado on toast. Maddy, there was a choice of jams, I chose apricot, you like that don't you?'

Maddy nodded. Internally reeling from Veronica's little pep talk.

'I am going outside for a cigarette. Don't wait for me if the food comes.'

'Are you sure?'

'*Absolument.*' Veronica pushed back her chair and sauntered out, people pausing their conversations as she passed.

'You OK, Mads?' her dad asked, pouring milk into his Americano.

'Yes, fine.' She nodded. Still stunned. 'I'm fine. Can you hold on a minute?' Maddy mumbled as she stood up. 'I just have to nip to the loo.' Then she scarpered in the direction of the toilets.

Once inside she put her hands on the marble sink and took a couple of calming breaths. Then she looked up at her reflection, saw the dark circles under her eyes, and whispered, 'He's not the victim. I'm the victim. I was the victim. Shit.' She ran her hand over her forehead. It had never really occurred to her that he'd missed her. He had Ella. He had given Ella every opportunity that Maddy hadn't had. He had let Maddy go. Yes perhaps making him choose between her and Veronica had been stupid but she'd only been little. All she saw Veronica as was a woman who drove a nail further into the possibility of him coming back. He had left them and she had kept him away.

Locking herself in a cubicle Maddy shut her eyes and saw him standing at the back of the crowd at her aunt's funeral. The sharp breeze making the ends of his scarf flutter and his overcoat flap open. She remembered the look of surprise on her mum's face when she saw him. Felt the jolt herself that he had come. All dressed in black, but still with his briefcase, straight from work.

The afternoon was freezing, not a cloud in the sky, just a pale icy blue sheet above them that stopped the frost in the graveyard from melting. The trees were painted white, the ground crunched underfoot. Up until the point she'd seen her dad, Maddy had been consumed by the fact she'd forgotten there was a hole in the bottom of her left shoe and her toes were frozen. She had avoided looking at anyone's faces just to block out the sadness. But as the crowd walked away from the grave, Maddy heard her mum sob so loud it made her cry herself. And her dad was there in a second, his arm around her mum holding her up, stopping her from falling. And to Maddy the moment had been magical, like a movie. The moment that would change everything. When he realised that he still loved their mum and would support her forever. He'd walked her back to his car as Maddy and Ella had trailed behind. Maddy hopping with pins and needles, her left foot completely numb, but not caring because she had watched, seen her dad's fingers press into the thick faux-fur of her mum's coat, and thought that this would be the moment he realised that he was wrong.

'Sorry,' Maddy said as she got back to the table. 'I just felt a bit queasy.'

'Are you OK? Do you want me to get you anything? A soda water? That's good for stomachs?' her dad asked, poised to jump up from his seat.

'No, no I don't need anything.'

The waiter had brought the breakfasts. In front of Maddy was a huge fluffy croissant and a little bowl of golden jam. Her napkin was green with The Ivy embroidered in white. If she hadn't been with her dad she knew she would have slipped it into her bag as a memento.

'God it's so nice to see you,' her dad said, just staring at her as she unfolded her napkin and laid it in her lap.

The best Maddy could do was a half-smile as she started spreading jam on her croissant.

At the wake Maddy had piled her plate high with mini sausage rolls and was popping them one by one into her mouth as she sat on a footstool in front of the fish tank. Ella was nibbling at a ham sandwich when she suggested they go in search of their parents.

It was their grandparents' house and while all the rooms were familiar, they felt like strangers as they watched people in black nodding and laughing softly as they ate off paper plates.

The door to the library at the far end of the corridor was ajar. Maddy recognised her mum's voice. Neither of them suggested they tiptoe but it seemed appropriate, and when they got to the door they stood silently, watching as their mum ran her hand down their dad's cheek, bit her lip and half-smiled, thanked him for coming and reading the tilt of his head as a lean in for a kiss, opened her mouth, closed her eyes and waited.

Maddy waited.

Ella put her hands over her eyes.

But he didn't lean in, instead her dad gently lifted his hands and put them on her mum's shoulders and holding her where she was – Maddy expecting a crushing *Gone with the Wind*-style embrace – took a step back and muttered, 'Sophie, don't.'

'Really?' Her mum's eyes had snapped open. 'I need you.'

'And I'm here.'

'Exactly!' her mum had said, her hands going up to her head, pressing into her temples. 'I thought that was...' She glanced to the door, seemed to see the kids but not see them. 'Ella said?' she paused. 'Oh God. I can't believe this is happening when my sister's just died.' She covered her face with her hands. 'I'm so stupid. It was just when Ella said you missed me–'

'Ella said what?' Her dad frowned.

'Nothing.' Her mum shook her head. 'Ella didn't say anything. It's nothing. It was me, I just thought, this woman's French for God's sake. You can't even speak French.'

Next to Maddy, Ella had started to cry.

'What have you done?' Maddy hissed.

Ella had cried more.

Maddy had run away and half the wake had been spent with her dad and mum trying to coax her down from their granny's apple tree.

When her dad had had to leave Maddy had refused to kiss him goodbye. She had said that she would never see him while he was with Veronica and her dad had taken a deep breath and said, *I can't do that, Maddy.*

And while her parents had a hushed argument at the front gate, Maddy had run to Ella, who for the first time wouldn't tell her that everything would be OK, who instead glared at her and said, *Why did you have to tell her about Veronica? Why couldn't you have just shut up. This is your fault. It's all your fault.*

And Maddy had narrowed her eyes and hissed, *It's not my fault, it's yours. You said something and now they hate you. We all hate you.*

Maddy had refused ever to visit her father again after that.

Now as Maddy spread jam on her croissant and her dad tried to make small talk, she thought about her mum wanting her to stay in Corfu. Wanting to hold everything just as it was. And Maddy so desperate to be set free.

It wasn't the same, she knew. But perhaps everyone needed to be given the chance to change. Perhaps, she realised, there were no victims. Just people. And what if it was no one person's fault, but everyone's?

CHAPTER 29

ELLA

'I thought you blamed me because I told you that he didn't love Veronica. I've thought that for ages but it's only as I'm saying it now out loud that it seems ridiculous. You knew, didn't you?' Ella thought about Max and Amanda, and about all the times she'd wondered if he was seeing someone else, kidding herself that everything was fine but knowing that it was just a matter of time before one of them acknowledged it was broken. 'You knew he loved her right from the beginning.'

Her mum huffed a laugh. 'Of course I knew. I knew.'

Ella got up and went back to sit at the table.

'Ella, you shouldn't have heard or seen that conversation, I should have talked to you about it, but to be honest I just wanted the whole day to disappear. We got stuck afterwards about Maddy refusing to go and see him and that was just horrendous and I suppose the moment passed to talk to you. I think because you were so strong and clever I thought you were more of an adult than all the rest of us put together.'

Ella had to press her fingers into her eyelids and hold them there.

'That's what I'm sorry about. I'm sorry that I didn't see you were a little girl still who held all this inside you. We should have done things differently – your father and I. But you can't just blame me. Yes I should have talked to you about what happened at the funeral but you should have talked to me. You should have said how you were feeling. And then you go and get all made over by Veronica–'

'Don't start that.' Ella held up a hand to stop her.

Over by the fireplace the wood cracked and bubbled as the flames started to die. Ella threw on another couple of logs and watched them spark. She could feel her mum watching her.

'OK fine,' Sophie went on. 'You became who you wanted, whatever, but that person was a complete stranger to me. You ran off with this boy who had no interest in any of us, then you jetted in and out of here like some film star and acted like we were all completely beneath you. Ella, I didn't even recognise you when you first showed up with him, my own daughter.'

As Ella threw the wood onto the fire the cat scarpered at the noise and the flames licked wild and red. She could still feel an anger tight in her chest that she just couldn't let go. Years of lonely rejection sat still burning. Years of isolation. Letters written in faux excitement about what a great time she was having at school. A life in two halves that never crossed. The churning in her stomach every time she thought about the lies she'd told her mum. The pressure. The confusion. The loneliness. Through the window the rain was unceasing. The leaves of the trees shaking with every drop. The cat was now pressed up against the wall under the dripping awning. The road was a river of stepping stones.

'What are you thinking?' she heard her mum ask.

Ella bit her lip. Dimitri had said that courage wasn't in acts of bravery but in facing your fears.

She saw her mum's reflection in the mirror above the fireplace. Saw her looking the way she wished she had looked at her for years. Realised how all the tiny unresolved things between them, the unspoken thoughts, had piled on top of each other and the wedge had got bigger and bigger until Ella had eventually become Ella-and-Max and a complete stranger to this life. To the smells and the tastes. Even, she thought as she saw the gold star hang too heavy for the branch and the fibre-optic angel wings glow, to the Christmas decorations. To the things that she had wanted to be hers but were so out of reach.

She looked at her mum's reflection again. Met her eyes in the mirror.

All that time she'd wasted. All that effort.

What was she thinking?

'That if I forgive you,' Ella said, turning to face her mum. 'I will be letting down the me that sat on the bed thinking you had forgotten me and spent hours willing you to come get me and sat on that rock on my own wanting you to find me. There's too much. There's too much there and–' she shook her head. 'I can't work out whose fault it is.'

'Does it have to be anyone's fault?'

'Yes,' Ella said. 'Yes because otherwise it's all just been a waste of time.'

What were the awards, the prizes, the small talk at flash dinners, the clothes, the polaroids, the flat, the car, the holidays, the hair, the everything – what was it all for?

'Ella, you can't control everything,' her mum said, reaching forward to touch her on the arm.

But where was she if she wasn't in control? Who was she?

CHAPTER 30

MADDY

Maddy watched as Veronica stalked back to the table. Her camel coat was draped casually over her arm, a light dusting of snow caught in the material, and she was pulling off matching tan kid gloves finger by finger.

It felt to Maddy as if her and her dad were just beginning to get somewhere. The small talk was becoming bigger talk and her spine was beginning to curve back into the leather chair. She didn't want Veronica to come back to the table, so when she turned to veer off in the direction of the Ladies', Maddy couldn't help but feel relieved.

'So you got a boyfriend?' her dad asked, scooping a forkful of scrambled egg into his mouth.

Maddy shook her head.

'No one?' he asked, incredulous.

'Uh uh.'

'It's because you're too pretty. They're intimidated,' he said, cup of coffee in one hand, slice of toast in the other.

Maddy laughed. 'Yeah right.'

He took a bite of the toast. 'It's true,' he said, mouth full. 'I could never ask a pretty girl out. I was terrified. Your mother had to make the first move.'

Maddy's smile paused on her face. She tore off a bit of croissant while her dad watched her and said,

'She was a massive part of my life, Maddy. I do talk about her.'

'Yeah, no I know.' Maddy nibbled on the pastry, not really sure why she had thought her dad had wiped that part of his life out of his memory but still uneasy with the casual manner with which he talked about her mum. 'Anyway. It's all tourists at home and I'm never going to go out with one of them.'

Her dad put down his cup in order to fork some more fluffy egg onto his piece of toast and said, 'I bet they're all running after you though.'

'Nah.' She shook her head. 'Well some are but you know… I'm trying to focus on other stuff at the moment.'

'So I hear.' Her dad nodded. 'You want to do more with your singing. I remember when you used to sing when you were little. And you'd do those cute dances for us all dressed up.'

'Yeah, it's not quite like that any more.' Maddy felt herself blush at the memory of dressing up as Ginger Spice, a Union Jack flag wrapped a couple of times round her and Ella's old Buffalo trainers stuffed with newspaper so they fit her feet. She'd wiggle around and dance like a maniac and have her parents in stitches.

'Do you know actually who you should talk to about this–' Her dad looked around the club.

'Dad, don't.' Maddy shook her head. 'I don't want you to help me.'

'No, no it's not helping, at all. It's just I–' He stood up and searched the room. 'I saw him come in… Rollo!' he called over to a man sitting at a table by the bar. Dressed in a blue suit, with thick blond hair and a face that looked like it had been ravaged in too many rugby games, Rollo held up a hand in greeting. When her dad beckoned him over, he pushed back his chair and ambled across to their table.

'Edward. Good to see you.'

'Rollo, I want you to meet Maddy, my daughter.'

Rollo turned Maddy's way, his brows raised as if intrigued to meet her, and drawled, 'Charmed,' as he held a hand out for her to shake.

Maddy sat up a little straighter, felt her fingers get crushed in Rollo's grip as she looked up at him, his shoulders so wide they were almost blocking out the light.

'Maddy wants to get into the industry,' her dad said, smiling proudly Maddy's way. 'She's got a great little voice.'

Maddy cringed.

'You could talk to her, couldn't you? Give her some advice, that kind of thing,' her dad said, before shaking his head and adding, 'She doesn't want my help.'

In the background the resident pianist started to play and Rollo looked over distracted. 'Always the same bloody music. Why do they do it? It kills me.'

'Oh I like it.' Her dad closed his eyes for a second to listen while behind him Veronica appeared, sidling up to the table in a haze of Chanel No 5, her lipstick freshly applied. 'I thought you hated the club, Rollo,' she murmured.

Rollo shrugged. 'A man's allowed to change his mind,' he said, then reached into his suit pocket and pulled out a business card and handed it to Maddy. 'Meet me here later,' he said, tapping the address on the card. 'We'll talk.'

Maddy reached up and took it from him as he buttoned up his jacket, ran his fingers through his hair and sighed, 'Right, I have to go. People to see and all that. Veronica, always a pleasure. Ed, call me later. Maddy, see you around three-ish.' With a quick salute he was stalking out the room, the fabric of his jacket straining over his shoulders, his head turned so that he could catch his reflection in the mirror by the door.

'What was he doing here?' Veronica asked, looking suspiciously at Maddy's dad as she folded herself into her seat.

'Having breakfast.' Her dad laughed.

'I can't believe you did that.' Maddy had to hold her hair up off her neck to cool down her blushing embarrassment.

'What?' her dad asked, mid-buttering another slice of toast. 'He was here. You take advantage of situations, Maddy. That's all. Go, meet him, have a chat. He's found some great talent in his time. He's got some big acts signed to his label. You have nothing to lose.'

'*She has a great little voice.*' Maddy mimicked her dad's earlier comment, rolling her eyes.

'Well you do? Or at least you did,' he said with a smirk. 'What did you want me to say?'

'I don't know.' Maddy shrugged. Felt the thick cream business card in her hand and couldn't quite suppress a rush of excitement. 'Do you really think he'll be fine with talking to me? I don't want him to do me any favours or anything but… Well.' She bit her lip. 'I mean, if he liked me, that wouldn't be a lie would it?'

Her dad shook his head. Smiling around his mouthful of toast.

She could feel Veronica watching, silently, but didn't look at her because she knew she would ruin the moment.

'OK. Yeah, I'll meet him.' Tucking the card into the pocket of her bag, she rolled her lips together to hold in a smile. 'Thank you.'

'I didn't do anything.' Her dad popped the last bit of scrambled egg in his mouth and laid his knife and fork down. 'He was here. That's all. It was an opportunity too good to pass up.'

'Well, thanks.' Maddy nodded, a thrum of excitement about the afternoon coursing through her.

'No problem. Here…' her dad said, chucking over a clean napkin that Veronica hadn't used. 'Put this in your bag while no one's looking. You can't come to The Ivy without a souvenir.' With a wink he leant back and crossed his arms, grinning, relaxed, looking suddenly like he did all those years ago.

CHAPTER 31

ELLA

In the morning Ella's bag was packed in minutes. Just as it had been when she left. Flung open and outfits from the wardrobe bundled together and rammed inside. She'd slicked her hair back in a side-parting low ponytail and donned black chinos and a black polo neck. She looked in the mirror and described her reflection as hard, maybe brittle. Then she thought back to her physics GCSE – Brittle: liable to break easily.

Hauling her case off her bed, she wheeled it out into the rain to the phone box.

'What do you mean there are no flights? This has been all week practically,' she said, trying to keep her voice even.

'I'm sorry madam. There's nothing because of the storms.' The travel operator sounded bored, like he'd explained this to a hundred people already that morning.

'Well how the hell do I get off this island?' She wiped some condensation off the glass in the phone box, looking out to sea at where her mobile was lying somewhere amongst the seaweed.

'You could make friends with someone with a helicopter.'

'Was that a joke?'

'Yes, madam.'

Ella made a face at the receiver. 'Well I don't find it very funny.'

'No, madam.'

'So when are the flights going to start again?' she asked, noticing Dimitri's bike pull up outside the taverna and watching as he wiped the rain off the visor of his helmet.

'We can't say, madam. When the storms are better.'

Ella huffed.

'Call back tomorrow,' the guy added with a sigh and hung up.

She was stuck.

The rain pummelled the glass of the phone box as she stood in what now seemed inappropriately smart clothing. Dimitri ran past her with his bike helmet in one hand, head down, leather jacket soaked. She could barely look at him because he said he liked her. It felt like a joke, something to help mend relations with her and her mum. A little something to sweeten the deal, she told herself. He would be expecting happy families inside the taverna. All made up, all fears conquered.

But it was still sitting like a balloon that wouldn't burst. She couldn't back down. Couldn't forget it. Couldn't just whitewash those years and walk in and let her mum be her mum.

But she was trapped. There was no way off the island.

Scrabbling around in her purse she found another couple of euros and dialled her dad.

'Ella! Honey. How are you doing?' His voice made her instantly calmer. She slumped against the phone box door.

'I'm OK. You know–'

'You'll never guess who I've just had breakfast with,' he said, cutting her off, his voice the most animated she'd heard it in years. 'Maddy,' he carried on without letting her guess.

The name was like a slap.

Ella sucked her bottom lip in and bit down.

'Isn't that amazing? We just bumped into each other. She's working at *Big Mack's,* that dreadful place in Soho. God knows how her mum can be happy with her working there. But anyway, it was brilliant. I took her to The Ivy, we had brunch. And Veronica was there. I think it was OK, Ella. I think they got on OK.'

Ella had to swallow away a lump in her throat that was just petty jealousy. How was Maddy in London having a great time with their dad? Where was her comeuppance? How could she have been a brat for fifteen years and it just be forgotten over Burford Brown eggs at The Ivy?

Maddy had cut their dad off and he could forgive her in seconds. Yet Ella was packed and ready to leave the moment their mum talked with any honesty about the past. She glanced back through the misted window at the taverna. At the painted sign on the wall. *The Little Greek Kitchen.* At the strings of fairy lights that her mum had obviously strung up last night all around the door, like glittering rain. And at all the olive trees that had red baubles now hanging from their branches and the wreaths of pine hanging on the loo doors. All the little windows had been sprayed with frosted snow and the nativity moved to a table by the doorway with a pot of what she presumed was *vin chaud* next to it and a stack of mugs. Overnight the place had been Christmas-ified. Ella looked at the date on her watch, surprised to see that there were only a few days to go.

'It's the best Christmas present I've ever had, Els. Just–' She heard him take a deep breath, wondered for a second whether he was going to cry. She pictured him at his desk, his PA glancing through the glass door to his office to see him patting his cheek with a handkerchief. 'I just never thought I would feel so God damn delighted to have breakfast with my daughter and my wife.'

'I'm glad,' Ella said, trying not to let the words stick in her throat.

'All I need now is you back and maybe we can all go out. I'm sorry about Max,' he added.

'It's fine.' She waved a hand. 'Almost a relief,' she said with a laugh.

'Come on, Els, I know you, don't be all poker faced about it. Have a good cry. If I remember your mum gives very good hugs.'

'Yeah.' Ella did a kind of laugh that she hoped would gloss over everything.

'Ella?'

'What?'

'Are you all right?'

'God yeah, I'm fine. Don't be daft. I was ringing to check you were fine. Not feeling like you and Veronica were going to be all alone at Christmas. But you've got Maddy so all's good. Is it snowing?'

'Buckets of the stuff. Can't go anywhere. And of course the trains are buggered, as always. I'm sorry I won't be seeing you this year.'

'One year off is OK.' She looked down and picked some of the fluff off her jumper, feeling herself start to get too emotional.

'It'll never be OK, Ella,' he said and she could hear him smile.

She sniffed back the possibility of tears and shut her eyes for a moment, then said, 'Well I'd better go. No more euros. Happy Christmas, Dad.'

'You too, sweetheart.'

When she hung up Ella had to put her face in her hands for almost a minute. When she looked up her granny and granddad were walking past in their Peter Storm jackets and a huge golfing umbrella. Her granny tapped on the glass.

'Everything all right, darling?'

Ella opened the door a crack, hoping her mascara hadn't run at all. 'Oh fine, fine. Just work stuff.'

'They work you too hard. It's nearly Christmas,' her grandfather called out from underneath the massive brolly.

'Do you want a cup of tea?' her granny asked.

Ella shook her head.

'Well don't stay out here too long. You'll get cold.'

'No, I won't.'

Her granny was about to walk away when she paused, turned back and opening the door to the phone box said, 'It's lovely to have you here, you know? Just lovely.' Then she smiled and hurried after Ella's granddad who'd marched off with the umbrella.

Ella watched them go. A rising sick feeling in her stomach of uncertainty. Lack of control. Of being trapped. The rain claustrophobic in its persistence.

She needed to sort this out. She needed to let go. She needed to find what it was about herself that was real.

She picked up the phone and dialled.

'Hi Max,' she said, leaning against the glass. 'It's Ella.'

CHAPTER 32

MADDY

Maddy didn't go home after breakfast. Instead she waved goodbye to her dad – Veronica had already left because her miniature schnauzer had been home alone too long – and headed blindly into London to do some Christmas shopping. If she went back to the apartment, she knew she'd just get nervous about her three o'clock appointment. So, A to Z in her pocket, she decided she wanted to just get lost and see what happened in the two hours before she was meeting with Rollo.

The snow was falling more heavily again. The pavements down side streets were thick with white and the roads a mess of carved-up black slush. Maddy tried to stick to the main thoroughfares where the grit had melted the snow and she didn't have to worry about ruining her shoes.

Following a couple of tourists, she turned a corner into Leicester Square, walked past the cinemas playing Christmas blockbusters and the queues of kids outside M&M World and, glancing at a signpost, decided to carry on in the direction of Piccadilly Circus. The flakes kept falling thick and fast as she walked. Shoppers barged past her with big bags up their arms from Hamleys and smaller ones from the Apple Store. Maddy had left a present for her mum back home but she wondered now if she should have got Ella something. They never had before but this year seemed different. And what if her dad asked her to come to his for Christmas? Would she accept? Did she want to spend the day with him and Veronica? She'd presumed it would be the first Christmas she spent alone but, with only a few days to go, it felt suddenly like he would ask her. And she would feel obliged to accept.

She'd have to get them presents…

The thought made her stop in the middle of the pavement on Regent Street.

'For Christ's sake! What's wrong with people?' A woman with a buggy barged past her.

'Sorry,' Maddy called, distracted, and ducked into Starbucks to get out of everyone's way. One red cup of peppermint mocha later and she'd decided that presents for her dad and Veronica were a necessity and she would do as the American couple sitting next to her were doing and head to Fortnum and Mason.

'Will you look at it honey? Will you just look at that window?' the American wife called out as they stood in front of the infamous Fortnum's Christmas window display, snow piling up around their feet, covering their jackets, landing cool on their cheeks. Her husband nodded and lifted up his camera to take a shot. They had no idea that Maddy was tagging along with them as she too paused and stared.

Lined with Christmas trees, standing proudly on the awning, the building sparkled. Behind each pane were little vignettes of fairytales, of Sleeping Beauty and the bejewelled red apple falling from her hand, Cinderella and her sparkling glass slipper, Rapunzel and her shimmering locks, Prince Charming waiting in the wings for them all. Maddy took out her phone and was about to take a couple of photos but paused, deciding instead that she would just look. Would take in every detail, every moment and remember it clearer in her mind than any photograph. This would be her trip to London. Her breakfast with her dad, the promise of a meeting with Rollo, her job at *Big Mack's,* her friends at Ella's apartment block. This was her Christmas. The snow falling on her face, her hands stuffed deep into her pockets, her toes frozen, the tourists next to her leaning forward and going, 'Hank is that a little mouse in this one, oh isn't that so dear. It's got a little collar and it's eating jelly fruit. We've gotta get some of that jelly fruit. Hank, I'm cold, let's go inside.'

Maddy watched them in their matching North Face jackets, hers pink, his blue, and then squeezed her eyes shut to bake the image onto her mind so she would never forget them because they had been part of her moment.

Inside, the shop it was warm and bustling. Beautifully colour coordinated Christmas trees almost touched the ceiling and great piles of turquoise boxes of champagne and truffles, and wicker hampers stamped with F&M bursting with festive treats lined the way. There was a chocolate counter with delicate truffles and glacé fruits with a queue snaking back across the shop. Pulling off her hat, she looked around unsure which direction to push her way through the crowd. Music drifted around her. The smell of chocolate and Christmas tickled her senses. People were loading up their baskets. Maddy saw a hundred things she could buy her mum but realised she had no idea what her dad and Veronica might like. In the end she grabbed a ceramic pot of Stilton for her dad and a miniature hamper of jams and headed to the till, then changed her mind about the jams and got some tea. Veronica seemed more Finest Black Leaf Tea Selection than strawberry jam. And when she was back out on Piccadilly, her turquoise carrier bag of presents in her hand, she took a big gulp of ice cold air and turned back to the lovely windows to take another snap with her memory.

'Maddy, great, so pleased you could make it.' Rollo was sitting behind a big glass desk when his secretary showed her in. 'Do you want anything? Tea, coffee, vodka? Line of coke? Kidding, sorry, just kidding.' He held up his hands and guffawed at his own wit.

Maddy shook her head. 'No thanks I'm fine.'

'Really? We have good coffee.' Rollo stood up, shrugged on his suit jacket that hung on the back of his chair and walked round to lean against his desk. When Maddy shook her head again, he said, 'Well I could murder one. Can't start the morning or the afternoon without caffeine.'

His secretary had waited by the door to hear if Maddy wanted a beverage and gave a quick nod before leaving to show she'd taken Rollo's order.

'So–' he said, seemingly patting down his jacket for cigarettes. 'You can sing?'

Maddy nodded.

The address on the card had been in Kensington. Looking on the map she had thought she could walk there but half way she was so exhausted and so cold that she'd got in a black cab and spent the rest of Veronica's fifty pounds. Now she was standing in the plushest office she'd ever been in. On the top floor of a vast art deco building, the inside had been gutted of all original features and the white walls projected with a different primary colour. As she'd stepped out of the lift and into reception the floor had lit up blue and the red walls changed to yellow. Television screens played videos on a loop of pop bands she'd vaguely heard of and winners of TV talent competitions smiling in awe as ticker tape burst from the sky. The receptionist had barely spoken to her when she'd said she had a meeting with Rollo, just stood up and implied that Maddy follow her clip-clop heels down the corridor to Rollo's office, watching as the squares beneath her feet changed colour.

As they reached Rollo's office his secretary had plucked Maddy's snow-covered coat and damp Fortnum's bag from her hand and handed it to a young boy who looked like he was on work experience. Maddy had watched him walk off with her stuff, half apologising for its wetness and half wondering where the hell it was going.

'Good. I'm looking for a singer,' Rollo said, voice muffled as he took a couple of puffs on his e-cigarette.

Maddy shook her head. 'Oh I didn't – I just came to ask some questions. Get some advice.'

'I'm sure you did.' Rollo nodded, then strode over to the door where his secretary was coming in with a mug of coffee. 'Thanks honey,' he said, wrapping one hand around the cup and taking a slug. 'Is everyone downstairs?'

'Yes, they're waiting.' The secretary handed him a file and an iPad and left.

'You want some advice?' Rollo asked, taking another great gulp of coffee. 'Do everything I ask and smile a lot. That gap-toothed thing you have going on is good – very Georgia May Jagger. Come on.' He stood waiting, cup in one hand, file under his arm, holding the door open with his elbow.

'Where are we going?' Maddy frowned, feeling like the situation was going out of her control.

'Downstairs,' Rollo laughed. 'Come on, move it.'

When she heard the office door click shut behind her, Maddy thought about backing up down the corridor and fleeing in the lift. Even if it meant leaving her Fortnum's stuff. Rollo was on the phone, marching ahead. His hair was freshly gelled and he smelt citrusy, like a Calvin Klein aftershave. As she trotted after him trying to keep up she wondered if he'd been to the gym since breakfast. There was probably one in the building. She glanced behind her and saw meetings going on in huge glass walled offices. All around people in beautiful clothes were tapping away at iMacs and laughing while they stood drinking coffee in takeaway cups at each other's desks. Geek-chic interns were rushing about with piles of papers while barking orders down mobiles. There were people everywhere, all confident, all stunning, all impeccably turned out. A girl sashayed past in skinny jeans that nipped in tight at the waist and an oversized kaleidoscopic print shirt slipping off one shoulder. Skin the colour of butterscotch and make-up perfectly invisible. Maddy wished she hadn't stood so long in the snow or walked so far in her shoes. She wasn't used to feeling so out of place. At home she was carefree, confident, easy but here she was intimidated, nervous, embarrassed of her appearance and daunted – by both Rollo and whatever it was he was leading her into.

'Down here.' Rollo summoned her with a wave of his hand.

They took the lift down to the basement. Rollo was on the phone the whole time. He said things like, 'I'll take the jet,' and 'Maybe but I think a helicopter wouldn't work.' He ended the call with, 'Money's no object, just get it done,' smiled at Maddy and then marched out into what looked like a car park.

'Rollo!' A girl with a clipboard shouted. 'Over here.'

Rollo got out his e-cigarette and the iPad as he walked over to where a group of people were sitting in fold out directors' chairs, ushering Maddy forward in front of him. The basement was all concrete. One of the walls was spray-painted with Banksy-esque stencil graffiti, another had a curtain strung up and scaffolding, guys in hard-hats were working on some set construction. The group they were walking towards were positioned in front a makeshift stage, a lighting rig suspended from more scaffolding and the floor was made up of scratched black boxes with big gaffer tape crosses on them. Either side of the stage were huge speakers and a scaffold platform from which a girl was securing black drapes as a backdrop. Just before they reached the others, a guy in black jumped on the stage and did a thumbs up to someone at the back of the room. Music blasted out, deafening French rap that made the whole place thump and Maddy almost cover her ears.

'Oh man!' Rollo shouted. 'Why are they testing with that shit?'

The guy on stage was grinning as the room vibrated. 'You no like?'

'I no fucking like.' Rollo shook his head and the guy signalled for the music to cut.

'You're such a killjoy, Rollo.'

'Yeah and I pay your salary. Now bugger off.' Rollo rolled his eyes and then summoned over a geeky looking intern to get him a macchiato.

The group lounging in the chairs were looking their way. Most of them looked like they worked for Rollo in some capacity. Three girls, however, sat slightly to the side. Much younger than the rest and dressed like they'd run wildly through Topshop grabbing whatever they could reach. The blonde of the three had pink shampoo highlights, the other two were brunette, one with alabaster skin and eyes like an alien, the other darker, possibly Spanish or Italian, and so pretty it was almost hurt Maddy's eyes, like looking at the sun.

'So I need a fourth,' Rollo said, nodding towards where the girls sat perched nervously on their chairs. 'I had a fourth but she's stuck in New York because no planes are flying because of the snow. It's bloody annoying and I'm unbelievably pissed off about it.' The intern appeared with the machiato. 'Thank you,' Rollo snapped. 'So, get up there, let's hear you.'

'What, now?' Maddy didn't have time to take the shock out of her voice.

Rollo had the takeaway cup up to his lips. 'Yes now,' he said before downing the espresso shot.

Glancing round the warehouse-like space she just saw people who were going to hear her. Workmen bashing at scenery, interns huddled together gossiping, the other girls in the group who eyed her suspiciously, all of Rollo's staff who were waiting – some looking Maddy's way, others deep in conversation unbothered.

'What do you want me to sing?' Maddy stammered.

'What do you normally sing?' Rollo raised his eyebrows and spoke as if Maddy was a toddler.

'Like, folk-y stuff. With my guitar.' Maddy bit her lip.

'Clarissa!' Rollo called out. 'Have you got a guitar?'

'Nope. No guitars, Rollo,' the girl with the clipboard shouted back from where she was pouring a cup of tea from a metal urn on a trolley. 'That's totally not the look we're going for.'

'Sorry hun, no guitars. This is more like female One Direction.'

Maddy chewed on her fingernail. She wanted to say, *'I'm twenty-four, d'you know that?'* but this was a crazy good opportunity and something most people would kill for.

'Can't you just do something by Rihanna or Katy Perry?' Rollo was scrolling through his emails on his phone, clearly starting to bore of the situation.

Contemporary pop wasn't Maddy's forte. For one, she was a rubbish dancer – and while she could belt out a

Mariah Carey or Christina Aguilera for fun in the shower, her voice was all gravelly emotion and frayed edges. 'Yeah I suppose so. Urm, what about Amy Winehouse.'

Rollo made a gun with his hand and pretended to fire a shot at her. 'Perfect.'

Maddy edged her way nervously to the side of the stage, hearing the chatter quieten as people looked up and started to watch her.

'You gotta climb up,' the girl hanging the drapes shouted. 'There are no steps yet.'

Maddy winced. Then as demurely as she could, hoisted her knee up and hauled herself up onto the stage, her trousers getting marked with chalk and dust.

'Can you stand on the cross in the middle, honey,' a guy behind a camera shouted. 'No not that one. That one,' he added, exasperated as Maddy moved between crosses, none of which seemed to be in the middle.

Her brain was still trying to catch up with her body. How was this happening? She was suddenly standing on a stage about to audition for a girl group in front of loads of record execs. Her hands were shaking. *Come on, Maddy. This is what you wanted.* She looked at the girls, one dressed in a multi-coloured crop top, lycra leggings and Nike hi-tops, the other in a vintage prom dress and the Spanish girl was in a black pant suit with huge fluorescent jewellery. They were like One Direction Spice Girls. Who would Maddy be? The old, out of place one? The idea of her actually being in this group made her smile to herself – it was so ridiculous, and that thought immediately relaxed her.

Standing on her cross she looked out at the impassive crowd.

'I'm 'er going to sing *Back to Black* by Amy Winehouse,' she half shouted.

She saw one of the women watching lean over to the guy sitting next to her and whisper something, making him snigger.

'Jez can you light her?' Clarissa with the clipboard shouted and suddenly the spots on the lighting rig flared to life almost blinding Maddy where she stood. 'Great, thanks, perfect.' Clarissa did a thumbs up to the back of the room. 'When you're ready, Mandy.'

'Maddy. It's Maddy,' Maddy said but Clarissa was already doing something else.

So Maddy coughed, brushed down some of the dust on her trousers, looked up over the heads of the people watching and out at nothing, trying to imagine she was in Dimitri's bar wearing her shorts and flip flops, her hair still damp from the shower, her skin freckled from the sun, bottle of Evian on the table next to her, bottle of retsina waiting in the fridge.

She could hear the waver in her voice when she started. Thought about starting again but carried on. Nerves made her slightly off key and she was suddenly far too aware of what to do with her hands with no mic and no guitar.

She battled through the song but knew it was terrible. Embarrassingly so. The workmen banging in the background kept distracting her and Clarissa and Rollo had a really loud conversation mid-way through. All she could think was that she was glad her dad and Veronica weren't there.

When Rollo's mobile rang and a couple of the crew started to build the staircase up to the stage she decided to put herself out of her misery and cut it off. Running her hand through her hair she stood waiting for someone to say something. Feeling naked. Foolish. Mortified that she'd been watched by all these industry professionals.

'Honey can you show us your dancing?' Clarissa called out over the drilling of the men putting the staircase together.

'Oh no I can't dance,' Maddy said.

Clarissa frowned.

'Sure she can,' said Rollo, his hand over the mouthpiece of his phone. 'Just bob around and do something, everyone can dance. We just need to see that you can move. Jez, put some music on.'

The French rap blared out again.

'Very funny. Not that crap. Something she can dance to.'

Maddy felt like she was in some sort of nightmare. Last time she danced had been the Easter festival when she'd got so pissed she couldn't say no when Dimitri and his friends had bet her fifty quid to dance Gangnam-style. The resulting effort had been videoed and screened in the taverna the next day while Maddy was lying on the cool tiles at the back trying not to be sick.

'Seriously I can't dance.'

'She says she can't dance, Rollo.'

'Can one of them not dance?' he shrugged. 'Like Posh Spice?'

'No.' Clarissa shook her head.

Lady Gaga boomed out of the speakers.

'Maddy, just do something. Pretend you're at a club.' Rollo sounded like he was getting annoyed. People in the audience were shifting uncomfortably in their seats. The Topshop girls were whispering, dubiously.

Maddy closed her eyes and started to shuffle her feet from side to side. Then her arms.

'That's it. Good girl,' Rollo shouted.

Dying inside, wishing she was on her balcony again in the snow, feet up, singing soft lullabies while her neighbour listened, Maddy carried on moving. Shuffling and side-stepping and trying to do interesting things with her arms without looking like she was writhing in pain.

'OK that's enough,' Rollo called in the end and she saw the interns cringing. 'Come down here, Maddy.'

Maddy sloped off the stage, feeling the amused glances of Rollo's staff follow her as she went to stand next to him, Clarissa jogging over behind her with her clipboard.

'I like her,' Rollo said to Clarissa. 'I like her look. It's different to the others and–' He shrugged. 'She's definitely got something.'

'The dancing is a problem. We can fix the singing, that's fine, but she's definitely not a natural mover.'

'She has good hair,' said a woman with a bright purple crop who'd been in the group watching and had strutted over to join them. 'And you're right about the whole gap-tooth thing. I think she has a look.'

Maddy went to say something but Clarissa just talked over her. 'You can definitely tell she's older than the others though,' she said. 'I mean do you see that as a problem, Rollo?'

He made a face. 'I don't know. I think we could get away with it, with the right styling. It could even work in our favour.'

'We just need to let something slip about her and Harry Styles,' the purple-haired stylist said, and Rollo boomed a laugh.

'Yeah, perfect. Love it,' he drawled. 'I think she could definitely work.'

Maddy was perplexed. No one had spoken to her and she felt like wheels were in motion that she couldn't stop.

But this was the dream, wasn't it? The blinding lights, centre stage? Styled, primped, made over? This was her as Ginger Spice dancing in the kitchen. This was why she was here.

'And I mean, if we have to take her–' Clarissa shrugged. 'It could be worse!'

Rollo shrugged, distracted by his phone bleeping.

'I'm sorry, what did you say?' Maddy asked, taking a step forward.

They ignored her.

'Excuse me.' She tapped Clarissa on the shoulder. 'What did you just say?'

'When?' Clarissa asked, already focused on the next item on her clipboard.

'Just then–' Maddy said, feeling her cheeks getting hot. 'If we *have* to take her.'

'Oh nothing.' Clarissa waved the question away and trotted over to where the interns were standing around attempting to look busy.

The purple-haired stylist was checking her lipstick in a compact and when Maddy asked her the same question she said, 'I don't know the ins and outs, sweetheart. Rollo just announced yesterday that the trio were going to be a foursome. God knows why, four never works. Look, can you pop by the dressing room before you leave, I need to fit you. I've got a lovely little pair of leather leggings that I think would work, they just might be a bit small. We can work on your weight though. Christ, I am dying for a cup of tea.' She snapped the compact shut and with a quick fake smile, strutted away in the direction of the tea urn.

Maddy stood watching Rollo as he talked into his phone. Waiting.

The other girls in the group were huddled together throwing her less-than-friendly sidelong stares.

What must they all be thinking? She could hardly bear it.

'Rollo?'

He held up a hand to make her wait. 'Yeah, yeah, definitely. Yeah I'm on it. OK, yeah gotta go.'

'Rollo?'

'Yes honey. That's all good isn't it? Exciting times. You'd better go out now and enjoy some incognito time, because in a couple of weeks you won't be able to walk down the street.' He cocked his head as he took a long drag on his e-cigarette, waiting for her to thank him.

'Rollo, why did Clarissa say that you *had* to have me?'

'Don't know what you're talking about.'

'The group, it's gone from three to four people.'

'Four's always better.'

'I can't think of a four person girl group.'

'*All Saints,*' he said with a raise of one brow. 'What's wrong with you? You should be delighted.'

'But I was awful. And I'm too old for this group. Look at them, they're like sixteen. I'm twenty-four and I can't dance.' She felt her voice choke on the last bit as annoyance started to build up inside her. 'He made you, didn't he? My dad.'

'No one made me, what are you talking about?'

Maddy shook her head.

There, handed to her on a plate, was international stardom. Waiting within her grasp. Even if the group didn't last long they'd at least have a decent shot at fame.

Take it, Maddy, don't question it. Just take it.

She looked at the girls, heads together giggling. Looked at the lighting rig, the scaffolding, the curtain held together with pins, the shabby tea urn, the bored interns, Rollo and his endless cups of coffee and inane phone calls, the backdrops for promos being built in the background, the wardrobe room with the tiny leather leggings and the idea of 'working on her weight.'

What was it Walter had said?

It's never going to be how you want it to be. The dream, it's all a mirage.

Taking a last look around, Maddy shook her head and said, 'Thanks Rollo, but I'm not going to do this.'

'What are you talking about?'

'The group, it's not for me.' She started to walk away in the direction of the lift.

'Are you crazy?' Rollo called after her.

She turned and walked a few steps backwards. 'Maybe.' She shrugged. 'But better crazy than a fool.'

CHAPTER 33

ELLA

'Wait one second, could you.' Ella heard Max bash into a couple of things then a long pause and then the sound of a door shutting.

'Sorry. Amanda's watching *Strictly* in the front room,' he said breathlessly.

Ella made a face at the window. 'I never realised you were such a TV watcher.'

'I know, me neither,' Max sighed.

Ella didn't know what to say next. She listened to the rain clattering on the metal roof of the phone box and imagined Max sitting somewhere in secret as he talked.

'I'm glad you called. Did you get my email? I'm really sorry, Els. I shouldn't have been such a coward. I should have said something earlier.'

Ella wound the phone cord round her wrist, then, with no rehearsals in her head, found herself saying, 'Max, do you think our time together was a half life?'

'Absolutely not. Why?' She heard him pour something in the background, maybe a glass of wine.

'Do you think we were ourselves?' she asked, staring out at the olive leaves she could see through the clearer sections of glass and the taverna, someone getting a *vin chaud* and pointing at the nativity.

'Well who else were you?' said Max, sounding confused.

'I don't know.'

'Ella, I used to have this bloody marvellous maths teacher who said to us, "Boys, it takes a lifetime to find out who you are. So go out, try everything and remember the body completely regenerates every seven years so you'll end up being someone completely different anyway." I think if you look at it that way, life's much less serious and a lot more fun. Us. We had a jolly good time. We loved each other. I doubt you learnt anything from me, but I think I learnt a whole lot from you. And now, well, we're regenerating.'

Ella tapped her index finger to her lips and thought about what he was saying. 'So you don't think our relationship was a lie?'

'Some of it probably. But isn't everything? El, you have to be a bit kinder to yourself. You're always so hard on yourself. Even what you wear you give yourself a beating over. You're not the girl I first met any more, you know that don't you?'

There was a pause as Ella considered it.

'Ella, you're a really successful woman now. You're funny, kind, pretty, much cleverer than me. You're strong. You're quite terrifying when you want to be. You could relax a bit more, smell the proverbial roses. Do they have roses over there?'

'I have no idea.'

'My case in point. Take some time out and go looking for some roses.'

Ella smiled despite herself.

Max paused, then said, 'You're you, Ella. I'm me and for a time we had the best time. Don't forget that. I just buggered it up by wanting all the cakes in the bakery.'

'Except our cakes were no longer compatible,' she said, while tracing the list of emergency numbers on the keypad.

'I think you'd be a cream horn,' he said.

Ella couldn't stifle her astonished laugh.

'Hard on the outside but soft and squishy in the centre.'

Ella leant back against the glass again. 'I can't work out if this is flattering or not. What's Amanda? A fondant fancy?'

Max snorted. 'Touché my petite cream horn. Touché.'

'OK, I'd better go.'

'That's a shame. I like talking to you.'

Ella was about to hang up, when she realised she had to ask him something else. 'Max are you still there?'

'Of course.'

'Can you drop in on Maddy? She's staying at the flat.'

'Maddy as in your sister Maddy? Who you aren't terribly keen on?'

'Yes that Maddy. My dad's just said she's working at *Big Mack's*. You know that dive in Soho?'

Max sniggered. 'Know it well.'

'She's meant to be at some flash place singing so I don't understand why she's there. Can you just check she's OK?'

'Absolutely pumpkin. It's the least I can do,' Max said, and she heard him take a sip of his drink.

'Max?'

'Yes?'

'Please don't make a pass at her.'

He made a noise like he'd just spat wine all over himself. 'I can't believe you'd say that. Don't you know me at all?'

'I know you too well. That's why I'm saying it. OK I'm going now.'

'OK. Bye.'

'Oh Max—'

'What?'

'Don't believe anything your parents ever tell you. They're awful and underneath it all you're OK.'

Max gave a booming laugh, 'I'm the chocolate truffle. Not quite to everyone's taste but delicious all the same.' He laughed again and then, just before he hung up, said, 'I'm going to miss you.'

Ella paused, her fingers tightening round the receiver. 'Me too.'

'I really loved you, you know? For you. Don't underestimate yourself, Ella.'

'Thanks,' she said, biting down on her bottom lip as she saw flashes of their time together before her eyes. 'I loved you too. I really did.'

'Bye Ella.'

'Bye Max.'

She held the phone to her chest for a second before putting it down, like they do in movies. And then she smiled.

Opening the door of the phone box she looked up to see a sliver of sun like a vein in the slate grey clouds. And over the path at the taverna, her mum was outside with a spray can, a green line through the *Greek* of *The Little Greek Kitchen* and *Christmas* graffitied in its place. Underneath was a pot of pale pink winter roses that Ella hadn't noticed before now.

CHAPTER 34

MADDY

When the lift doors opened on the ground floor Maddy just strode straight out the building. She ignored the lights changing colour underfoot, ignored the receptionist and was more than happy to leave her Fortnum's presents wherever they'd been put because she sure as hell wouldn't be giving them to her dad now.

Outside however the snow was bucketing it down, swirling like a ripped pillow, feathers all over the place. Her coat was with the Fortnum's bag, along with her gloves and hat. But she didn't want to go back in. Couldn't face the idea of standing around in reception waiting, remembering her hideous audition, the sniggers as she'd danced, the whole lot of them working out how to make the best of a bad deal.

Why would her dad ever think that this was the way she would want it to be?

There was no denying that she was freezing though. Her jumper was getting damp from the snow and her legs shook from the cold as she waited under the building's awning deciding how best to get home.

'Maddy!'

She turned and saw Rollo striding out of the revolving door.

'I won't tell him,' she said. 'Don't worry. I won't let him know that I know he set it up.' Her teeth chattered as she spoke.

'Wait.' Rollo held up a hand, dismissing what she was saying. 'Just come inside, we'll go up to my office, have a coffee. Christ at least get your coat.'

'I don't want to.' She shook her head, her arms wrapped tight around her. 'I'll buy another one.'

Rollo laughed. 'That's ridiculous. Come on.' He walked over to her, put his arm around her shoulders and ushered her inside.

'Only to get my coat,' she muttered through frozen lips.

'And for me to have a coffee.'

'You know caffeine's a drug?' she said as they entered the warmth of the day-glo foyer.

'And your point is?' Rollo asked, then chuckled to himself as they waited for the lift.

Inside Rollo's office it was toasty warm. The secretary had looked on bemused as he'd asked her to go and get a hand towel for Maddy to dry her hair. Maddy had walked over to the window, unable to look Rollo in the eye and instead stared down at the view of Kensington Gardens and The Royal Garden Hotel, the people in the snow tiny like toy town.

'So that was all very dramatic,' Rollo said with a snigger. 'You don't want to be in my group, that's fine, just say so. You don't have to run away.'

The secretary came in with the towel and a tray of coffee and biscuits.

'Here have one of these, it'll warm you up,' Rollo said, pouring out a coffee and then adding a slug of brandy that he had in his desk drawer.

Maddy took it from him, wrapping her hands round the scolding hot cup. 'Rollo?' she asked, chewing on her lip.

'Yes Maddy,' he said, munching on a bourbon biscuit.

'What would you have thought if my dad hadn't made you take me?'

He shrugged, mouth full of crumbs. 'I'd have thought you were ok,' he said. 'That you had some way to go but that you might get there.'

Maddy nodded, took a sip from the alcohol-laced coffee and tried to hide her disappointment. Even though her audition had been crap and she didn't want to be in the group, a tiny part of her had hoped that Rollo would say that he thought she was marvellous, just not quite right for the pop world.

'I would probably–' Rollo went on, popping a custard cream into his mouth, 'have left it at that. In fact I definitely would. I'm a busy man.' He laughed. 'But!' he said, holding up a hand as Maddy hung her head a little and putting down her cup went to start patting her hair dry. 'But I will add, because you're Ed's daughter and I can give you–' he looked at his watch, 'a few more minutes of my time, and tell you that I don't think this is what you want. There's not the hunger or the fight. I need commercial and people who are willing to do whatever it takes. Whether it's mainstream pop or hippy-dippy folk. Those girls down there, one of them has been making tea here for three years. Another sang on the doorstep every morning at the exact time I was coming to work. It was bloody annoying but I liked her tone. You see, I think you enjoy what you do and that should be enough. You have a really lovely voice, but I don't think you have what it takes for all the rest. A lot of shit comes with this job.'

Maddy tried to hide her disappointment by towelling her hair a bit more vigorously.

'You want validation?' Rollo asked, filling his cup with just neat brandy. 'Stick yourself on YouTube and get a couple of thousand likes and as many hates. Can you do hates on YouTube? Christ I'm so out of date. That's why I have so many bloody interns. They do all our "social media".' He did air quotes around the phrase, spilling some of his brandy. 'Listen Maddy, you don't need validation. You know you're good. You enjoy it. But did you enjoy *that*?'

She put the towel down on the back of one of the club chairs next to the window and thought about standing on that stage in front of people who didn't really care what she sang and how she sang it. She shook her head.

'Exactly. Now go and live your life. This–' he pointed round the office at the posters of pop stars and framed platinum albums. '– is not for you.'

One of the interns knocked on the door and came in carrying Maddy's stuff. 'Thanks.' she mumbled, taking it from him, then turned to Rollo and said, 'I really appreciate you talking to me. Thank you.'

'You do? I haven't broken your heart? Trodden on your dreams?' He raised a brow.

'Maybe.' She pulled on her still damp coat. 'But it's probably for the best,' she said, draining the last of her coffee, coughing from the brandy, and walking away to the big glass door.

'Hey and Maddy,' Rollo called out as she was just about to leave.

'Yeah?'

'Don't go hating on your dad. He was just trying to help.'

She didn't reply. Just gave him a quick wave and walked out of his office, down the light-up corridor and out the building. There was a tramp sitting outside High Street Kensington tube who asked if she could spare any change. She handed him her Fortnum's bag, the stilton and the black leaf tea, and said that it was all she had.

CHAPTER 35

ELLA

Ella wheeled her case over to the taverna entrance.

'You're not leaving are you?' her mum asked.

'No.' Ella shook her head, then remembered Dimitri saying when she'd first arrived that her mum might think she was just using the place to escape, and said, 'I was thinking about it but actually I'd like to stay for a couple of days if that's OK with you?'

'It's always OK, Ella. You are always welcome.'

'Thanks.'

'But there's a big party here Christmas Eve and a lot of work to do so you'd better go and get changed.'

In the kitchen it seemed that all hands were on deck. Dimitri had been set up at the kitchen table to prepare the filling for cheese pies and the taramasalata, while her granny was chopping herbs for the mini meatballs and checking the oven every couple of minutes for her sausage rolls.

'Ella, do you still know how to roll *dolmades*?'

Ella nodded. 'I think so.'

'OK, well start with that. I've rinsed the vine leaves so if you make the stuffing now you can wrap them and we'll put them in the fridge.' It was like a military operation, there was none of the flap and panic of the impromptu self-service dinner, this was Ella's mum on fire. Christmas was her forte. Ella remembered big parties at home with all the neighbours, them working like mad to get all the canapés ready – chopping vegetables for dips and skewering cheese and pineapple onto sticks were her and Maddy's jobs and they took it so seriously, while her mum and aunt whipped up plates of delicacies that disappeared in a flash when the guest arrived. The whole village would come. Their's wasn't the biggest or grandest house but with the fire burning and the big table laden down with treats it was a date in the Christmas calendar that no one missed.

She looked up at her mum, her hair pulled back neatly, no make-up on, white chef's apron wrapped double around her waist and thought of when she'd stand in the kitchen at home, cup of tea in one hand, list in the other calling out orders just as she was doing now. But then, when it all got too fraught, her dad would come in, pinch a sausage roll and swap the cup of tea for a glass of champagne and her and Maddy would shut their eyes and make faces when he kissed their mum under a sprig of mistletoe.

'Dimitri, are you going to make the cheese pies? Because if you are, they need to be neat.'

Dimitri swivelled round in his seat and did a mock salute, which made Ella's mum roll her eyes and walk away towards the larder to get supplies for the next dish on the list.

'Why are you here?' Ella whispered across the table to Dimitri.

'Because I wanted to spend the day with you,' he replied.

'Really?'

He laughed. 'No.'

'Oh.' Ella felt herself blushing as she diced some onions.

'I got roped in. I only came in to talk about the alcohol for the party.' He shrugged then leant forward, his elbows on the table and rested his chin in his hands. 'Would you like me to want to spend the day with you?'

Ella had no idea. What good would a holiday fling do her now? She was barely out of her relationship. But… She looked up, he was watching her, thick dark lashes blinking slow like a lizard in the desert, smile lazy on his face, like he had all the time in the world and wasn't fussed either way. Maybe this was new Ella. The one that, as Max said, was regenerating. One with the memories of a past but no longer the same person. One who paused to smell the winter roses and the Christmassy sap of the pine.

Ella raised a brow. 'Would you like me to want you to want to spend the day with me?'

Dimitri sat back and laughed. 'I can't even work out what that means.'

When she thought back to that morning as evening fell it actually seemed calm in comparison. As the day had unfolded Ella's *Dolmades* had been deemed too baggy so she had had to roll them all again. Her gran tripped, dropping the bowl of finely chopped herbs all over the kitchen and half onto the fire making the whole room cloud with smoke. Dimitri made an amazing taramasalata but lost concentration when it came to the cheese and spinach pies and the filo pastry stuck to the table, the fine sheets tearing as he tried to salvage them. As water continued to pour down the wind picked up and there were murmurs of the *mistral*. Her mum burnt two trays of mince pies and the yellow-eyed cat nabbed a dish of battered anchovies that he crunched on the doorstep until her granddad shooed him away.

'This is ridiculous!' Her mum ran her hand over her forehead and looked like she might cry as she pulled out the second of the charred little mince pies.

It felt to Ella like the *mistral* had already come.

'Sophie, honey,' her granddad called as he came back from shooing the cat away. 'I think you'd better come and see this.'

'What?' Her mum rubbed her hands with her apron and walked over to the doorway, a frown on her face.

Her granddad nodded towards the toilet block outhouse. 'The roof's coming up.'

'It can't be, it's new.'

He shrugged. 'Then they did a bad job, but the wind's got the under the felt.'

'Shit.' Her mum slapped the wall with her hand.

They all stood in the doorway looking out through the fairy lights at the roof, flapping away in the wind.

'It's going to leak into the toilets. Who the hell is going to want to fix it in this weather? Oh God! Why? Why now?'

Ella watched as her mum turned away and went and slumped down in her granddad's hideous old chair. She looked old suddenly, worn out, worn down. When Ella had first arrived and they'd cooked together for the dinner feast she'd seemed vibrant, scatty, fun. Now it was like the life and energy had been stripped out of her.

She thought of her dad just forgiving Maddy. Of wanting her in his life so much that it didn't matter what had happened in the past.

She thought of her dad handing her mum a glass of champagne. How her face would brighten. Her shoulders would soften. Who handed her champagne now? Ella didn't even know if she had a boyfriend, if she'd ever had a boyfriend. She looked at her, remembered how beautiful she'd always thought her, how funny, how kind. How she'd always aligned her with Maddy but actually there was a softness, a vulnerability that Ella felt in herself.

Her mum shut her eyes and she watched her take a couple of deep breaths, her hand gripping the arms of the chair. She caught sight of the list sticking out of her apron pocket. Two sides of A4, really small loopy writing. They had so much to do.

Outside the wind knocked over an oil can of geraniums, she heard it roll over the concourse and out into the road. Bashing and clattering against the stones. Dimitri and her grandparents were sheltering in the doorway talking about the roof.

Ella had told her mum that she needed someone to blame otherwise it all meant nothing. But maybe it wasn't that she needed someone to blame, it was that she needed the courage to forgive. Perhaps her fear had been how to move on from this point, how to admit that she was perhaps too afraid to stand up on her own with nothing in the past to blame for her mistakes.

She'd stayed in a relationship that she knew wasn't working. In a company that was safe, where she was a big fish. She was too scared to rely on her own fashion sense, for Christ's sake. Was she strong?

She looked from her mum to the rain lashing down outside, the wind tearing more of the felt from the roof, the path almost a flood of brown mud, the waves smacking the beach, the sound of the pebbles crushed and thrown in the surf. Up the road the decorations across the street were tossing in the wind like birds, their ropes holding steadfast against the growing gale.

'I'll go up,' Ella said suddenly. 'I'll go up the ladder and fix it.'

Dimitri almost choked on a laugh. 'Don't be ridiculous. You can't go up, I'll go up.' He shook his head like she was bonkers.

'You can't, you'll have to hold the ladder. I'm not strong enough to hold the ladder,' Ella said.

'Well we'll get one of the guys down here to help.' Dimitri frowned at her.

'There's no time. Look at it.' Ella pointed to where the nails were being ripped out one by one as the wind got stronger.

'Ella–' Her mum sat up from the chair. 'You're not going on the roof.'

'Why not? You need it done. Dimitri can hold the ladder. It'll be fine. There's no other choice.'

They all looked at each other.

Her granddad took a couple of steps back from the doorway. 'I think she's right.'

'Michael!' Her grandmother slapped him on the arm. 'Don't be stupid.'

He shrugged. 'Give the girl a chance. For God's sake. Dimitri'll hold the ladder. She's sensible. Come on. Like she said, there's no other choice. I can't do it.'

Ella could feel her legs trembling. 'It's really high,' she shouted over the sound of the rain as Dimitri held the ladder in place – he only had his leather jacket with him so had her granddad's yellow fisherman's mac on with the hood up.

'It's OK, just hold onto my hand for the first couple of steps. You won't fall, I promise.'

Ella gave him a look. 'How the hell are you going to help me from down there?'

'You don't have to do it,' he shouted.

Ella had a hammer and nails in a bag over her shoulder and her mum's Millets pack-a-mac on. She put her foot on the first slippery rung. 'Yes I do.'

'She's missed you, you know?' he said, his hand on her back.

'Who?'

'Your mum. She talked about you all the time. How well you were doing at work and stuff.'

Ella could feel the rain hitting her face, sliding down her collar and her back. 'She did?' she asked, gripping onto the bars.

'Uh-huh.'

She hoisted herself up another couple of feet, the ground seemed really far below her. She'd never imagined her mum talking about her when she wasn't there.

'When you're at the top just hammer it in at random. Just as long as it stays, don't worry about it. Just do it quickly, don't take any risks or anything,' he instructed.

'I can't hear you,' Ella shouted as she neared the top.

'It was nothing.'

'What?'

'Just–' he shouted, '… just take care.'

She looked down at him, his face upturned, lit by the outside light, his brow furrowed, his mouth tight with worry. She smiled, taking a hand off the rung to push back her hair that was falling in her eyes. 'I will – Oh shit.' Her foot slipped at the same time as she tried to put her hand back on the ladder. 'Shit.'

As she slid down the cold metal Dimitri shot up the ladder, holding onto her waist while she flailed about getting a new grip on the slippery rung.

'Thank you.' Ella turned her head and was level with his. She could see the water on his eyelashes.

'You're welcome.'

A couple of beats of silence passed. The ladder swayed.

'I've got to go back down and hold this thing. Don't take your hands off again, OK.'

She nodded. 'Except to hammer in the nails.'

'Just get on with it and get yourself back down.'

'OK.'

She thought that maybe he was about to kiss her from the way he paused and looked at her. The way his eyes narrowed and his grip on her waist loosened, like he was going to move his hand up to her shoulder. But then the ladder wobbled again and he slid like a fireman to the bottom and held it tight.

Ella didn't know if she was relieved or disappointed. All her family were watching from the doorway. 'Right,' she said to herself. 'Let's get this bloody done.' Then as she hammered the nails in, all skewiff and haphazard, all she could think was that she'd just thought of them as her family.

CHAPTER 36

MADDY

There weren't many people in *Big Mack's* but enough to cause a stir when Maddy sent her dad packing.

'I don't need to talk to you.' She'd waved a hand in his direction and started to walk away towards the swing doors.

'Maddy–' he'd pleaded.

'Please just go. Honestly. I just feel like you set me up. Why couldn't you have listened to what I was saying.' She paused, her hand on the bar top. She could feel Walter watching as he sipped his Guinness. Could see that her dad was embarrassed, wanted her to come back towards where he stood so they could have a private conversation.

'Maddy,' he said, trying to keep his voice neutral. 'I just wanted to help you.'

'But I didn't want your help.' She shrugged and walked out to the back room where she waited for ten minutes until she knew that he had gone.

'God you're a spoilt brat aren't you?' Betty, the other barmaid, muttered as she came out the back to get her cigarettes.

'You know nothing about me,' Maddy said, chin jutted out defensively.

'I can see you're a little rich kid who gets whatever she wants.'

Maddy shook her head but didn't reply, just walked past her back out to the bar.

Walter held up his hand for another drink.

He watched as she poured the thick black liquid, the white foam swirling around the glass then rising to settle while she waited to top it up.

'I think you owe your dad a thank you.'

'And why is that Walter?' Maddy sighed.

'Because fame is just a drug habit and an addiction to your own self-importance.'

Maddy rolled her eyes.

'Honestly. It doesn't come to those with the most talent, but those who want it the most. You should just go and find yourself. You've watched too much *X-Factor* on that tiny island of yours and think that's it.'

'I do not,' she huffed.

'There's always something else, Maddy,' he said, leaning forward, his arms crossed on top of the bar. 'You're never done. There's always another door.'

'Please don't start.' Maddy kept her eyes fixed on the Guinness.

'I'm just saying that most people have such a fixed idea about what their dreams are and spend so long chasing them that when they get them it's nothing like they hoped. But there's always another door.' He took the drink from her and put it down on his beer mat. 'That's all I'm saying.'

'Oh yeah?' Maddy said, hand on her hip, one eyebrow raised. 'And what's your other door? You're just in here every day. You hate Christmas, you hate your books. What was your dream? I think you're too afraid to write anything else in case you fail.'

Walter scoffed. 'Don't psychoanalyse me.'

'I'm not, I'm just stating the obvious!' she said, shaking her head while she went to go and get a cloth to wipe down the spirits at the back of the bar.

'Tell me about your Christmases,' he said.

'No.' She didn't turn around.

'OK, I'll tell you about them. I think they were probably lovely. All cosy and warm around the fire, lots of food and crackers and presents.'

Betty walked past with a crate of Cokes and added, 'You probably got a puppy or a pony.'

Walter sniggered. Maddy's spine stiffened.

'And yeah your parents split, but that probably meant you had two Christmases. Two sets of presents, both of them trying to gloss over the fact they weren't together and make sure you were happy. Maybe they took you to a show or to see the Christmas lights being turned on? Am I close?'

She didn't reply.

'Sounds pretty perfect to me. And now you've got your dad in here begging for you to talk to him, probably wishing you were coming to his for Christmas.' Walter took a big gulp of his drink, Maddy could just see him in the mirror behind the vodkas.

'I grew up in a caravan illegally parked just off the Hanger Lane gyratory. If you don't know what it is Google it, it's the most depressing place on earth. I don't know my mum, my dad was a bastard, my step-mums were often lovely, my brother was a bully, my sister ran away when she was thirteen and–' he held his hands out, 'I've seen her once since, when I was at a book signing – she was asking me for money. For Christmas I got a satsuma and some crap from a car boot sale up the road.'

Maddy paused, her hand stilling on a whiskey bottle as she listened.

'And from the window of that caravan I could see a church – and at Christmas a nativity and lights around the door. Every Christmas Eve I would sneak out the window, after my dad would lock me in and go to the pub, and I'd sit in the back of that church and listen to the carols at Midnight Mass. I'd be right at the back in the dark and I'd look at everyone in their coats and wonder what they were going to do when they got home. How many presents they all had waiting and how many turkeys there were in people's fridges. But right there in that moment I was just like them. We all sang, we all said those prayers that no one knows the words to, we all shook hands, we all smiled, we all took a chocolate from the vicar at the end. For me, that was Christmas. None of this shit.' He pointed outside with the hand not holding his pint. 'None of these Christmas lights advertising Disney cartoons and sponsored skating rinks and queues for spoilt brats to get XBoxes or whatever it is they get. It was that magic. That sound. The white lights and the candles. The unity. And that's what I wrote about. My books were that feeling. They were my escape. But they're done. I'm old and I can't cling onto a childhood dream forever.'

Maddy turned around, her hands behind her back holding onto the counter. 'Maybe like you say, you need a new dream.'

He shrugged.

She watched him as his fingers toyed with the beer mat and then saw him look up, the wrinkles round his eyes crease as he smiled.

'There's always another door,' he said. Then sat back and crossed his arms. 'Perhaps we're both afraid of the same thing.'

Maddy scrunched the cloth in her hand. 'What's that?'

'Letting go of the past.' He shrugged. 'Stepping into the unknown.'

'Or–' Betty said as she pushed passed Maddy, this time struggling with a crate of Fanta, '… growing the fuck up and stop feeling so bloody sorry for yourselves.'

Walter snorted into his Guinness and white froth went all over his face.

'I mean the two of you.' Betty shook her head, after slapping down the crate with a bang. 'Whine, whine, whine. That's all you do. Maddy, you're a fantasist. Walter, you're a procrastinator. Life is what you make of it. Dreams, doors… it's bullshit.' She took a cigarette from behind her ear and nodded to Mack who had walked past pointing towards the front doors to say he was going out for a smoke. 'It's going to be done and gone by the time you two stop moaning.' She shook her head at the two of them like a headmistress. And as she strutted out the bar, Walter looked guiltily at Maddy and they both giggled like school kids.

Maddy cycled home in the snow. She found herself looking at the churches – the ornate and the plain. The redbrick spire of St James's, Piccadilly, and the sound of carols drifting through the still night air, Westminster Abbey lit up in the moonlight, Christmas trees sparkling on the path. St Saviour's in Pimlico, its stained glass shining like Quality Streets. She thought of Walter seeing hope in those shimmering lights. And it suddenly didn't matter about her missing suitcase with her presents or her embarrassing dance routine on stage. It was about possibilities.

Hope.

Perhaps the mistakes and choices in her past didn't have to suffocate her future.

Maybe Maddy, it was *time to grow up*.

As she clicked her bike into one of the docking stations, the path in front of her seemed suddenly as clear as the fresh white dusting of snow. Maybe her dream had been wrong or maybe she had tried and it simply didn't fit. Maybe what she thought as a child didn't have to rule her life as an adult. And if it was like that with her dreams, maybe with her dad there could be similar infinite possibilities.

'So you've done it again!' She heard a French accented voice snap from the steps of her apartment block.

'Veronica?' Maddy pulled off her hat as she climbed the steps, looking up at her step-mum dressed in a big black astrakhan coat and a red cloche hat pulled down over her ears with a curl of hair peeking out the side.

'Don't you Veronica me, all innocent. What did I say to you? You decide if you are still nine or not. You're a little devil, you know that. Why? Why did you come here? Why not New York or Paris? Anywhere. You come here to play your stupid, selfish little games. I'm not having it any more. You don't come near him. Enough.' She crossed her hands in front of her. 'You are the worst kind of person, Madeline. You play games, you are spoiled, you are weak and selfish.'

Maddy swallowed. Veronica looked like there might actually be tears in her eyes.

'You know, after the breakfast it was like a spell it was broken, there he was, normal again. And then–' She shrugged a shoulder. 'Yes he probably makes a mistake but you think the world should circle around you, that you are the only right one? I told you before, but I don't think you listened. People, Madeline, they learn to forgive. They learn to accept faults. You–' she started to walk down the steps past Maddy, her boots crunching in the snow. '…you see only your way. Your world.'

Veronica gave a slight shake of her head and then, pulling on her leather gloves, was about to cross the road when a van drove up and pulled into a vacant space in front of her with a skid of tyres in the slush. As the driver got out he apologised for startling her and Veronica waved a hand dismissively as if it was nothing. He nodded and went to open the back doors of his van.

Before she went, Veronica turned back to Maddy and said, 'I will do whatever I can to stop him from seeing you. Do you understand?'

Maddy nodded.

The van driver paused, embarrassed to have overheard the exchange and watched as Veronica stalked away across the road and got into a sleek grey Mercedes parked opposite.

'Erm–' the driver glanced at his clipboard and then up at Maddy. 'I've got a delivery. Flat Three. Madeline Davenport.'

'That's me,' she said, still shaking from Veronica's tirade. Cold, embarrassed, shocked, she tried to compose herself to talk to the driver.

'Right, great. One suitcase,' he said, dragging it out the boot and up the stairs, plonking it down where she stood. 'Sign here please.' He held out a tablet for her to sign. 'That all sounded a bit fierce,' he said, eyebrows raised.

'Yeah.' Maddy tried to keep her voice light. 'Families, you know, Christmas.'

'Say no more, darling. Totally understand. Well, hope there's something in there that'll make you feel better.' He grinned and then jogged away down the steps, jumped into his van and drove away.

CHAPTER 37

ELLA

The roof fixed, they all huddled round the fire, fingers wrapped around hot chocolate and towels round their shoulders. When she'd seen the ladder wobble, Ella's mum had run out into the rain to help Dimitri hold it steady and got completely soaked in the process. She was upstairs getting changed.

The yellow-eyed cat wound his way around Ella's legs, his damp fur against her ankles.

'You're growing on him,' said Dimitri, nodding towards the cat.

'Should I be honoured?' Ella asked.

'He only usually likes Maddy.'

Ella refused to align any symbolism to the choices of a cat, but all the same, couldn't deny a feeling of triumph that he was getting ready to sleep on her toes.

'So I thought the moment called for this.' They all turned to see her mum holding up a bottle of Krug champagne. 'I've been saving it for a special occasion and it's time it was drunk.'

'What a marvellous plan,' her grandmother said, going over to the cupboard to get down as many champagne flutes as they had and a couple of wine glasses when she realised there weren't enough.

'Ella–' her mum said, handing her a glass, the tiny bubbles popping on the surface.

'Thank you,' she said, taking it from her, realising that her mum didn't need anyone to bring her champagne any longer, she could give it out herself.

'I think it's more like, thank *you*!' Sophie smiled. 'I'm sorry today was such a palaver. Please come back tomorrow and help me and I promise it'll be better.'

Dimitri laughed. 'Especially if there's more of this.' He held up his glass of Krug.

Once all the champagne had been drunk, Dimitri ventured back out into the rain to ride home but came back claiming it was too wet and windy even for him to try it. Her grandparents didn't think they could make the walk either so Ella told them to stay in her room. Dimitri would have the sofa in the living room, and Ella would share with her mum.

As she went upstairs to get her toothbrush and pyjamas, Ella found herself being purposely slow. Deliberating about what she might need. It was nerves she realised, the idea of being so close to her mum, the politeness when it came to getting washed and changed, the silence when they turned off the light, the sound of her breathing. Like all the time there would be a feeling that she should say something. That their thoughts were so obvious and huge that they would fill the room to bursting. Pressure mounting on her chest.

When she finally stuffed what she needed into a carrier bag and went down the corridor to her mum's room, she was so nervous, so awkward that she could barely reply when her mum showed her where everything was and went out to use the bathroom down the hall.

There was a blow-up airbed on the floor with a sleeping bag and a blanket that her mum said she would sleep in but

Ella got changed quickly and zipped herself into it before her mum came back in.

'What are you doing? You take the bed!' her mum said, dressed in the same nightshirt that Ella remembered from when she was a kid. Threadbare now in places and so worn the blue cotton was soft. 'You've been up a ladder in the cold.'

'Honestly, it's fine,' Ella said, almost snapping because she wanted her mum to keep the bed.

Her mum nodded, and climbed under her duvet without saying anything else, turning off the main light and flicking on a side light.

'Sorry,' Ella muttered. 'I didn't mean for that to come out the way it did.'

'That's fine, don't worry.'

'OK.'

'OK. Night Ella.'

'Night.'

Her mum turned the light off and the room was so dark Ella couldn't see her hand if she held it in front of her face. She could hear the waves though, crashing against the shore. Could hear the wind in the chimney and the rain on the roof.

'Maddy used to be so afraid of this kind of weather,' her mum said into the darkness. 'Do you remember? She'd climb into our bed and we'd have to convince her how great the rain was.' She laughed. 'Like *The Sound of Music*. And then you'd appear at the door, not wanting to be left out and clamber in as well.'

Ella smiled at the memory of being all curled up and cosy, snuggled up between her parents in their big bed.

'I am sorry you lost that, Ella. I'm sorry you lost that security.'

Ella stared up at the ceiling, seeing the pattern on the wallpaper come into focus as her eyes adjusted to the darkness.

'I was thinking–' her mum went on. 'That maybe, perhaps, I could become your friend? I know it sounds a bit stupid and sitcom-y, but I thought it might take the pressure off a bit. Off both of us. You're a grown-up now, and I don't think you need me as a mum.' She paused. 'I'm not explaining this very well. I know you need a mum, but I would really like to get to know you. As a person, not necessarily as a daughter. And I would like you to get to know me. I understand it all. Everything you said, and I'm sorry I wasn't who you wanted me to be, I'm sorry I didn't see you – but I see you now. Ella, I'd really like to be your friend.' She stopped, Ella heard her roll over in her bed and face where she was lying on the airbed on the floor. 'I would look out for you, Ella, unconditionally.'

Ella was still staring at the ceiling. Her eyes pooling with water, her chest tight. The anger in her like the wind, sweeping away over the ocean.

'I would look out for you, too,' she said in the end. 'I would like to do that.'

She thought she heard her mum laugh, but it could have been the echo of the wind in the chimney breast. When her mum spoke again her voice was lighter. 'Good. I'm glad. Thank you.' She heard her take a sip of water and then put the glass back down on the old chair she used as a bedside table. 'Good night, Ella.'

'Night, Mum.'

CHAPTER 38

MADDY

Maddy's suitcase seemed like an odd reminder of a distant time. She'd survived adequately without it and now as she hauled it up onto the bed and unzipped it, everything inside seemed weighted down with jovial expectation. The travel-sized shampoo and conditioner bottles. A pressed black shirt for her defunct first day at *Manhattans*. A rain coat because it supposedly always poured in England. And then she discovered a present from her mum nestled amongst her clothes and one from her gran wrapped up and stuffed into one of the inside pockets, tied with a bow and a plastic holly leaf. She shook the box, it sounded like jewellery. There was a card from Dimitri and, at the bottom of the case, her mum had slipped in her recipe book. Old and tatty and sauce stained, Maddy held up to her face so she could breathe in the smell of the pages. It was the smell of home.

She put the book down carefully on the bed, along with the gifts and carried on unpacking. It was as she was unfolding her pyjamas that she found something else. A pink and white striped paper bag. She presumed it was something else from her mum. Unfolding the edge she looked inside to see a thin beige notebook, the edges of the pages the same silver as the flowers that were embossed on the front. It looked expensive, like it would have been at home in the stationery department she'd fallen in love with at Liberty.

Opening it up she saw immediately that it wasn't her mum's.

Instead it was Ella's.

The first pages were clipped together with a paperclip – on them were random workings out, to-do lists, phone numbers – but then on a fresh page there was a note written to Maddy:

It's daunting sometimes being in a city on your own. (I'm always a bit lonely on business trips so please don't see this as me being patronisingly big-sisterish). So I've made you a list of all the places I like in London. Especially near the flat where there are lovely little cafes and shops, there's a car boot at the school on a Sunday and some weird outdoor aerobics class (if you go, good luck!). Then over the bridge, I've drawn you a really bad map of Vauxhall and the gems that sit amongst some of the rougher places (don't go there on your own at night!)

Anyway, it's all there. You don't have to use it. I just thought I would have liked it when I first moved to London.

Enjoy. Look up more than you would normally (some bloke said that to me on the tube). And if you get lonely give dad a ring – he'd love to hear from you.

Ella

Maddy was so astounded she had to read it over and over again. Flicking through the pages of lists and scanning over the best restaurants, theatre shows, bars, cafes. Ella had put her favourite spa and physio, good routes to jog, exhibitions she'd enjoyed, flea markets, food markets, must-see tourists attractions that she'd like but might miss like the Harrods food hall or the top floor restaurant at Harvey Nichols. Maddy turned page after page smiling at hastily drawn maps and crossed out mistakes.

It was almost impossible to align the Ella that had turned up in Corfu with this Ella – the Ella who had made this list to make sure her sister was OK.

She sat crossed legged on the bed, a pillow across her thighs, and stared at the notebook. She took the paperclip off and looked at Ella's scribbles – her life; her handwriting.

She realised then how much she'd underestimated her. How she'd thought the old Ella gone. How she'd thought the breakdown of their relationship went right to the core when perhaps it was only skin deep. Perhaps underneath it all her sister would always look out for her; Ella may not like her but she would always protect her.

That thought made her hold the notebook to her lips for a moment as a smile spread across her face.

A couple of minutes later a sharp knock on the door drew Maddy's eyes away from the pages of looped, slanted script that she knew so well as Ella's, and pulling on the cardigan from her case she went to answer it.

'Margery! How are you?' Maddy asked when she saw her standing in the hallway.

'Yes, I'm fine Madeline.' Margery was holding her hands clasped to her front, dressed smartly in grey woollen trousers and a peach sweater and pearls. 'I wondered if you might like to pop in for a glass of sherry? Not for long, I have to go to bed soon, but just a quick glass.'

Maddy felt herself smile. Could think of nothing she'd like more than a distraction from all the circling thoughts of family in her head. Grabbing her keys she pulled the door shut and followed Margery into her apartment.

Inside it smelt like her granny's house, of wax polish and coffee brewing. The dim lighting in the front room cast a warm glow, sparkling off the crystal decanter and prisming on the Laura Ashley wallpaper, classical carols were playing on an old tape deck while the tatty Christmas tree was trying its hardest to live up to expectation as too few baubles and ancient fairy lights weighed down its dying branches.

'Sweet or dry?' Maddy heard Margery ask and when she shrugged that she didn't mind, Margery said, 'Well I prefer dry so why don't you start with that and if you don't like it you can swap.'

'OK.' Maddy nodded, looking round the room at the little ornaments, the black and white photos on the side table, the antimacassars on the sofa. When she looked at Margery she thought her hand was shaking as she took the stopper out of the decanter. She was nervous, Maddy realised and, as Margery handed her a little sherry glass, tried to make casual small talk by picking up the nearest photo frame and asking, 'Who's this, Margery?'

Margery paused mid-pour. 'My husband.'

'How long have you been married?'

'I'm not. He left me for his secretary. Probably for the best. He drank too much. Cheers,' she said, holding up her glass and clinking with Maddy.

Maddy had to stifle a smile at Margery's curt matter-of-factness and moved onto the next picture. 'Aw, and what about this one? Is this you?' she asked, looking at a photo of two girls and their mother standing in front of an ivy covered cottage, a big labrador asleep at their feet.

Margery put her specs on and came over to have a look. 'Yes that's me on the right. That's my sister. She lives in Australia now. And that's my mother. Very cold woman. Oh and there's Bonnie. I loved that dog.'

As Maddy stared at the picture it suddenly occurred to her what the washed-out faded photograph was of in Ella's drawer. It was the last summer they'd had all four of them. They'd just come back from Corfu, just picked the cat up from the cattery and there'd been a fight about who got to hold her. Maddy had won but the cat had scratched all up her arm. Ella had made a face like she deserved it but then helped her to hold it tighter. Their mum had held out the camera and taken a snap just before the cat had bolted. Afterwards they'd had lunch in the garden, pretending they were still on holiday, and the cat had crunched on fish heads. It was the last time that there were no cracks. It was before the bickering turned to proper arguments. Before they'd become two pairs. Her and her mum. Her dad and Ella. Gradual at first and then a divide like a tear between them.

Margery took the photo frame from her and put it back on the shelf. 'It's always a little more lonely this time of year. I don't really look at these.'

'What are you doing for Christmas?' Maddy asked.

'Oh nothing, I just watch a bit of TV and then go to bed.'

'And Christmas Eve?'

'Nothing. Never do.'

All these people, all lonely, Maddy thought. Families and friendships with tears in them just like hers.

She took a sip of the sherry and watched as Margery rearranged her photos. Thought of Veronica on her doorstep and Ella's notebook in her bag. She could fix this, she realised suddenly. Not for everyone, but maybe for a few. If Ella could watch over her from a different country, and Veronica could defend her father so staunchly, then Maddy could swallow her pride. She could patch over what was torn and make it stronger.

CHAPTER 39

ELLA

Ella had never enjoyed cooking so much. The rain had lightened as the wind had picked up, and the fire crackled and glowed as it howled down the chimney. Her mum had got up early and left her to sleep, so when she appeared in the kitchen there was freshly baked bread, homemade fig jam and a big silver coffee pot with a napkin tied around the handle to stop anyone getting burned. There was yoghurt and bowls of stewed fruit, pomegranates bursting with ruby seeds, orange juice and crushed tomatoes to spread on toast.

Dimitri was sitting at the table already in his boxers and a t-shirt. His hair was all skew whiff from sleep and his eyelids heavy. She had this strange urge to go and curl up on his lap but instead grabbed a piece of bread and jam, poured a thick, strong coffee and asked her mum where she should start.

'Well I'm thinking redo the mince pies and some more sausage rolls,' her mum said, glancing up from her crumpled list. 'There's gazpacho out of wild greens but Dimitri needs to pick them from his garden. I have started the stuffed peppers – look at these, aren't they sweet.' She held up some miniature little red ones. 'You could do the caper salsa. I have the recipe for it written here. Then–' she turned over the paper and exhaled, blowing her fringe up out of her eyes. 'We've got more *Kourabiethes* and *Amygdalota* – you remember them don't you?'

Ella shook her head.

'They're my favourite. Make double,' Dimitri shouted over.

'Those little almond biscuits that your dad liked.'

When she thought back, for the first time Ella didn't have a bittersweet memory of the past, instead she just remembered her dad ramming them one after another in his mouth until he couldn't talk and them all tickling him so he nearly chocked with laughter, and she smiled. 'Yeah I know the ones.'

Her mum looked up from her list and smiled back. 'Maybe you can take him some when you go home.'

'Yeah maybe.'

She heard Dimitri shift in his seat. There had been no talk of Ella going home.

'And that, I think, is nearly it.' Her mum scanned the list. 'Oh shit, no there's a massive moussaka, mini chicken souvlaki–' she peered at her writing trying to decipher it. '…morello cherry liqueur. Dimitri will you bring that with you?'

Dimitri nodded.

'It's divine. We left it out on the roof during the summer and the heat from the sun just makes it–' she kissed her fingers. 'It's wonderful. Oh and here, I added this this morning just for you – pineapple and cheese on sticks.' She turned the paper round so Ella could see, a big beaming grin on her face.

Ella laughed. 'Sounds good to me.'

'OK, so why don't you start on the capers? And then when you're done with that maybe the quiches? That OK?'

'Perfect,' Ella said, taking a bite of her bread and jam, the sweetness of the figs melting in her mouth and the freshly squeezed orange juice tart on her tongue.

When she took the seat opposite Dimitri he looked up. 'What's happened between you two?' he whispered.

'Nothing.' Ella frowned. 'Same as it's always been.'

He scoffed. 'Yeah right.'

Ella looked down at her bowl of capers, hiding a smile on her face as she started to crush them in the pestle and mortar.

As the food piled up and the space in the fridges decreased, the list was predominantly words crossed out and empty cups of coffee and tea were replaced with red wine, Ella sat back and took a moment to look round the taverna. Moody Agatha and head waiter Alexander had been drafted in for decorations, ordered around by her grandmother. Crepe paper concertinas had been draped from the poles supporting the roof, out and over to one of the olive trees that stood between the tables, a hole in the concrete floor allowing room for the ancient trunk. More strings of fairy lights hung from the eaves, kissed by the wind they danced against the plastic storm walls.

On every table were jam jars tied with ribbon, bunches of hellebore lolling over the fresh white tablecloths, their dusky pink petals drooping too heavy for their stems. Strings of mussel shells, their insides gilded, had been looped across the windows and the mantle piece, the gold shimmering as it reflected the flickering lights. Ella's granddad had been given the task of festooning the railings with silver tinsel while Dimitri had had to stand on a chair, his t-shirt pulling up to reveal his hairy belly as he stretched out to screw in a new bulb on a string of coloured lights. As he did, her granddad had flicked the switch so they buzzed on in his palm, the shock knocking him back down to the ground – making her granddad snigger.

Ella watched, feeling like if she breathed it in deep enough it might stay with her better once she was home.

CHAPTER 40

MADDY

Maddy cooked all day. All her mum's specialities from the ancient recipe book open in front of her, the food splattered pages completely incongruous in the sparkling kitchen. She sent texts and emails to everyone she'd met in London as she queued at the fishmonger for white fish that she baked in garlic breadcrumbs in Ella's never-before-used oven. Rifling through Ella's bureau she found a packet of cream and gold notelets that she made a silent promise to replace before she left and scrawled out some hasty party invitations. When she dashed out again in the heavy snow because she'd forgotten to go to the butchers for rabbit, she posted invitation cards through the doors of the apartment block, and, miscounting how many there were, popped out again to post more as red wine and cinnamon from the *stifado* scented the kitchen. Then she made all her mum's usual mezze and added some that she found in one of Ella's glossy, untouched cookbooks: crispy shallot and basil fritters and bite-sized Yorkshire puddings that she filled with turkey and redcurrant jelly. For dessert she made florentines, cupcakes with mixed spice and cranberries and *Melomakarona* cookies that she couldn't help eating as they cooled.

Then at lunchtime she took off her apron and knocked on Margery's door with her guitar in her hand and asked if she might be able to use her tape player.

'Certainly.' Margery opened the door wider to let her in. 'Doesn't your sister have one of those fancy new ones?'

Maddy nodded. 'Yes, but I want to use a tape. It fits better with what I want to do.'

She'd been thinking about it since last night, lying in bed staring out the window at the snow, the flakes picked out perfectly by the street lamps, trying to come up with the strongest link she had with her dad and Christmas.

'Do you have a cassette?' Margery asked.

Maddy shook her head and made a face of apology. 'I was hoping you might have one of them as well.'

Margery smiled and, leaning forward, proudly threw open the doors of a black lacquered cupboard in the front room to reveal stacks and stacks of tapes and about ten packets of blanks ones still in their cellophane. 'I can't abide any of these MP3s and things. If it works, why change it?' she said, then, as Maddy bent to get a cassette, added, 'Lovely invitation by the way, thank you. I'm really looking forward to your party. Picked out what I'm going to wear already. Do you want me to bring anything? I've got the rest of the bottle of sherry.'

'That would be perfect.' Maddy smiled, unwrapping a blank tape and slotting it into the machine.

'So are you going to play the guitar?' Margery asked.

Maddy nodded. 'I'm actually going to sing something for my dad.'

'How lovely.' Margery made herself comfortable on the sofa. Maddy had intended to ask her to leave because she was nervous and embarrassed and didn't want an audience, but Margery seemed delighted to be able to watch. 'Off you go. Do you want me to show you how it works?'

Maddy shook her head. Her dad had had one just like it in the nineties and she knew exactly how it worked, she'd spent hours lying on the living room rug listening to his music. To his Joan Baez, Cat Stevens, Bob Dylan. Now she sat on a stool in Margery's front room and leant forward to press the record button, her fingers strumming for the right key, and her voice singing the words to *White Christmas* without her having to hardly think about it, she knew them so well.

She closed her eyes and saw the Christmas table laid with candles and crackers, presents stacked as high as mountains under a tree that touched the ceiling. It didn't matter so much suddenly what came after those Christmases, it was that she had them – unlike Walter – there in her memory to be called on when needed. Snapshots of her dad, mayonnaise round his mouth as he ate his Big Mac and pushed the tape into the machine for the last song of Christmas, her mum carving the turkey with her eyes half shut, anxious that she hadn't burnt it, all her grandparents arguing during midnight mass because some of them wanted to sneak out early to go to the pub, her and Ella singing in stupid voices at the village carols and comparing their presents to check that neither of them got more. Boxing day in their pyjamas watching films all day on the sofa while munching on turkey sandwiches so big that they could hardly get their mouths round them. Trudging round the sales while their dad winced at all the people and their mum took back half her Christmas presents. Everything tinged with the rosy glow of nostalgia, more sweet than bitter. The first slice of fruit cake thick with marzipan, thimblefuls of their great grandmother's morello cherry liqueur, hot coffee and the sweet cinnamon *kataifi* and *baklava* on Christmas morning. Poorly remembered Greek blessings and guilt from their great-grandmother for not trekking to the orthodox church in Bayswater on Epiphany. All of it played like the strip of tape in the machine, a ghost of the past laid finally to rest in a better place.

When she opened her eyes the song was finished. The only sound the whir of the tape player, Maddy hardly able to believe it was done, and then after a few seconds Margery started to clap.

'I adored that, Madeline. I simply adored it.'

Maddy rested her guitar against the cupboard and pressed stop on the machine. She glanced over to where Margery sat, her feet tucked underneath her, her palms pressed together and resting over her lips, and saw her eyes shimmering wet in the low light.

'You think so?' Maddy asked, tentatively. 'You think it's OK?'

'Madeline, I think it was simply stunning.'

Maddy couldn't stop herself from smiling as she clicked open the tape deck and slotted the cassette into its case.

'I'd better drop this off then,' she said slipping it into the back pocket of her jeans.

Margery looked at her watch. 'Not too long till the party kicks off.'

'Do you think people will come?'

'Maddy darling, I know people will come,' she said, standing up and brushing lint from her trousers, 'There was much talk about it down in the laundry room. I just hope you have enough food.'

'Oh believe me.' Maddy laughed. 'I have enough food!'

Wrapped up in Ella's coat and scarf and gloves, Maddy took a taxi to her dad's office and handed the parcel to the receptionist letting them know that it was urgent. She had slipped one of the notecards into the jiffy bag and had almost crossed her fingers when she handed the package over.

'You will make sure he gets it, won't you?'

'Yes, madam,' the woman behind the desk said with a tight little smile.

'It's really important.'

'As you said. He is very busy, especially at this time of year, but I will make sure he sees this as soon as possible.'

'Thank you.' Maddy walked backwards a couple of paces, 'Thanks, it's really important.'

'Yes.'

When Maddy stepped out into the snow-drenched Soho street, giant silver baubles strung from one building to the next, a man selling roasted chestnuts on the corner, people spilling out of pubs with pints in their gloved hands, she looked at her watch and saw that she still had four hours till her party started.

Four hours to get out Ella's little notebook and get to know her sister's London.

CHAPTER 41

ELLA

The tourists started to arrive in the early afternoon. Ella stood at the door of the taverna to greet them holding a big umbrella and ushering them inside for a glass of champagne topped with a dash of morello cherry liqueur or, for those needing a little warming up, a glass of Metaxa brandy. Everyone had dressed up. Ella had decided the occasion called for her kaftan, which she wore over skinny blue jeans and flip flops, the rain soaking between her toes. Her mum was wearing a black dress that stopped mid calf and a big yellow necklace of beads threaded on wire, all her hair piled on top of her head, she looked straight out of *Vogue*. Ella looked over at her really proud as the tourists oohed and aahed over the decorations, the food and the roaring fire as they sipped their bubbly and procrastinated over the mezze that Alexander and Agatha were carrying on trays. When they popped the little quiches into their mouths or dipped the meatballs into the caper salsa they closed their eyes and shook their heads and proclaimed how much better this was than their hotel.

'Are you open tomorrow?' some of them asked, sidling up to Ella's mum so their holiday rep didn't hear.

'Sorry, tomorrow's for my family.'

Hand on their hearts they'd look downcast and say, 'Such a shame.' Before having another champagne and moving onto the taramasalata and plump purple olives.

As evening fell the clouds thinned and a glimmer of sun set over the navy water. The wind still howled down the chimney making the flames dance like imps.

Agatha had arrived in her raincoat and predicted an end to the rain, saying the *mistral* would whip through the island and take the bad weather with it. No one quite believed her as they stared out at the pouring rain and when lightning forked on the horizon, Alexander chuckled at her predictions.

'You wait,' she said, grumpily, picking up another tray of cheese pies that the tourists demolished in minutes.

Just as the tourists were sitting down – to plates of lamb slow-roasted with orange and oregano, butterflied pork stuffed with chestnut and prunes – the children of the village arrived in their anoraks and wellingtons to sing carols. Six of them worked the room, belting out the words while two boys hung back and hit a tambourine and a triangle. The tourists were entranced, clapping and laughing, handing out coins like candy, while Ella's mum took the kids inside for baklava and hot chocolate.

Out on the water the boats moored along the jetty had been decorated with with fairy lights and further out, the decorative model ships made from wire and light bulbs swayed precariously in the wind.

Then, once the main courses were devoured and dessert was brought out, the locals started to arrive – kissing Ella's mum, bringing her gifts as they marvelled at the trouble she'd gone to and nibbled on new plates of soft creamy cheese pies and crispy tentacles of calamari. As the tourists savoured as many of the sweet options as they could cram into their already full bellies, the artists turned up in their mini-van fresh from a wet, windy excursion to the other side of the island. Soon there was loud singing and exuberant dancing. Music echoed tinnily out of speakers along the far wall of the restaurant and carafes of red wine were poured, bottles of retsina flicked open and glasses raised to everything – Christmas, good health and wealth and happiness. Then the artists insisted that Dimitri bring out more Metaxa and set fire to the brandy in giant glasses, the fumes merging with the wood smoke and the rain and an exuberant new toast made to *The Little Christmas Kitchen* which made Ella's mum blush and have to go inside to make some coffee.

'Hey.' Dimitri strolled over to where Ella was sitting at one of the tables, twirling the hellebore flower between her fingers and looking with awe at the community and friendship that her mum had on this island.

'How are you feeling?' Dimitri asked, hoisting himself up to sit on the railing and squashing a bunch of tinsel under his bum.

She glanced up at him, at his big, droopy eyes and crazy wild hair, the stubble that was on the verge of a beard, the tan, faded, but still like caramel against his black t-shirt and saw the same relaxed, comfortable ease she had seen when her mum greeted the friends who arrived. The casual chatter with the artists, the long mornings spent drinking coffee with her grandparents, the food that brought such pleasure, the boat that bobbed just metres away that in seconds could take you to the middle of the deep blue sea.

'I feel jealous.'

'Seriously?' His eyebrows drew together as clearly he'd been expecting a lighter, more frivolous reply given the evening's festivities.

'I just wonder what it would be like to have this forever.' Ella swept her hand around the taverna, her eyes narrowed, her head tilted as she considered it, absorbed the dancing, the drinking, the laughter. 'I think I'm jealous. I'm jealous of you. Of my mum. Of Maddy. Of what you have and what makes you happy.'

There was a pause. The party boomed on behind them. Dimitri rubbed his hand along the back of his neck, watching Ella as her eyes darted from one thing to the next. 'Do you want to go for a walk?'

'In the rain?' she asked, unsure.

'Yeah.'

'Do you have an umbrella?'

'No.'

'I'm in my kaftan.'

'Ella you're kind of ruining the moment.'

'Oh. OK, yeah. Can I get a coat?'

'Jesus.' Dimitri blew his hair up out of his eyes. 'If you must.'

Leaving the celebratory commotion, Ella wrapped in an ungainly yellow mac, they started up the muddy path towards the olive trees. Unlike the desertion of previous nights, tonight the road was lined with cars parked for the party and people jogging to get to the taverna and out of the rain.

To Ella's surprise, Dimitri took her hand in his, his warm fingers curling round hers and holding tight as they trudged silently into the torrential weather. Christmas lights hung above them, draped between the branches and blue and white bunting rattled in the cold north wind. The mistral was here.

Almost oblivious to the swirling gale, Ella could just feel Dimitri's rough palm against hers. People smiled and waved as they ran past and Dimitri waved back but never let go of her hand. Completely comfortable for all to see while Ella was glancing back over her shoulder like a dog chasing its tail to check if anyone was watching. Behind her she could see the taverna, lit up through the plastic storm shutters, laughter and music carried in the wind, the warm glow through the front doors, the strings of lights blowing about like kites' ribbons, and she could just make out the Christmas branches and the big gold star, tipping slightly to one side.

But then the road changed to a path and the trees thickened, their shadows dancing on the stony ground. As they entered the dark, quiet, sheltered land of the groves up at the highest point of the coastline they could stand on the lip of the cliff and gaze out over the wide black water.

Ella felt the weight of Dimitri's arm as he rested it across her shoulders and realised that all she wanted was what she'd seen in that photo, heard in that story. And now he was there next to her, relaxed and uncomplicated.

'See over there–' Dimitri pointed towards the lemon groves further round the bay. 'See how the leaves sparkle?'

Ella nodded, only half able to look, focusing mainly on the proximity of him, the feel of his body next to hers, the outline of his face in the darkness, the rain on his skin. 'Why is that?'

'They're Christmas lights, they keep the trees warm in winter.'

'You're kidding?'

'No.'

She stared out over to the glittering grove, the lights like glowworms dancing round the leaves. 'It's lovely.'

Dimitri nodded. 'It is pretty special.'

She felt him turn away from the view and towards her, his fingers sliding down the plastic of her over-sized mac and searching under the cuff to take her hand again. She couldn't be a hundred percent sure that he was going to kiss her, didn't want to ever make the mistake of presuming again, but the more it seemed like an actual possibility the more her body suddenly tensed up. Because as much as she liked him, as much as he made her whole body light up, it was all happening too quickly, more quickly than she was comfortable with, it felt like she was frantically peddling, trying to catch up. She'd only just left Max, only just found her mum. She thought back to the photograph of Dimitri's wedding, the exquisite fantasy of being looked at the way he looked in that picture, and she knew immediately that if this was to happen it was something she wanted to savour. To know that it wasn't rushed and unconsidered. That she was choosing it for herself. A self that she was confident in.

The scary thing was that faced with the reality as his hand squeezed hers, his eyes looking down at her with the look she had dreamed about, she suddenly felt like this actually might *be* the real her – just Ella – or at least a sliver of her, exposed.

And that made her nervous. So instead of closing her eyes and going with the moment she quipped, 'Is that why you brought me up here, to look at the lemon trees?'

He tucked her hair behind her ear, his thick black eyelashes opened and closed, she looked anywhere she could but at him while her brain was desperately scrambling through possible things to say.

'Do you think that's why I brought you up here?' Dimitri said, wiping the rain from her cheek.

'Do you think that I think that's why you brought me up here?'

'Not this again.' He shook his head. 'Ella, do you want that to be the reason why I brought you up here?'

She paused, felt the rain splash through the curtain of branches above them, heard the waves lash against the cliff edge, the wind rustling the leaves and clashing against a metal roof in the distance, saw his eyes, bright green and glistening as they watched her, seemed to see right into her brain and how it worked.

When she didn't answer she felt his grip loosen on her fingers and she wanted to shut her eyes tight and wish herself away.

'I'm just worried,' she said in the end. 'I don't know what this would achieve.' Dimitri looked at her for a moment, then running his hand through his wet hair took a step back and laughed.

The tree branches silhouetted behind him looked like broomsticks, the shadows like witches' fingers. All around the noises of the rain dripping through the leaves made it feel like creatures were moving in the darkness.

'You don't know what it would achieve?' he said, smirking. 'What the hell do you want it to achieve? It doesn't have to achieve anything. It's Christmas for God's sake, it's raining, it's a nice view. I like you.'

Ella looked down at the big cuffs of her mac, the yellow plastic iridescent in the moonlight, not one of her polaroid outfits but her granddad's fishing coat with her sparkly kaftan just poking out underneath. 'It would just make it more painful to go home.'

'So don't go home.' Dimitri shrugged. The shadows of the branches danced. The moonlight splintered through the leaves, catching on spider's webs spun in the grooves of the tree bark.

'Oh don't be ridiculous,' Ella snorted.

'I'm not,' he said. 'What have you got to go home to? Here you have your mum, you have your family, you have the bloody sun three quarters of the year, you're less stressed, you seem much happier and well–'

'What?' she stood, eyebrows raised like he was talking nonsense, arms crossed tight.

'Well *I'm* here.'

Ella shook her head. 'Dimitri, you don't want me to stay here for you. It would be weird.'

'No.' He took another step away from her. The branches creaked and groaned in the wind, the waves smashed below them and the rain trickled down their faces and splashed in heavy drops to the floor. 'No I want you to stay here for you. I would just have been a bonus.'

Ella watched him retreat through the shadows of the trees, back towards the path. She glanced behind her at the lemon trees with their sparkling, glowworm lights, the vast coal black sea, the clouds like bruises on the horizon. As she turned back a pair of yellow eyes lit up on the path ahead and the white cat came into view, pausing to lick his paw and watch them from the tangled roots of an olive tree. Could she stay? 'It would feel like I was running away.'

He shrugged a shoulder. 'It's not running away if you find out where you fit,' he said, then smiled – the same neutral, closed, easy smile that she saw him give to tourists – and beckoned her to follow him back to the taverna. The moment was gone. 'Let's go. It's freezing out here.'

CHAPTER 42

MADDY

The first of Maddy's guests arrived as she was tying the belt on a gold Diane Von Furstenberg wrap dress that she'd picked after trying on everything in Ella's wardrobe. Hair loose, make-up light, St Christopher round her neck, she felt excited but nervous. Nervous no one would come, anxious they wouldn't like the food, jittery about what she would say to her dad if he turned up on the doorstep after listening to the tape, but most of all worried about how she would feel if he didn't.

There was a second impatient knock as she started slipping on her shoes and she ended up doing a sort of hop across the living room pulling them on as she went.

'Hugo!' She beamed as she threw open the door, buckling up the strap round her ankle. 'Come in.'

'Great idea this Maddy. I've had a shocking week.' He stepped inside, handing her a bag with a couple of bottles of flash white wine but keeping tight hold on a six pack of Kronenbourg.

At the same time the front doors of the block crashed open with a bang as Rollo strode into the hallway accompanied by Clarissa, one of his interns and the three girls from the new group, 'Maddy! Darling. I brought this lot, hope you don't mind, have to take them everywhere with me at the moment to stop them getting pissed in Bouijis and trying to get off with Prince Harry.' Rollo ushered his troupe in in front of him and then took a big wicker basket off his intern and said, 'This is a hamper Sony sent us. Full of luxury stuff, not my kind of thing really. Thought you'd like it. Hi there, I'm Rollo–' He cut off from talking to Maddy when he saw Hugo. 'Don't you play squash at The Hurlingham?'

'When I get a moment.' Hugo laughed, mouth already full of *Dolmades*. 'Great spread, Maddy.'

Maddy felt her shoulders relax as she watched them chatting, hoovering up her food, glugging back the alcohol. She looked around at the decorations – the red and gold lanterns that she'd picked up from a backstreet shop in Chinatown that Ella had noted wasn't too touristy, bright paper concertinas from the Conran shop that she'd said was her favourite for decorations, the vanilla cinnamon candle from Anthropologie on Regent Street that filled the hallway with the sweet smell of a Christmas sweetshop, pine cones she'd picked up while walking through St James's Park to see Ella's secret view of London from a little bridge over the stream and sprigs of red berries from the flower stall outside Liberty that Maddy had bought when she'd popped in to buy a notebook. One exactly the same as Ella had given her, but this one with bright pink edges to the pages, that Maddy would use to start her own list of favourite places. Maybe one day they wouldn't just be of London and Greece but be filled with secret hideaways and little gems that she might lend to Ella when she needed it.

As Hugo was handing Maddy a glass of champagne, Margery arrived wearing a blue Chinese silk dress and carrying a poinsettia and her half-full bottle of sherry. She beckoned Maddy into the bathroom and whispered, 'Can you just button this up? It's a bloody hook and eye and my fingers just won't do it!'

'Margery how many outfits have you got that you haven't been able to do up?'

'Oh hundreds, Madeline, I'm just getting started.' Margery laughed.

Stella from upstairs popped in and brought her twin sister with her who was visiting for Christmas. They didn't stay long, neither of them seeming to want to take up too much space or overstay their welcome. Walter pulled up in a giant cream Rolls Royce dressed in his white suit and shiny shoes.

'Is that your chauffeur?' Maddy asked, peering through the hallway doors.

'Yes.' Walter nodded without a backward glance.

'Don't you think you should invite him in?'

'Why?'

'He'll get cold out there. And it's Christmas Eve, Walter. For goodness' sake.'

Walter paused and then turned around to look out at his chauffeur who was reading the paper where he sat at the steering wheel. 'God, maybe I should.'

'Unbelievable.' Maddy shook her head.

'Yes, how miserable I am.' Walter laughed. 'Oh I brought you these,' he said, handing her a box before striding back outside to get his chauffeur.

Maddy untied the string and opening the flaps gasped when she saw inside a complete set of Walter's books, hardback, first edition. Carefully opening the cover of the first in the series, she saw he'd inscribed it, *To old dreams and new adventures. The door will never be closed for you, Maddy.*

'Oh Walter, that's lovely. Thank you,' she said, tracing the ink with her fingertip.

Walter was coming back in, followed by his chauffeur who actually looked like perhaps he might have been quite looking forward to sitting in the car and reading the paper. 'Yes, whatever, don't make too much of it,' Walter said. 'Just– Well– Yes– OK. Martin, go and have something to eat and be jolly.' He ushered the chauffeur into the flat, ignoring Maddy's thank yous as best he could.

More people from the apartment block arrived and then at ten-thirty Mack and Betty and the others from the bar appeared. 'Closed early,' Mack boomed as he found Maddy in the kitchen where she was desperately piling more food onto serving plates. The canapés were being devoured quicker than she'd thought possible. People were scooping *stifado* out of little paper bowls and someone had polished off the fish leaving behind just a dish of garlic breadcrumbs. 'Didn't want to miss this,' Mack said as he slapped down a bag full of cheap Russian spirits and helped himself to a glass of red from the side table that Maddy had turned into a makeshift bar, 'Is that Rollo?' he asked. 'Christ, what are you doing here old man?'

Betty twisted the cap off the bottle of *Christmas Spirit* that Mack had brought with him and, pouring a slug into a glass, handed it to Maddy. 'You look like you might need this.'

'Thanks,' Maddy said, gulping down the firewater.

'I'm sorry if I've been a bit of a bitch to you,' Betty said, pouring another glass for herself.

'Don't worry about it.' Maddy coughed, the liquid burning her throat.

'You were just so perky and eager.'

'Yeah, honestly, don't worry about it.' Maddy waved a hand.

But Betty carried on regardless, toying with her tongue stud as she spoke, 'And so innocent. Like, I couldn't believe someone could be that naive without it being an act.'

'You can stop now, Betty, thank you.'

Betty sniggered and then spying Hugo, who was lounging against the French windows, muttered, 'Blimey, he's a piece of all right.' And grabbing the bottle of *Christmas Spirit,* headed his way.

'Sterling work, Maddy,' Walter said, sidling up beside her and nabbing a miniature Yorkshire pudding off the plate she was holding.

'Maddy can I do anything to help?' Margery appeared on her other side, looking as if she'd polished off a good portion of the sherry.

'No, I'm fine, honestly. Have you two met?'

Walter stepped forward. 'No, haven't had the pleasure, I'm Walter Brown.'

Margery giggled at his outstretched hand and said, 'And I'm a bit squiffy.'

'Marvellous.' Walter squeezed his way past Maddy, pushing her back so he could stand closer to Margery. 'So what is it that you do Margery?'

Maddy rolled her eyes as she watched him loop his arm around Margery's waist and with the other hand pluck a glass of champagne from the bar and take a sip.

'Since I retired–' Maddy heard Margery say as they swayed together out into the living room. 'I spend a lot of my time writing letters of complaint.'

'Margery, you sound exactly like my type of woman,' Walter drawled.

After Maddy had topped up all the canapés, opened more wine, popped more champagne, she leant with her back against the sink and watched as everyone around her chatted, laughed, drank, some even danced. Outside it was snowing lightly like a pattern of lace in the midnight sky. It couldn't have gone better.

But no matter how much she tried to enjoy it, Maddy couldn't forget the fact that her dad hadn't arrived. Every time the doorbell went her breath caught but it was never him.

The one time she convinced herself it might be him, dashed over to the door when she saw a black cab pulling away in the street, held her breath as she turned the latch, she was surprised to find Ella's Max standing in the hallway instead.

'I came to check–' he started, then peering round the door said, quite astonished. 'Are you having a party?'

Maddy cringed. 'Yeah. Sorry! I know this is your flat.' She held her hand up to her forehead. 'Sorry.'

'Absolutely nothing to be sorry about, darling. There's nothing I adore more than a party,' Max said, strutting inside. 'Nice work with the tree,' he added, before heading over to the makeshift bar.

The last of the guests left at two in the morning. Margery and Walter seemed to have sloped off together much earlier in the evening. Maddy, who was checking outside every ten minutes to see if her dad might be about to ring the bell, had just caught the cream Rolls as it slipped away.

Hugo, Rollo, Max and the girl group were going on to some club somewhere and tried to persuade Maddy to join them but she shook her head. By that stage she had finally admitted that her dad wouldn't be coming and just wanted to go to bed.

As they kissed her goodbye, thanked her for the party, told her to look them up next time she was in London and wished her a Merry Christmas, Rollo suddenly turned back and said, 'Oh Maddy, sorry I forgot, Ed said to tell you he's coming in on the red eye. Had a business meeting yesterday in New York. Wanted you to go to his tomorrow. Don't know why he didn't text you himself, but–'

'Because he doesn't know my number,' Maddy said slowly.

'That'd be why.' Rollo laughed.

'He's been in New York?' she asked.

'Yeah, I think it was just for a day, sorting some shit that had hit the fan with one of his acts.'

'So he hasn't been in his office?'

'Not the London one.'

'And he wants me to go tomorrow? For Christmas?'

'Maddy, I can't keep repeating myself. I'm hammered. I can barely see you. I have to either keep drinking or pass out, there can be none of this in-between stage. OK? Go to him tomorrow, you're invited. Blah blah blah. Great party, great food. You know actually, that's what you should do – keep the singing as a hobby but blimey, I'd pay to eat your cooking.'

'Really?' Maddy said, distracted from the thought that her dad hadn't listened to her tape, hadn't got her invite or her apology and still he wanted her to go for Christmas Day.

'Yeah. These–' Rollo said, leaning forward to nab the last mini spinach pie, '… these have star quality.' When he popped the pastry into his mouth she heard the filo crack against his teeth. 'Amazing. OK, I'm off. Sure you don't want to come?'

Maddy shook her head. 'No.'

'Your loss,' Max shouted from the hallway, and they all fumbled out into the snow and the waiting taxi.

The news about her dad created such a flutter of excitement in Maddy's tummy that she couldn't go straight to bed. Instead she cleaned up, loaded the dishwasher, thought back over the evening and without the cloud of worry about her dad, took a moment to enjoy the memories, wondered what Walter and Margery were getting up to and then decided she didn't want to know. Opening the French windows she pulled over a chair and sat looking out at the snow-covered patio with a shot of *Christmas Spirit* and the remains of the bowl of *stifado*. Spooning the stew into her mouth, savouring the flavour, she wondered if Rollo was right, maybe this was another path? Her cooking another possible dream?

As she was picturing her name in lights above a chic little restaurant a male voice pulled her out of her reverie. 'Hey.'

Startled, she looked up to see the guy from the balcony next to hers.

'Sorry I didn't make it to your party. I had a work thing–'

He looked different without his baseball cap on. His hair falling forward almost over one eye. He looked like he'd just got in, wearing scruffy jeans but a smartish navy shirt and was clearly freezing standing out on the balcony.

'That's cool. Don't worry.' Maddy shook her head. 'Enough people came, I wasn't billy no mates.'

'Yeah I didn't think you would be.' He laughed, he had amazing teeth she noticed, and when he leant forward so his forearms rested on the lip of the balcony she studied his face, the shadow of stubble, his eyes sort of sleepy but bright, bright blue like the sky at home in summer.

'You didn't?' she said.

'Well you seem to have managed to get all of this lot talking.' He nodded towards the windows of the other flats. 'That's a miracle. I got a leaflet the other day about starting up a committee for the block.'

'Oh God.' Maddy made a face. 'What have I started.'

'I know. I hold you personally responsible.'

Maddy laughed. He smiled, looked down at his hands clasped together in front of him and then back up at her from underneath dark lashes.

'Are you going to play your guitar again?' he asked.

'I wasn't going to.' Maddy shook her head. The snow had started to fall again, drifting softly down and disappearing as it touched her skin.

He nodded.

'Do you want me to?' she said after a moment.

He smiled, shrugged. 'Yeah. Yeah actually I would.'

Maddy felt herself blush, a bit nervous, excited. 'I'll erm– go and get my guitar.' She nodded back towards the flat.

'OK. I'll go and get a sweater,' he said, pointing inside.

Maddy stood up to go back in but paused with her hand on the doorframe, 'You know, there's still loads of wine and beer, not much food, but some, if you, you know, maybe wanted to come–'

'Yeah.' He cut her off. 'Yeah that would be really nice.'

'OK, well. See you in a second. Flat three.' Maddy smiled.

'OK. Right. Yeah. I'll be right there,' he said, running a hand through his hair and then nodding as his mouth spread into a big wide grin.

Maddy backed up a couple of steps and then as soon as she was out of view bolted to the mirror to check her reflection, frantically combing her hair with her fingers, rubbing her cheeks then running to get some lip gloss from the bathroom.

When the doorbell went she bit down on her bottom lip and scrunched her eyes up tight with excitement. This was the dream. The parties, the people, the friendships, the snow, the possibilities.

Taking a deep breath, she opened her eyes and pulled open the door.

CHAPTER 43

ELLA

Ella smiled her way politely through Christmas lunch. The mistral hadn't blown the rain away, it was still pouring. The drains had flooded and there was a truck outside the window pumping out the water as they ate.

The food was beautiful. Pink lobsters with pots of melted butter that dripped onto their chins as they ate. Then red mullet wrapped in vine leaves and garlic infused rice. Followed by Christmas pudding, at their granddad's request, lit and flaming when it was brought to the table. But Ella hardly tasted anything she ate.

Distracted, she watched Dimitri across the table chatting happily with her mum and gran while she half-listened to a story her granddad was telling. Behind Dimitri she could see the fibre-optic angel sparkling and candlelight flickered over the nativity.

When Ella stood by the door later in the day, her granddad having a snooze in his armchair, Dimitri outside helping the guys with the drain, her mum came over and rested her hand on her shoulder. The feel of her so close was something Ella hadn't realised quite how much she'd missed. The smell of her perfume, the same Penhaligon's that Ella would sneakily dab a drop or two of behind her ears when she was small.

'So you're going home tomorrow?' Sophie said.

Ella nodded.

'I'm going to miss you.'

Ella kept her eyes focused on the rain, and the men as they battled with the torrents of water streaming over the road.

'I'll come and visit.'

'It's not the same.' Her mum sighed. 'I feel like I've just got my daughter back.'

Ella laughed. 'Maddy'll be home soon.'

'You could stay you know. Work from here? You could do that, couldn't you? Become a consultant or something? You're so experienced,' Sophie said, following Ella's gaze over to where Dimitri was having a hectic looking discussion with one of the workmen, the rain battering them as they shouted above the noise.

'I don't belong here.'

Her mum shrugged. 'Maybe. Maybe not.'

When Ella didn't say anything her mum added, 'Surely belonging is just a matter of where you're happy?'

'It's not that simple,' Ella said with a shake of her head.

'Ella honey.' Her mum tucked a strand of Ella's hair behind her ear. 'Things are as simple as you want to make them.'

CHAPTER 44

MADDY

As Maddy cycled through the snow to her dad's flat in Battersea she tried to quash her nerves by remembering the night before. Her evening with Leo, the boy next door, who had nearly choked on *Christmas Spirit* but then sat up with her talking till dawn, listening to her as she played the guitar, telling her about how he was going to South by Southwest music festival in Austin and awkwardly asking her if she might want to come along. She'd never been to America she'd told him. He'd looked surprised. She'd told him she'd never been anywhere. He'd been everywhere. And when he told her stories they painted pictures in her mind like bright patterned quilts and she found herself wanting to go every place he'd been.

And then they'd kissed for hours like teenagers and slept side by side on the charcoal velvet sofa. In the morning he'd smiled when he'd opened his eyes.

They'd had breakfast together at the little cafe table in the kitchen. Freshly baked chocolate croissants and hot, bitter coffee.

'So can I call you and stuff?' he'd said, leaning forward, his fingers tracing patterns on her bare leg.

'You can call me and stuff.' She'd smiled then said, 'You can come and visit me if you like?' But then had to look away, shy.

'Yeah?'

'Yeah, definitely'

'And you'll come to Texas? I'm totally serious about the invite. You'd love it.'

'Yeah, I'll come to Texas. I'm going to as many places as possible,' Maddy had said with a laugh.

'Can I join you?'

'Of course.'

He'd bitten his bottom lip as he smiled.

The memory made her skin tingle.

But as she docked her bike and struggled through the snow in her inappropriate ballet pumps that she'd worn because they were pretty and it was Christmas, no amount of reminiscing could counter the anxiety of what was to come. What would Veronica do when she saw her? What would Maddy say to her dad? The invitation she'd been so excited about last night in the stark morning light seemed impossible, the day could only be one of awkward, polite chitchat and narrow-eyed glares from Veronica.

By the time she'd walked up the steps to the front door, Maddy was practically shaking. She'd had to grip onto the front garden railings because she was struggling to walk in her shoes on the icy pavement. She hadn't had enough sleep, there was a touch of a hangover and she'd managed to work herself up into a frenzy about the day ahead. She pictured herself being pulled aside by Veronica and reminded acidly that she'd warned her to keep away.

The snow was getting thicker and heavier, Maddy's hair was wet, her face frozen. Her toes had gone numb in her thin leather pumps and as she reached for the doorbell her foot slipped on a patch of ice on the top step making her fall forward and bash into the front door with a thump.

It opened as she was scrabbling around on the ice trying to stand up, but as her shoes had nothing to grip she kept slipping, unable to right herself.

'Madeline?' She heard Veronica's voice, saw her stiletto clad feet from where she was bent double on the doorstep.

'Yep, hang on. I'll be–' But Maddy's feet just slid back and forth on the step, the thin soles of the ballet pumps unable to get purchase.

She felt Veronica reach down and take hold of her arm to help her up, but as she tried to yank her forward Maddy slipped again, grabbing onto Veronica's hand for support. The next thing she knew she'd hauled Veronica down on top of her and they were lying in a heap in the snow.

'Ah *merde*!' Veronica's face was inches from Maddy's. So close she could see the lines around her mouth from smoking, the mascara on her eyelashes, the foundation on her skin. Smell the heady mix of Chanel and cigarette smoke.

'Oh God I'm so sorry.' Maddy put her hands over her eyes as Veronica pulled herself up using the doorframe as support, thick flakes raining down on them. 'I'm really, really sorry.'

'It's fine,' Veronica said flatly, wiping the snow from her trousers and rubbing her elbow where she must have fallen on it.

Maddy tried and failed once again to get up and in the end just slumped against the stair rail. 'I'm really sorry. It wasn't meant to go like that.'

Veronica didn't say anything.

Maddy looked up at her. 'I know you hate me.'

Still Veronica didn't reply, just stared impassive, irritated.

'I've just got myself really nervous about seeing you,' Maddy went on, felt the tiredness of no sleep make her eyes sag heavy. 'And worried about what you're going to say.' Then she looked down at her feet and shook her head. 'I shouldn't have worn these shoes, and I'm just really sorry, I suppose. God, look I've ruined your trousers.'

'You haven't ruined the trousers, Maddy,' Veronica sighed.

Maddy put her face in her hands again. Closed her eyes for one blissful second, imagined the white all around her was the duvet not the frigid snow. 'I'm really sorry.'

'Madeline–'

But Maddy couldn't stop, she felt nauseous and exhausted, and cutting Veronica off moaned, 'I'm sorry. I'm sorry that I didn't come here sooner. I'm sorry that I got so cross about the audition, I just… I made such a fool of myself at it. It was so embarrassing.' Then she paused, traced a line in the snow with her finger and said, 'I'm sorry for what I did to your lives.'

She looked up at Veronica who was staring down at her, one eyebrow raised. Maddy couldn't tell if it was a look of pity or disparagement. Then she heard the music in the background – her tape recording of *White Christmas* playing on the machine. Glancing past Veronica and into the hallway she saw on the side table her jiffy bag, her invite on the cream notelet, her apology.

'They couriered it over from the office and he has played it non-stop since he got back,' Veronica said as she took a cigarette out of her case and lit it.

Maddy swallowed.

'You have a lovely voice,' Veronica added, her hand going back to rub the bruise on her elbow.

'Thank you,' Maddy said quietly. She felt the cold of the snow seep through the bum of her black skinny jeans. More flakes were falling as she sat there, the sun picking up the flecks as they swirled in the breeze.

'Would you like a hand up?' Veronica asked.

Maddy looked down at the icy floor and then up at Veronica who put her cigarette between her teeth and then proffered her hand.

'Yes.' She nodded. 'Yes I would. Thank you very much.'

CHAPTER 45

ELLA

On Boxing Day Maddy and Ella's planes crossed in the sky.

Maddy happily tucked into the weird chicken fricassee concoction that came with a roll and triangle of Dairylea and knocked back a miniature bottle of red wine, closing her eyes between mouthfuls and remembering her Christmas Day – the oysters and champagne on the balcony, her dad chinking her glass and looking at her like she was the crown jewels. Veronica offering her a pair of black patent wellingtons when Maddy discovered they were going out for lunch. The restaurant with the big glass windows and starched white tablecloths. The fish course with a crisp Chablis, the beef served with a Malbec the colour of blackberries, the fluffy white meringues with passion fruit coulis and a miniature glass of sweet Sauternes. Nothing in the way of a cracker or Christmas hat, but a few discreet glass jars of silver-sprayed fir cones. Maddy had drunk it all in like a wide-eyed tourist, mesmerised.

When it was time to leave Veronica had kissed her on both cheeks, a wariness lingering still between them but there had been a noticeable thawing in their relationship. Her dad had asked if he could drive her to the airport in the morning and when he'd come to pick her up he'd come alone.

Maddy had climbed into the huge Porsche four-wheel drive, snuggled into the heated leather seat and savoured every minute of the half-hour drive with just her dad.

At the airport he'd glanced over to her and said, 'I think there's just enough time for a Maccy D's. What do you think?'

'I think I'll have chicken nuggets and a vanilla milkshake please,' Maddy had replied with a grin.

They had sat in the car watching the planes, some dreadful boy band version of *White Christmas* playing in the background – *'Sorry it's all I have on this, it's my work iPod'* her dad had laughed. *'They may be awful but they make me a lot of money'* – and they had talked about nothing in particular. She had mentioned the music gig in Austin, Texas, he'd said he'd be in New York around that time and she could come and stay at his apartment, if she wanted to, otherwise he could get her a hotel. She'd said she thought she would like to stay with him. And he'd nodded, turned back to his Big Mac and she'd watched out the corner of her eye as he'd tried to hide a smile.

While Maddy was reminiscing about all things Christmas however, on the other plane Ella was doing exactly the opposite. She had shaken her head to refuse the tray of airline food and was using the time to scribble down ideas for the Obeille mobile phone presentation, blocking out all and every memory of her Christmas. It was done, over. She'd smoothed things over with her mum, now she could move on and start afresh. Anything else was just fantasy.

Unlocking the front door of her apartment however she was confronted by a smell that hit her like a punch. The fresh, sharp tang of the Christmas tree mixed with her mum's brand of washing powder, Maddy's citrusy perfume and maybe even the lingering scent of food that she'd cooked while in Greece. It didn't smell like her apartment.

Yet at the same time it smelt exactly like her home.

Leaving for work in the morning dressed in her favourite polaroid outfit of cobalt blue pencil skirt, white shirt and leopard print belt, but with her hair exhibiting a slight wave, Ella was just locking her front door when the elderly woman next door came out and waved.

'Oh you're back, hello. Did you have a good time?'

Ella glanced over her shoulder to see if there was someone behind her that this woman was talking to.

'We had a lovely time with your sister, she's fabulous.' As the woman chatted on, a man with white hair and glasses who looked faintly familiar appeared next to her.

'So you're the sister are you?' he said, inspecting her through narrowed eyes.

Before she could reply the door opposite opened and Hugo stepped out. Ella had exchanged the odd 'Good morning' with him in the past but nothing more.

'Hey, how's it going?' Hugo asked, big bright smile. 'I think I'll probably have some kind of New Year bash so you and your sister, if she's still around, more than welcome.' Then he looked over his shoulder at Margery and Walter and grinned, 'Well look at you two! Love this–' Hugo waved a hand between the two of them. 'Never too old.'

Margery raised a brow. 'Thank you for that, Hugo.'

Booming a laugh, Hugo patted his laptop case and said, 'Anyway, gotta run, no rest for the wicked. Good to see you back, Ella.'

Ella just nodded, stunned by this new hallway camaraderie.

'You really do have a fabulous sister,' Margery said, reaching down and picking the newspaper up off her mat. 'Really fabulous,' she said again, and as she started to close the door added, 'You're very lucky. I wish I'd had family like that.'

CHAPTER 46

MADDY

'So you just let her go?' Maddy was sitting crossed legged on the jetty, holding a brolly, watching as Dimitri bailed out his boat.

'I didn't just let her go,' he said angrily without looking up. 'She didn't want to stay.'

'Well why don't you go after her, you doofus?' Maddy twirled her umbrella, enjoying this conversation with Dimitri immensely.

'Because she made it quite clear, *Maddy,* that she didn't want anything to happen. Said it wouldn't achieve anything.' Dimitri hurled the water in his bucket violently out into the sea.

Maddy had to stifle a laugh.

'I'm so pleased you find my suffering so amusing.'

She picked at the hole in her red jumper. 'I'm sorry.'

Dimitri raised a brow as if to show that he knew she didn't mean it.

'Well what did you offer her? What did you tell her it would achieve?'

He paused. In the distance it started to thunder. 'Nothing.'

'Good one.'

'But she said–'

'Dimitri–' Maddy stood up, rested the brolly on her shoulder. 'What do you know about Ella?'

'What do you mean?' The thunder got louder.

'List what you know about her.'

'She's clever. Smart.' He started to walk to the stern of the boat, 'Sharp. Pretty. Strong.'

Maddy rolled her eyes. 'Think back, Dimitri. People don't change that much. This bit–' she pointed to her chest, her heart, '…this bit stays the same.'

She watched Dimitri as he narrowed his eyes, watched him roll his thoughts back into the past. See the Ella who did her ridiculous wiggle-walk down the jetty to try and seduce him, who waited on the steps of the supermarket to catch him as he went in to buy cigarettes, the Ella with the trousers that flapped around her ankles, the hair that stuck out like an tent, who sat patiently playing Sylvanian Families with Maddy – her cheeks pinking when him and his friends sloped past.

'Shy,' he said softly.

Maddy gave an encouraging nod.

'Soft.'

She nodded again.

Lightning forked, the crack breaking the sky in two.

'Sensitive?' he added with a shrug, lost in his daze of thoughts.

'You betcha.' Maddy laughed then leant forward and hooking his upper arm with her hand said, 'Come on, we'd better get you off this boat before you get fried. Can't go on a mission to rescue anyone if you're struck by lightning.'

CHAPTER 47

ELLA

Ella sat in the boardroom watching the work experience girl twirling a pen with a pompom on the top that she'd clearly got for Christmas. She looked like she was about nineteen, Ella thought, and noticed she was surreptitiously checking her emails, probably organising her New Year's Eve.

Ella had no plans for New Year bar Hugo's hallway invite.

'So–' Adrian tapped the table top with his pen. 'Any thoughts from anyone about the Obeille campaign?'

There was silence around the table, uncomfortable shifts in seats. The exec opposite her was focusing on trying to separate a bourbon biscuit while keeping the chocolate bit in the middle whole.

'Come on!' Adrian said, exasperated. 'Someone must have something. I know it's Christmas but–'

Ella looked at her pad. Her ideas were terrible. She listened as a couple of people chimed in with the same pat stuff that they'd been throwing around before the break. She watched Adrian sigh, the work experience girl's phone beeped. Ella wished she had her own phone for distraction but it was still sitting at the bottom of the Mediterranean.

'Oh–' she said suddenly, sitting up straighter.

Everyone turned to look at her, she could see the desperation in their eyes, the hope that she might be about to crack it as she usually did.

'What about if the phone gets thrown away?'

Adrian sighed.

'No hang on, bear with me,' Ella said. 'There's a girl on holiday, amazing view out in front of her, totally picturesque, but she's not seeing it because she's on her phone. She's so distracted that she doesn't notice anything, the beautiful food put down in front of her, the lavish cocktail, the really gorgeous guy strolling towards her. And the viewer is just willing her to look up, to take in everything that she's missing, but she stays tapping away at her screen. Then as the guy sidles up and she just gets a glimpse of him over the top of her phone and she gets excited that he's about to say something flirty but instead of saying anything he plucks the phone from her fingers and hurls it into the sea. After that he just strolls on by. It could end on a line something like, *When you're on holiday be on holiday. All other times, enjoy your phone.*'

Adrian narrowed his eyes.

Katya leant her chin on her hand and said, 'Like a kind of, enjoy your phone responsibly campaign?'

'Yeah, if you want.' Ella nodded.

All eyes in the room turned and looked at Adrian.

'I'm not convinced,' he said in the end, 'I just don't think they'll go for something that puts their brand in a negative light. It's a clever idea, Ella, I like the setting. Can we have her on her phone, same setting but finding some hidden restaurant or private island because of augmented reality?'

'But she'd be missing the view,' Ella said, sitting forward in her chair. 'That's the whole point.'

'You've been on holiday too long,' Adrian laughed. 'We're selling the phone, not the view.'

Ella was about to reply but paused, her mouth slightly open, and then when Adrian raised his eyebrows in expectation of her saying more she shook her head. 'No you're right. Crap idea. Someone else have a go.'

As the others threw some more ideas around, Ella found herself staring off into space, her pen doodling on her pad. All she could see was Dimitri chucking her iPhone into the wide blue water, his eagerness for her to enjoy what was right there in front of her. She thought about him coaxing her back so she'd make up with her mum. Constantly checking to make sure she was happy. Holding her hand and leading her to see the lemon trees warmed by the lights.

All of it had been for her. To make her happier.

He had pushed her to step back into her family, and he had waited on the outskirts making sure she didn't trip.

She looked at the work experience girl playing with her pompom pen, at Katya writing 'augmented reality' down on the flip chart, at Adrian, tired and pissed off, rubbing his hand across his forehead, at the shabby bunches of tinsel along the wall and the bunches of baubles that had come untied and been bashed and broken by people walking past. Then she glanced down at her pad and saw that she'd written: *We're selling the phone not the view* and wondered what the hell she was doing there.

CHAPTER 48

MADDY

Maddy was just driving back from breakfast having dropped Dimitri at the airport at the crack of dawn when she saw Ella step out of a taxi.

'No, no, no,' Maddy shouted from the window. 'You can't be here.'

The air was heavy, the clouds hanging low, exhausted.

Ella frowned then said, 'It's OK, Maddy. I'll stay out of your way. I'm not here to upset you.'

'No you idiot,' Maddy sighed. 'He's gone to get you.'

'Who's gone to get me?' Ella paid the taxi driver, opened her brolly against the drizzle and started to wheel her case over to where Maddy was sitting in the Jeep.

'Dimitri! He's on a plane.'

'He can't be.'

Maddy scrunched up her face and said, 'He is. He's up there now.'

They both glanced up at the sky, the rain pattering down lightly on the Ella's umbrella.

'Oh,' Ella said and they just looked at each other, surrounded by the noise of water plinking on plastic, the swish of the windscreen wipers and the throaty growl of the Jeep engine.

'Yeah, "Oh" is about right.' Maddy had to hold in a smile. 'Get in.'

'No I can walk, it's fine.' Ella gave a little shake of her head.

'Ella–' Maddy drove forward a few feet as Ella started to walk away. 'Get in the car.'

'Honestly I can walk.'

'You're so stubborn,' Maddy shouted as Ella got further away and the rain started to fall harder, pounding the drooping dead leaves of the bougainvillea and tapping on the cars parked along the roadside. 'Can't we just get over this? Can't we just be friends? It's over. We can make it over and done with.'

She saw Ella's pace slow. She was wearing straight legged blue jeans, a yellow scooped-neck sweatshirt, green converse and a beige trench-coat. Maddy didn't recognise the outfit from any of the Polaroids. Taking her foot off the brake, she let the Jeep roll forward till it was level with Ella.

'It's over. It's no one's fault. We were little. I was little and stupid and selfish and you were a bit bigger and stubborn and stupid.' Maddy paused, watched Ella's lips tighten, saw her hand grip the brolly. 'What is it Veronica would have said? *This is our time to show whether we're still spoiled children or finally grown women.*'

Maddy watched Ella's head turn and held her breath.

'I can't believe you're quoting Veronica.'

Maddy exhaled on a laugh. 'I know! Silly cow. No don't look at me like that, we've made up, sort of. Well, we understand each other. Respect each other. I respect her. I don't think she respects me. But–' she shrugged. 'What can you do?' As they spoke, the rain was drenching the windscreen faster than the wipers could push it away. 'So are you getting in or not?' Maddy shouted above the sound of the downpour.

Ella ran round to the boot and chucked in her case, then coming round to the passenger side flung open the door and clambered in.

'Are you soaked?' Maddy asked.

'Not too bad,' Ella said, pulling off her mac and throwing it onto the back seat.

'So–' Maddy grinned. 'You and Dimitri, eh?'

CHAPTER 49

ELLA

'Are you sure it'll work?' Ella asked Maddy nervously, pulling at the hem of her jumper.

'It'll work.' Maddy nodded before heading into the kitchen to help their mum.

As they'd driven up to the taverna in the Jeep and seen the look of surprise on Sophie's face as the two of them jumped out, Maddy helping Ella with her case, Ella holding the brolly over both of them, the rain had stopped. Like God had clicked his fingers, just like that.

Now Ella was sitting on her own at the end of the jetty. She was wearing her jeans, her St Christopher and a pale blue woollen jumper. She had thrown all her Polaroids away when she'd got back to her flat after the bad work meeting. Had decided it was time to trust her grown-up instincts.

Next to her on the jetty was a jam jar filled with hellebores, their pale pink leaves squashed together as she'd crammed in as many flowers as she could. Chilled retsina sat in a bucket decked with sprigs of olive and a handful of candles were dotted about, burning bright in the low winter sun. From the wooden post she'd tied a fishing line, the float bobbing in the water ahead of her. Next to the jam jar was another line, still in its plastic

The dinner was amazing. They had smoked salmon canapés with little dollops of caviar followed by turkey and sage and onion stuffing, chipolata sausages wrapped with bacon, cranberry sauce and brussel sprouts that Ella had brought over with her in her suitcase. Ella made a toast to her mum and Maddy for cooking it all so beautifully and when she leant back from chinking glasses Dimitri's arm was draped along the back of her chair, his fingers toying with the fabric of her top.

When Sophie came back from the pantry carrying a tray of baklava, Maddy nipped up to her room and reappeared holding a bottle of *Christmas Spirit*. 'Here's something that'll probably remind you of the war, granddad,' she said, sloshing some into a glass. 'Either that or it'll kill you,' she laughed.

'I can't think of a better way to go,' he said, and downed the shot in one. When he'd finished coughing all he could mutter was, 'Christ alive, that's some liquor.'

By evening they were all fairly merry but Dimitri and her granddad had taken it one stage further and the resulting *Christmas Spirit* competition had got the better of them both. Her granddad was asleep in his chair while Dimitri was passed out on the sofa in the living room. The rest of them ate mince pies and had a cup of tea.

When her gran yawned and Maddy went upstairs to bed, Sophie insisted that they clear up in the morning but Ella said she would do it now. When she stubbornly started to tidy her mum rolled her eyes and stayed to help, refusing to leave her to it.

'Do you feel better now?' Sophie asked when the kitchen was sparkling.

Ella nodded. 'I just like things tidy.'

Her mum raised a brow. 'Yes but there's no hurry. You're going to have relax into island life at some point, you know?'

'Yeah that might take me a while.' Ella made a face.

Sophie laughed, 'I think you'll get there sooner than you think.'

Ella looked over at her mum. 'Thanks.'

'What for?'

'For this–' Ella pointed round the room, to the fibre-optic angel and the nativity, the champagne flutes dripping on the draining board, the plate of mince pies covered in cling film. 'For Christmas.'

'You're more than welcome.' Sophie smiled then picking up her mug of camomile tea asked, 'Am I allowed to go to bed now?'

'Yes.' Ella nodded.

'Thank you. Good night.'

Ella stood for a second on her own, glanced around the kitchen, dried up the glasses and put them away in the cupboard, then went to check on Dimitri. He was lying on his back snoring away. She sat down on the edge of the sofa and leant over to put her cheek next to his, felt the roughness of his stubble against her skin, took a breath in and inhaled the scent of him, then, pulling the blanket up so it was almost touching his chin she went upstairs to sleep in the spare bed in Maddy's room.

CHAPTER 51

MADDY

'Hang on, I'm in the bath,' Maddy called as Ella pushed open the door to the en suite.

'Oh sorry.'

'That's OK. Come in if you want. I'm covered in bubbles.'

Maddy waited to see what Ella would do, assumed ~~she'd~~ close the door and go and use another bathroom. But she didn't. Instead she walked in and, squeezing some ~~toothpaste on her~~ toothbrush, sat down on the tiled floor next to the bath.

'I've got the new Grazia in my bag if you want it?' Ella said, her toothbrush sticking out of her mouth.

'Thanks.' Maddy nodded. 'I'll read it in bed.'

'OK.'

The curtain was open in the bathroom and through the window Maddy could see the stars. Millions of them like pinpricks in the sky.

'So?' she asked, looking from the view back towards her sister.

'So what?' Ella frowned.

'Is he a good kisser?'

Ella blushed. 'Yeah he's OK.'

'Only OK?'

'No.' Ella shook her head. 'Not only OK. He's amazing.'

Maddy smiled, glanced back to the stars. 'Don't break his heart.'

'Unlikely!' Ella laughed.

'He won't break yours, don't worry.'

Ella nodded.

Maddy watched her as she cleaned her teeth.

'I can't believe you made friends with all my neighbours?' Ella said, standing up to rinse out her mouth.

'They're lovely.'

Ella made a face. 'They're all a bit odd.'

Maddy laughed. 'You're a bit odd.'

'I'm not odd.'

'Ella, we're all odd. That's the beauty of it.'

Ella paused as she wiped her face on the white fluffy hand towel, considered the possibility.

'Do you want a Quality Street?' Maddy asked. 'I've got some in my bag. They were giving them out at the airport.'

'I've just cleaned my teeth.'

'So? Clean them again later. It's Christmas.'

Maddy watched Ella think about it, weigh up the pros and cons, remembered stealing the shiny-wrapped chocolates out of the tin when they were little and shovelling them into their mouths as they giggled under the duvet. Remembered standing side by side at the village carol singing and Ella reaching into her pocket and sneakily pulling out a handful, then silently arguing about who would get which one. Remembered coming downstairs in the morning and discovering that their dad had eaten all their favourites.

Maddy watched from the bath as Ella's mouth stretched into a smile and grinned when she said, 'Have you got any of the purple ones?'

Inspired by the Davenport family's delicious holiday
traditions, here is Jenny Oliver's guide to
Christmas eats—with a Greek twist!

The Little Christmas Kitchen Guide to Festive Feasting

Melomakarona

You won't believe how addictive these honey-drenched little cookies are! Bonus: when these babies are in the oven, your house will smell like Christmas heaven.

- 1½ cups light olive oil
- ½ cup butter
- 1 cup beer or orange juice
- 1 tbsp ground cinnamon
- 1½ teaspoons ground cloves
- 2 oranges, zest of
- 1 cup sugar
- 2 cups fine ground semolina
- 6 cups flour
- ½ tsp baking powder
- ½ tsp baking soda
- 1 tsp salt

For the syrup:

- 1½ cups sugar
- 1½ cups Greek thyme honey
- 1 cup water
- ¾ cup walnuts, finely chopped

Method

1. Put the oil, butter, beer (or orange juice), cinnamon, cloves, orange peel and sugar in a mixing bowl and beat until thoroughly blended.
2. Sift one cup of flour with the baking soda, baking powder and salt and blend into the oil mixture. Add the semolina, a cup at a time.
3. Add the remaining flour, a cup at a time, and mix with your hands until you get a rather firm dough. Roll the dough into cylinders, about two inches long and one inch in diameter, and

flatten them with your hands. Then place on olive-oil–greased cookie sheets.

4. Bake at 180C for 30 minutes, then remove the cookies from the oven and cool. Lay the cookies out in a rimmed baking pan large enough to contain them and pour the hot syrup over the cookies, sprinkle them with the chopped walnuts and let them soak overnight.

5. For the syrup: mix the sugar, honey and water, and bring to a boil. Cook on low heat for four minutes and skim off the foam that forms on top.

6. The next day put them on your prettiest platter, sprinkle each layer evenly with the finely chopped walnuts and and serve.

Christmas Morning Kataïfi

These cinnamon-dusted treats look like little birds nests and are the perfect way to start Christmas morning on a sweet note. Serve with hot coffee and, if you fancy a little extra indulgence, sticky baklava.

- 450g kataïfi dough, defrosted per package instructions
- 225g butter, melted

For the filling:

- 1 cup walnuts, coarsely chopped
- 1 cup almonds, coarsely ground
- ½ cup fine granulated sugar
- 1 tsp ground cinnamon
- ½ tsp ground cloves
- 1 egg white, lightly beaten

For the syrup:

- 2 cups sugar
- 1¼ cups water
- ½ tsp lemon juice
- Thin strip of lemon peel
- 4 whole cloves
- 1 tbsp thin honey

Method

1. Preheat oven to 180C.
2. To prepare the syrup, heat the water in a saucepan over low heat. Add the sugar and stir to dissolve. Add the lemon juice, peel and cloves and bring to the boil. Reduce heat and simmer for 10 minutes. Stir in the honey. Remove from heat, strain and set aside to cool.

3. In a mixing bowl, combine all the ingredients for the filling and blend well with a wooden spoon.
4. To prepare the kataïfi dough, lay the long strip out on a clean work surface and divide into 18-24 pieces.
   Take care not to let the dough dry out by covering unused dough with parchment paper and a damp towel.
5. Brush each strip with melted butter. Place a tablespoon of the filling at one end of the strip and roll into a cylinder, tightly tucking in any stray pieces of dough. Place the rolls seam side down in a lightly buttered baking dish, close together but not squashed, and brush well with remaining butter. Bake for 45-60 minutes, until golden brown and crispy.
6. Remove from oven, pour cool syrup over the pastry and cover with a clean tea towel. Let cool for 3-4 hours as it absorbs the syrup.
7. Sprinkle with cinnamon or icing sugar for the perfect festive look!

Alexander's Saginaki

If, like me, you worry that trying Alexander's method and setting cheese on fire would end in catastrophe, here is an easy way to make saginaki without the sizzle. A delightfully different Christmas starter—and no singed eyebrows!

- 450g haloumi
- Flour (for dredging)
- ½ cup olive oil
- 2 lemons, cut into wedges

Method
1. Cut the cheese into strips (2 inches wide and ½ inch thick).
2. Run strips one by one under the cold water tap and coat lightly with flour. Set aside until all the strips are coated.
3. Heat oil in a heavy skillet and pan fry the cheese, turning once until golden brown on both sides.
4. Remove, dab with paper towels and serve immediately with lemon wedges.

Disappearing Dolmades

Serve these gorgeous stuffed vine leaves as part of a mezze platter. Be warned: these tasty morsels will vanish in no time.

- 115g long-grain rice, cooked
- 250g minced lamb
- 1 tsp dried oregano
- 1 onion, finely chopped
- 3 tbsp parsley, finely chopped
- 3 tbsp celery, finely chopped
- Salt and black pepper
- 1 tbsp tomato purée
- 250g preserved, drained vine leaves
- 2 tomatoes, sliced
- 2 garlic cloves, sliced
- 1 lemon, juice only

Method
1. Preheat oven to 180C.
2. In a bowl, combine the rice, meat, onion, herbs, celery, salt and pepper. Fold in the tomato purée.
3. Place one vine leaf on a plate, vein side up. Take a heaped teaspoon of the mixture and place in the centre of the leaf near the stem edge. Fold the stem end up over the filling, then fold both sides towards the middle and roll up like a small cigar, but don't roll too tightly as the rice will expand.
4. Line the bottom of a large ovenproof dish with tomato slices or leftover vine leaves. Pack the stuffed leaves in layers on top, pushing small pieces of garlic in between. Sprinkle with lemon juice and add 150ml cold water. Cover with oiled foil.
5. Place the leaves in the oven for 45 minutes, adding extra water if necessary. Serve.

Ella's Mum's Stifado

There's nothing like mum's cooking—especially Ella's mum's!
The sauce for this dish is absolutely divine: rich and full of
flavour. Serve with roast potatoes or just some really good crusty
bread.

- 800g-1kg lean beef, cubed
- 500g shallots
- 1 large onion
- 2 tomatoes
- 4 garlic cloves
- 1 vegetable stock cube
- 1 small wine glass of extra virgin olive oil
- 1 glass of red wine
- 2 tbsp red wine vinegar
- 2 tbsp tomato purée
- ½ cinnamon stick
- 3 sprigs of rosemary
- 1½-1 tsp of ground nutmeg
- 4 bay leaves
- Black pepper and salt, to taste

Method

1. Sear the meat in a frying pan and then add the olive oil,
   onions and garlic. Leave for about five minutes until the
   onions start to soften.
2. Add 2 tbsp of red wine vinegar and red wine, then cover and
   leave for 5 minutes.
3. Add the nutmeg, cinnamon, stock cube, bay leaves,
   rosemary, tomato purée and salt and pepper, stirring

constantly. Then add in chopped tomatoes and continue stirring for 5 minutes.

4. Transfer to a clay pot or casserole dish and add about ¼–½ litre of water, then cook for at least one hour in the oven on a moderate heat. Keep checking, as you don't want it to dry out, adding water as needed.

5. Whilst the stifado is cooking, place the shallots into hot water to soften and peel, then fry in a little olive oil.

6. After the stifado has been in the oven for an hour, add the shallots to the pot and cook for a further hour until the meat is tender.

Ella's Great-Grandmother's Morello Cherry Liqueur

There's a reason the recipe for this sweet and spicy liqueur has been passed down for generations. A little thimbleful of this ruby-red liquid is the perfect offset to a heavy Christmas dinner. Don't forget to make in advance!

- 1kg sour cherries
- 500g sugar
- 12 whole cloves
- 4–5 cinnamon sticks
- 250ml vodka, or alcohol of your choice

Method
1. Stem the cherries, but don't pit them. Rinse.
2. Put the cherries and sugar in a big glass jar in alternating layers. Screw on the lid tightly and let sit in a sunny spot for one month.
3. After a month, it will be juicy in the jar and you can add your spices. Tie them up in a cheese cloth and throw them in. Then close the jar and let it sit for another month.
4. After two months, your liqueur is ready to drink. Dig out the spices in the cheesecloth and then pour in the vodka. Save the cherries—they make a decadent decoration to any cake!